**TIME SEEMED TO HANG SUSPENDED
FOR A MOMENT AS HIS HAND
STALLED IN HER HAIR, AND THEN HE
PULLED HER GENTLY FORWARD**

Lark came willingly, knowing that this was what she'd wanted since last night. This time Stone didn't kiss her cheek.

The kiss was softer than she expected—almost shy and tentative, but incredibly warm, and unbelievably erotic. She had never been kissed like this before.

And in a corner of her mind she knew, without question, that she had more experience in kissing than Stone Rhodes did. But somehow that didn't matter. This kiss was not about recreational sex, or passing the time, or having fun.

No, Stone Rhodes was not a guy like that. And when he decided to kiss someone he moved in like a Marine, with clear intent. His kiss was deliberate, as if he'd been thinking about it for some time...

"Full of small-town charm and southern heat...humorous, heartwarming, and sexy. I couldn't put it down!"
—Robin Wells, author of *Still the One*

"A sweet confection...This first of a projected series about the Rhodes brothers offers up Southern hospitality with a bit of grit. Romance readers will be delighted."
—*Library Journal*

"Hope Ramsay delivers with this sweet and sassy story of small-town love, friendship, and the ties that bind."
—Lisa Dale, author of *Simple Wishes*

"Ramsay has created a great new series... Not only are the two main characters compelling and fun, but as you read, the entire town of kooky but very real people become part of your life...I can hardly wait until I visit Last Chance again."
—FreshFiction.com

"Touching...funny...Ramsay's characters were endearing and lovable, and I eagerly look forward to the rest of [the series]."
—NovelReaction.com

"A sweet romance...sassy and fun characters."
—Book Hounds (maryinhb.blogspot.com)

"Captivating...great characterization, amusing dialogue...I am glad that the universe sent *Welcome to Last Chance* my way, and I am going to make sure that it does the same with Hope Ramsay's future books."
—LikesBooks.com

~LAST~
CHANCE
Christmas

~LAST~ CHANCE
Christmas

HOPE RAMSAY

FOREVER

NEW YORK   BOSTON

Copyright © 2012 by Robin Lanier

Forever
Hachette Book Group
237 Park Avenue
New York, NY 10017

www.HachetteBookGroup.com

Printed in the United States of America

First Edition: September 2012
10 9 8 7 6 5 4 3 2 1
OPM

Forever is an imprint of Grand Central Publishing.
The Forever name and logo are trademarks of Hachette Book Group, Inc.

The Hachette Speakers Bureau provides a wide range of authors for speaking events. To find out more, go to www.hachettespeakersbureau.com or call (866) 376-6591.

The publisher is not responsible for websites (or their content) that are not owned by the publisher.

For Pop

Acknowledgments

I would like to thank my wonderful critique partners: Robin Kaye for helping me with the plot of this book, and Carla Kempert for helping me with a teenager's point of view. I would also like to give a shout-out to the wonderful Ruby Slippered Sisterhood, who encourage and amaze me every day. Also, many thanks to my wonderful editor, Alex Logan, for every drop of her red ink. Thank you Elaine English, for all your help and support. And finally, my eternal gratitude to my husband, Bryan, who is not a man of many words, but it doesn't matter because his heart is so very large.

~LAST~
CHANCE
Christmas

CHAPTER
1

Jesus looked like he'd been hit by a Mack truck. The statue of the son of God lay on its side, its fiberglass infrastructure torn and ragged. Scattered on the gravel beside the bleaching carcass were the remnants of a sign that read "Golfing for God."

Lark Chaikin hugged her elbows and tried to keep warm against the December gust that blew her bangs into her eyes. Who knew South Carolina could be so cold. She looked up at the tops of the pine trees, swaying in the wind. She shivered.

She had to be crazy to have driven all the way from New York on this fool's errand. Roadside America was littered with the corpses of mini-golf courses, their windmills suspended in time, their giant Paul Bunyans toppled. And it sure looked like Golfing for God had gone the way of all the fiberglass dinosaurs.

Pop should have checked before he made his last request. But, of course, Pop had been sick for a long time.

Lark turned back toward her late father's SUV, a giant

silver thing that drove like an ocean liner and guzzled gas like one, too. She opened the back door and stared down at the cardboard box containing Pop's ashes. The box was eight inches square with the words "Chaikin, Abe" scrawled across its top.

She pressed a couple of fingers against the ache in her forehead that had been growing all day. "Why'd you make a big *mahgilla* about being buried here in the middle of nowhere on a closed-up mini-golf course?" She couldn't go on. Her throat closed up, and tears threatened her eyes. She swallowed back the grief that was too new to be expressed yet.

Lark leaned on the tailgate, her gaze shifting from the box to the canvas camera bag sitting beside it. Her fingers itched to pick up the Nikon, maybe shoot a few photos of the broken statue. She might be able to capture the Picasso-like perspective of its smashed face. Maybe shooting a few photos would help her get back the balance she'd lost during the Libyan civil war. She had experienced a lot of heavy fighting during the battle for Misurata.

But she couldn't find the courage to pick up the camera. She slammed the tailgate and turned toward a gravel path clearly posted with "No Trespassing" signs.

Something violent had damaged the stand of pines growing on the right side of the path. The trees looked as if they had been blasted by napalm or something. A wave of nausea gripped her. Man, she was really losing it. The nightmares were bad. But the waking flashbacks were worse.

She took a few calming breaths and focused on the noise of her feet crunching on the gravel. She looked up. Clouds, heavy with rain, scudded across the sky, and a lone hawk circled, watching and waiting. She felt light-headed. She couldn't remember the last time she'd eaten or slept.

She lowered her gaze. A medium-sized structure resembling Noah's Ark loomed ahead of her. Scaffolding had been set up around it, and it looked as if someone were giving the Ark a fresh coat of paint. Still, for all that, the place seemed sad and abandoned. A few dead leaves, driven by the wind, swirled across the path.

She turned right and made a circuit of the place, hole-to-hole, past Adam and Eve, the Tower of Babel, and David and Goliath, feeling as if she'd slipped through the bounds of reality. She stopped at the tee box labeled "Plague of Frogs." Something terrible had happened here. She remembered Pop talking about how the frogs used to spit water over the fairway. But there weren't any frogs left. Just random frog legs stuck onto concrete lily pads.

She turned and walked past the undamaged Jonah and the whale, then cut through the Wise Men with their bobbing camels and Jesus walking on water, until she reached the eighteenth hole.

She halfway expected this hole to be the much-laughed-about Tomb of Jesus. It would be just like Pop to want to have his ashes installed in the ersatz tomb of a messiah that wasn't his. She could see him laughing his ass off as people putted golf balls across his grave. After all, Pop had a murderous short game.

But the eighteenth hole wasn't a tomb.

It was a statue of Jesus. The sign beside the tee box displayed a quote from Mark 16: "Go into all the world and preach the gospel to every creature."

Apparently the eighteenth hole was a celebration of the resurrection.

• • •

Stonewall Rhodes, the chief of police for the incorporated city of Last Chance, South Carolina, drove his cruiser south on Palmetto Avenue, taking his second-to-last circuit of the day. It was nearly five o'clock, and the light was fading quickly into dusk. It would be dark by the time he drove out to the edge of town and back.

He got about halfway to the Allenberg County line before he saw the silver Cadillac Escalade parked in the lot at Golfing for God. The New York tags caught his attention.

Cars with New York plates didn't come through this neck of the woods very often—unless the folks in them were lost tourists searching for the road to Hilton Head, or people making a pilgrimage to Golfing for God.

At one time, Golfing for God had attracted a fair number of pilgrims. The place was listed on RoadsideAmerica .com and had made it into a couple of tour guides. But the place had been closed up for more than a year—ever since its propane tank had been struck by lightning.

Of course, Hettie Marshall and the Committee to Resurrect Golfing for God had just hired a contractor to begin fixing up the place. They were aiming for a big reopening in the spring. In the meantime, though, the "No Trespassing" signs were designed to keep the pilgrims and the pranksters away.

Stone pulled his cruiser into the golf course's parking lot, the gravel crunching under its wheels. He eyeballed the Cadillac. It appeared to be unoccupied, but appearances could be deceiving. Before getting out of his car, he keyed the plate information into his cruiser's computer. An instant later the Cadillac's history came back to him. There were no outstanding warrants involving the vehicle, which was registered to one Abe Chaikin of Kings Point, New York.

Stone stared at the name for a long moment as the little hairs on the back of his neck stood up on end.

The past had come back to haunt his town.

He snagged his Stetson from the passenger's seat and dropped it on his head as he left the cruiser. He pulled his heavy-duty flashlight from his utility belt as he cautiously approached the vehicle. He shone the light through the driver's side window and confirmed that the car was unoccupied.

The SUV was a late model, clean and fully loaded, with a GPS system and satellite radio in the dashboard. A well-worn canvas bag in army green occupied the cargo area, loaded with what looked like expensive camera equipment. The SUV was locked.

He turned away from the car and walked up the charred remains of the main walkway. He saw the woman as soon as he turned the corner by the first hole. She sat on the wooden bench at the feet of the resurrected Jesus on hole eighteen, with her head bowed as if deep in prayer. For a brief moment the Savior's hand seemed to move outward toward the praying woman, as if He were trying to comfort her.

A shiver inched down Stone's spine, and he blinked a couple of times. Only then did he realize the deepening dusk had played a trick on him. A little sparrow sat in the hand of Jesus. It turned its head this way and that and gave the appearance of the statue's hand in motion.

The woman was as tiny as the bird, with short-cropped dark hair that spiked around her head. She wore jeans and a peacoat. A stiff wind might blow her away.

She looked up, turning a pair of dark, hollow eyes in his direction. All the breath left his lungs as he found himself caught up in her stare. For an instant, he felt as if he might be looking at a ghost from some forgotten past. Her face was oddly gray in the fading light, the skin beneath her eyes smudged with the purple of exhaustion.

She looked hopelessly lost, like a small waif or street urchin.

A hot, tight feeling slammed into his chest. The unexpected intensity of the emotion was tempered by the immediate clanging of alarm bells in his head. She was trouble.

She had arrived in a car registered to Abe Chaikin—a man who had so upset the balance of things in Last Chance that practically everyone still remembered the incident.

He couldn't shake the feeling that the woman was here for the same purpose. This tiny person was going to rend the daily fabric of life in his town, and he couldn't let that happen.

She looked up at him, and he recognized his doom right there in her hollow eyes, just as he recognized something about her that he couldn't even put words to. He had this odd feeling that he had known her for a long, long time.

Lark gripped the edge of the bench and stared at the fiberglass Jesus. This had to be the Excedrin headache to end all headaches. Was this Pop's idea of a joke?

The sound of boots on gravel drew her attention to the walkway by the Ark. A policeman came into view.

Holy crap, she was in trouble now.

"Ma'am," the cop said. "What part of 'No Trespassing' do you not understand? Golfing for God is not in business, and I'd be obliged if you would move on."

She stood up, feeling dizzy and disconnected as she focused on the cop's face. She recognized the green eyes, dimpled chin, and meandering nose. Crap. She *was* going crazy.

"Carmine?" she asked. Her throat hurt.

"Ma'am?" The cop went on alert. His shoulders stiffened, and his body coiled in that ready-for-action pose she'd seen in the marines patrolling the streets of Baghdad.

She blinked a couple of times, trying to clear her vision. He wasn't Carmine, of course. And she was not losing her mind. She cleared her dry throat. "I was wondering if you could tell me where I might find Zeke Rhodes. I need to speak with him about something."

"Ma'am, Zeke Rhodes has been dead for more than forty years. I would have expected you to know that."

"Oh," Lark said as she fought a wave of disappointment. "More than forty years? Really?"

"Yes, ma'am. He died the day Abe Chaikin left town."

Her head throbbed, and her face went from hot to cold. "You knew my father?" That seemed unlikely.

"No, ma'am. But I've heard the stories about him. He hightailed it out of town the same day Zeke Rhodes died. They found Zeke's body right where you're standing now."

She took a reflexive step backward as if to avoid the long-dead body of Zeke Rhodes.

"Of course, not everyone thinks Zeke was murdered. There's a big debate on that topic."

"But you think he was."

The cop's shoulders moved a little. "Maybe. It happened before I was born. So you're Abe's daughter?"

"Oh, yeah, I'm his daughter." The world started tilting sideways.

"Well, ma'am, some folks think *your daddy* murdered Zeke."

Abe Chaikin's daughter gave Stone one wide-eyed look before her eyes rolled up in her head and she crumpled. He caught her before she planted her face in the Astroturf.

He hoisted her up in his arms and realized that she was burning with fever. No telling what kind of bug she'd brought to town. She could be carrying anthrax or some deadly virus for all Stone knew. But that was nothing compared to the fact that she was Abe Chaikin's daughter.

He lugged her deadweight up the gravel walk. She regained consciousness before he laid her in the backseat of his Crown Vic. She cracked one bloodshot eye.

"I passed out, didn't I?"

"Yes, ma'am."

"Where are you taking me?"

"To the clinic, you're sick."

"But my car and cameras and—"

"I'll make sure they're safe. You need medical attention. You just rest there for a minute." He opened the trunk and pulled out an emergency blanket, which he wrapped around her.

"Thanks," she said through chattering teeth. "I'm so sorry. I never get sick. Really." Her eyes closed. Her chest rattled ominously when she took a deep breath.

Just his luck. He needed this like he needed a hole in the head. She was the daughter of the most notorious man to ever set foot in Last Chance. What the hell was she doing here?

He slid into the driver's seat, dropped his Stetson on the seat beside him, and radioed back to main dispatch. He gave them his location and an outline of the situation. Winnie, his night dispatcher, replied that she would give his momma a call to let her know he would be late for supper.

Momma would call Miz Polk, and Miz Polk would call Miz Hanks, and Miz Hanks would call Miz Bray, and pretty soon every member of the Christ Church Ladies' Auxiliary would know that Abe Chaikin's daughter had just arrived from New York.

By this time tomorrow morning, the entire county would be in an uproar. And wouldn't that be fun?

"You think you can stand?" he asked Abe Chaikin's daughter when they arrived at the urgent care center five minutes later.

The woman tried to push herself up, but flopped back onto the cruiser's seat. He hopped out of the driver's seat, opened the back door, and pulled her up into his arms.

She was as delicate as a dragonfly's wing. Not his type of woman at all. But when she looked up at him out of those glassy brown eyes, something pressed hard against his chest, and he had trouble breathing.

"I'm so sorry," she murmured as her head fell against his shoulder. For some inexplicable reason, the weight of her head against him felt impossibly good.

He needed to run this woman off just as soon as he could. She was big trouble.

Winnie had already alerted Annie Jasper, the night nurse, who directed Stone into one of the half dozen exam rooms. He eased Abe Chaikin's daughter down to the exam table. "You'll be fine, ma'am. Do you have your car keys? If you do, I can see about moving your car to a safer place."

She dug into the pocket of her jeans and handed him the keys.

"Thank you, ma'am. Now, what's your name?"

"Lark."

"Lark? Like the bird?"

She nodded and swallowed hard. "Yeah. Mom and Pop were nonconformists."

Now, there was an understatement. Folks of a certain age in this county still remembered her daddy. They mostly referred to him as that Yankee hippie.

"Is your last name Chaikin, too?"

She nodded. "Who runs the golf course these days?" she asked.

Stone hesitated. "That's a complicated question. Elbert Rhodes holds the deed to the land, but there's a committee that has taken over the rebuilding and expansion of the place. Hettie Marshall chairs that."

Her bloodshot gaze wandered over his face and then down to the name badge on his chest. Her eyes widened a little. "Deputy Rhodes?" she said.

"That would be Chief Rhodes, ma'am."

"And the 'S' is for . . . ?"

He tried not to grimace. "Stonewall. Everyone calls me Stone—Stony if they know me well."

The corner of her mouth twitched. "And you thought I had a strange name? So, are you related to Zeke and this Elbert guy?"

He didn't want this interview to get personal, but it

was heading in that direction. It wasn't as if he could lie. "Yes, ma'am."

"I need to talk to Elbert."

"About what?"

She closed her eyes, and the shivers took her for a long moment. Stone took off his uniform jacket and draped it over her legs.

He was about to shout for Annie when Lark said through chattering teeth, "My father wants to have his ashes scattered on the eighteenth hole. He died a week ago."

Holy crap.

"I can tell that I've surprised you," Lark said. The shivering seemed to be passing.

"Well, as a matter of fact, yes, ma'am, you have."

Lark's eyes flew open. "Look, I heard what you said, before. But my father didn't murder Zeke Rhodes. Pop always said he 'found himself' on the eighteenth hole at Golfing for God, whatever the heck that means."

"Really? That's hardly evidence of his innocence, is it?"

She stared at him like he was an alien. "No, I guess not. But, to be honest, Pop never explained why he used to say that."

"There you go. There is also the fact that your father left town suddenly on the same day as my granddaddy died."

"Zeke Rhodes was your grandfather?"

The Last Chance chief of police stared down at Lark out of a pair of oddly familiar green eyes. "Yes, ma'am," he drawled in a deep voice that sounded like it came right up from the earth itself.

"And you think my father murdered him?"

He shrugged. "I don't know. My granddaddy's death was ruled an accident. But my daddy always said it was kind of hard to explain how a man gets that beat up by accident."

She must be having a fever dream because the gorgeous policeman was saying stuff about Pop that made no sense whatsoever.

Just then, a thin, youngish nurse wearing blue scrubs and bearing a badge with the name "A. Jasper" bustled in. The nurse interrupted the mutual interrogation. "Ruby called," she said to the cop. "She's holding dinner for you. You need to be getting along home."

"It'll keep. I need to ask the patient a couple of—"

"Your questions can wait." The nurse advanced with a digital thermometer, which she pressed into Lark's ear. It beeped inside of thirty seconds.

"Uh-huh, you see? One hundred and three." Nurse Jasper looked down at Lark. "You take any medicine?"

"A couple of aspirin about four hours ago, when the headache started." Lark sank back into the pillows. Her head felt like an anvil. Every muscle screamed in agony if she so much as twitched, which was problematic because she was twitching all over with the shivers.

"All right," Nurse Jasper said. "Let me go get Doc Cooper."

"I'll just stay here and ask a few—"

"I told you, Stony, the questions can wait. Now, you go on home to your girls." Nurse Jasper's voice knifed through Lark's head and sent pinpricks of pain shooting behind her eyes.

The chief folded his big arms across his chest. He

didn't look very impressed with Nurse Jasper. "Can she drive?" he asked.

The nurse gave the cop an imperious stare before replying, "The patient has a hundred-and-three fever. She isn't going anywhere anytime soon. What's the problem?"

"Y'all gonna keep her here, then?"

"Depends on what Doc Cooper says. He'll either send her up to Orangeburg or see if Miz Miriam can nurse her."

Lark was not entirely sure, but this news didn't seem to make the chief of police happy. Truth to tell, it didn't make her happy either.

"Um, no hospitals. It's just a virus," she managed between her trembling jaws. "And as soon as I'm feeling better, I'd be happy to leave. Is there a hotel nearby with room service?"

The nurse and the cop laughed. Lark's head pounded.

"This ain't like New York," the cop said.

The nurse put on a professional smile. Lark would give her points for her bedside manner. "Honey, don't you worry," Nurse Jasper said. "We'll take good care of you."

Then the nurse turned toward the cop. "And you quit harassing her. What's she done, anyway?"

"She's Abe Chaikin's daughter."

That stopped the pretty nurse right in her tracks. "You're kidding?"

Chief Rhodes glanced toward Lark. "Am I kidding?"

Lark shook her head.

Big mistake. Her stomach roiled, and her brains rattled. She must have made some kind of gagging noise, because when her stomach heaved an instant later, Nurse Jasper was there with a basin.

"Aw, honey," the nurse soothed, "there aren't any hotels

worth staying at around here. So I reckon you'll be sent to the nursing home in Orangeburg. Or maybe Miriam Randall and the Ladies' Auxiliary will look after you. But don't you worry. And don't you listen to Chief Rhodes, now, you hear? Because there are plenty of folks in town, like Nita Wills, who think your daddy was a hero."

CHAPTER 2

Stone and his family sat at Momma's dining table. Elbert, Stone's father, sat at one end, and Ruby, his mother, at the other. Stone and his two daughters, Haley and Lizzy, occupied space in the middle. Stone and his girls actually lived in a small rented house down the block, but they always took their meals with Momma and Daddy. Momma had been helping Stone raise his girls ever since Stone's wife, Sharon, had died in a car wreck six years ago.

Predictably, the dinner conversation turned to the stranger in town.

"She wants to do what?" Daddy said. He looked up from his plate of pot roast and gave Stone his pale-eyed, scary-Daddy look.

Stone was impervious. Daddy might look scary, but he was about as gentle as a kitten. Today he wore his "Global Warming Is Nothing Next to Eternal Damnation" T-shirt. The garment was black with white block letters and hot-rod flames curling across the chest.

"Well, I think it's nice that Abe Chaikin's daughter

wants to scatter his remains out at the golf course," Ruby said.

"What's nice about it?" Daddy asked as he scooped up a fork of butter beans and rice.

"Well, it's nice that a person of the Jewish persuasion would want to have his mortal remains scattered at the feet of Jesus. You think he accepted Our Lord as his savior before he died? You know if he did kill Zeke, but accepted the Lord, we ought to forgive him, because I know the Lord has."

"Uh, well, I don't know, but I reckon it's something to think about." Daddy chewed for a few moments as if giving the matter serious thought. "Nope, I don't think I can forgive him for beating up my daddy."

Like a bass rising to the bait, fifteen-year-old Lizzy leaned forward in her seat, her long dark hair hanging down over her face as if she were trying to hide herself behind a veil. "Granddaddy, you don't actually know that this man killed Great-Granddaddy. I mean the official cause of death was accidental, wasn't it?"

"Who knows what the official cause of death was. The fact is that Andy Bennett made the official ruling. And you can't ever trust a Bennett." Daddy gave Lizzy one of his scary stares. It bounced off Lizzy, too.

"And besides," Elbert continued between chews, "that Yankee hippie was the last person to see my daddy alive."

"That's not evidence. Is it, Daddy?" Lizzy looked up at Stone.

He was going to get drawn into this argument whether he wanted to or not. "No, it's not," Stone said.

Elbert turned his stare at Stone. "Don't encourage her, son. She's already too big for her britches."

Stone swallowed his food. "Daddy, just because you have a long-running grudge against the former sheriff of Allenberg County doesn't mean everything he did was totally wrong."

"No? I don't see you singing the praises of his idiot son any."

Stone should have seen *that* coming. Andy Bennett had been sheriff of Allenberg County for decades. And when he retired, his son ran for the position. Of course Billy was elected, seeing as his last name was Bennett. But Billy wasn't much of a cop. Stone had reserved his opinions about Billy's father, though. Andy Bennett had been sheriff when Stone was a kid.

He gave his father a pointed stare. "I know you were angry when Granddaddy died, but that's not a good reason to go off blaming folks for his death when you have no proof."

"He was only fifty-four. He should have lived for a long time."

Stone heard the unmistakable note of anger in his father's voice. Daddy was a pretty mild-mannered man. He was a good man. But he was a little eccentric. Most folks believed that Daddy's oddities were a result of his war injuries. But Daddy believed something else. The first time Daddy ever saw an angel was the night Zeke died. And Daddy had been seeing angels pretty regular ever since.

So naturally, Daddy held a grudge. Especially since Zeke died so young.

"You can believe what you want," Stone said. "But there isn't any evidence that Abe Chaikin killed Granddaddy. And to be honest, I have to believe that, if there had been proof, Sheriff Andy would have pursued it. Besides,

Chaikin's daughter was pretty surprised when I suggested that her father might have committed murder. In fact, she didn't even know that Zeke was dead. She asked to speak with him."

"Did you tell her what Nita's folks think about her father?" Momma asked.

"No, ma'am, I didn't."

Haley, Stone's eight-year-old daughter, suddenly stopped fidgeting in her chair. "Granny, did you mean Miz Wills? Miz Wills is really, really smart. All librarians are really smart."

Momma laid her fork across her plate and smiled at Haley. "Yes she is, darlin'. Now eat your pot roast." Momma rolled her eyes in Daddy's direction. "I think we've had enough of this conversation, don't you?"

"Well, maybe," Daddy grumbled.

"I'm serious, Bert, we need to let this go once and for all. Maybe letting that woman scatter her father's ashes at the golf course would be a good first step."

"I ain't letting her scatter anything there. So don't even start."

"All right." Momma turned toward Stone. "Once this woman is well enough to travel, I think maybe it would be best if you would explain the situation to her and send her on her way. It's clear that scattering her father's ashes out at the golf course is going to upset your father."

Daddy snarled at the other end of the table.

Stone nodded. All in all, that would probably be best.

Lizzy let go of one of those eloquently annoyed teen-aged sighs. "Daddy, are you just going to agree? I mean there's a big question here. Maybe her father actually did murder Zeke. Or maybe someone else did. Or maybe—"

"He fell off the roof of the Ark, honey. That's what happened," Stone said.

"Ain't no way," Daddy said. "They found him on the eighteenth hole, and there was no way his body would end up there if he fell from the roof."

"Maybe the angels put him there," Haley said.

Lizzy glared at Haley. "No one asked your opinion so—"

"Keep a civil tongue, young lady," Momma said.

"Yes'm." Lizzy looked down at her plate and hid behind her hair. Stone thought the matter was settled. But a minute later, Lizzy looked up.

"I'll try to be civil, Daddy, but there's something wrong here. I mean, if old Sheriff Andy fudged something, we ought to find that out. We didn't have a policeman in the family back when Great-Granddaddy died. You could investigate this and lay it to rest."

"It was more than forty years ago. As cold cases go, this one is practically frigid."

"But if there was an injustice done, if Zeke was murdered by someone, don't you want to know that? I mean, it probably wasn't Abe Chaikin, but what if—"

"Lizzy, this is like a stick of dynamite. Pushing an investigation would upset things in town, and I don't think Miz Chaikin came here to have her father's reputation posthumously trampled."

"She probably didn't, but that shouldn't be a reason not to find out the truth."

"No. But the timing isn't good, honey. We've got a new mayor who might object to my spending time on a forty-year-old case in which her mother played a prominent role. Right now, I want to be friends with Mayor LaFlore, not alienate her. My contract with the city comes up in the spring."

"That's not a good reason." Lizzy gave him one of those heartrending stares that convinced him he was no good as a father. He could see the disappointment in her green eyes.

But there was nothing he could do about it. Agreeing with her wasn't an option.

Haley Rhodes sat up in her bed, listening carefully. Lizzy was asleep in her bed across the room. Haley could tell by her sister's little snores.

The wind rattled the windows a bit and moonlight came through the curtains, making the room look kind of silvery.

The house made a few creaky noises. Daddy said it was just the old place settling on its foundations. Haley wasn't so sure. When the house creaked, it was kind of spooky.

Haley listened to the wind sounds, and the house sounds, and the sound of Lizzy's breathing. And she heard it—the noise that had really pulled her from sleep.

The Sorrowful Angel was weeping. Again.

The Sorrowful Angel had been with Haley for a long, long time. Haley had been trying to get her back to Heaven, but that was proving to be really hard.

Haley slipped out of her bed and padded down the hallway toward Daddy's bedroom. The door was ajar, and the flickering light of the television lit her way. Daddy often fell asleep with the television on.

She tiptoed into his bedroom.

The angel was waiting. She stood in the corner, all

twinkly and pale, her long white hair coming down to her shoulders. She always shimmered like that when the moon was shining or in the TV light. She looked the way an angel was supposed to look.

Except for the wings, of course. The Sorrowful Angel didn't have any. She was kind of like that angel in the Christmas movie that Granny always watched about the angel needing to do a good deed to get his wings.

Maybe that's what the angel needed.

Haley crossed the carpet and took the Sorrowful Angel's hand. Her hand was cold, but the angel's long fingers curled around hers and squeezed.

Haley felt safe with the angel's hand in hers. Nothing could hurt her when the angel was there. She knew this from experience. Sometimes she wondered if maybe the angel was a kind of guardian, in which case Haley probably shouldn't be working all that hard to get her back to Heaven.

On the other hand, having a weepy guardian angel was kind of a pain. People thought Haley was crazy because most of them couldn't even see the angel. So Haley had come to a firm decision this Christmas. She'd written a heartfelt letter to Santa Claus and mailed it down at the post office. And she'd written a letter to her mother and left it in a Christmas wreath down at the graveyard.

She figured, if anyone could help get the angel back to Heaven, it would be Santa. And since Momma was in Heaven with Jesus, maybe she could put in a good word, too.

Getting the angel back to Heaven was the only thing Haley wanted for Christmas. Except, of course, for the Barbie Glam Vacation House. She had kind of mentioned that in her letter to Santa, too. But only in the PS.

The angel bent down so that she was at Haley's height. She wrapped her arm around Haley's shoulder and drew her close. The hug made Haley feel all shivery inside. But it wasn't scary or anything like that.

"Your daddy needs to make room in his heart for love," the angel whispered. Her breath had no warmth to it. In fact, her whisper seemed to have come without any breath at all.

The shivers down Haley's spine got a little bigger. The angel had only spoken a couple of times before, and what she said usually didn't make much sense.

But this time, the angel had given Haley a clear mission. A really easy one, too.

She could do this. It would be simple.

Maybe she didn't need Santa after all.

The next morning, everyone in town knew that Abe Chaikin's daughter had come for a visit. So Stone wasn't at all surprised when the county dispatcher's voice crackled over the radio in his Crown Vic just as he finished his first patrol of the day. "Alpha 101 to Lima 101."

He toggled his radio. "Go ahead, Alpha 101."

"You've got a 10-25 for a signal-17 out at Lee Marshall's place."

"Ten-Four," he acknowledged.

He'd just been summoned by the big man in town.

He motored up Palmetto Avenue and headed north. Five minutes later, he turned up the drive that led to the old Marshall home place, which had been built on the foundations of Heavenly Rest, the old plantation that had once belonged to Chancellor Rhodes before the Civil War. The house, with its colonnade and wrought-iron balconies, left

Stone feeling like a poor relation, especially since it was supposed to be a replica of the earlier mansion—the one that had belonged to Stone's forebears.

The place looked decidedly festive. The five Doric columns that spanned the front of the Greek Revival home were swathed in red ribbon, making them look like candy canes. Holly swags topped every one of the six-over-six double-hung windows. A wreath the size of Alaska hung on the door.

Lee was waiting for him on the porch, sitting in a straight-backed rocker with a plaid blanket across his lap. Last night's rain had given way to a bright, sunny, and unseasonably warm day, perfect for porch sitting.

Lee was in his middle sixties, but the years had not been kind to him. He was fond of bourbon, and the booze had taken a toll on his face. Broken blood vessels gave his nose a red sheen. It was a well-known fact that Momma had turned down Lee's proposal of marriage more than forty years ago in order to follow the advice of Miriam Randall.

And for that reason, Lee Marshall had never been particularly friendly to Stone. Not that Lee was a particularly friendly man.

"Nice porch weather for December," Stone said with a little deferential tip of his hat.

"Don't talk to me about the weather," Lee growled. He waved toward the rocking chair beside him, but Stone ignored the invitation and leaned back on one of the porch columns.

"What can I do for you, Mr. Marshall?"

"You can run that woman out of town."

Stone thought about playing it straight and asking

Lee who he was talking about. But he just didn't have the
energy for one of Lee's cat-and-mouse games.

"Lark Chaikin is sick right at the moment. Can't
exactly do anything about her until she recovers."

"Well, it's damnably inconvenient."

Stone said nothing. Arguing with Lee about the state
of the Chaikin woman's health was just a waste of time.

"When she recovers, you need to tell her what's what."

"Okay, Lee, you mind telling me what's what first, so
I get it right?" Damn. He hadn't bothered to disguise the
sarcasm in his voice.

"You're asking me that seriously? After what happened? I would think your people would be happy to see
her leave."

Stone made no comment on the snide reference to his
people. "I get why my daddy wants her gone, but why you?"

"You know as good as I do that this woman is a walking time bomb. We don't need to revisit that sad time in
our history. It would be a distraction."

"A distraction from what?"

Lee glowered. "Don't be stupid. Last Chance has a new
mayor who doesn't want to deal with this woman. And I
don't want Kamaria to have to. So, if you know what's good
for you, you'll run her out of town. You got that, boy?"

Stone fixed his expression. There was no point in
letting Lee know just what he thought of him. Lee was
an a-hole, but he was powerful. His son, Jimmy, owned
Country Pride Chicken, the biggest employer in the
county. And the Marshalls had been running this town for
as long as anyone could remember.

To make matters even more complicated, Daddy was
now beholden to Jimmy Marshall's wife, Hettie, who

chaired the Committee to Resurrect Golfing for God. Jimmy and Hettie had been estranged for the last several months, but the scuttlebutt around town was that they had reconciled. So making nice to Lee, Jimmy, and Hettie was in Stone's best interest.

Not to mention the fact that Kamaria LaFlore, the mayor-elect and soon to be Stone's boss, had her own good reasons for wanting Lark Chaikin gone.

"I hear you, Lee," Stone said.

"That's good. You keep me apprised of this situation, and you have a real nice day."

Stone knew a dismissal when he heard one. He turned and headed back to his cruiser, his annoyance growing with each step he took.

He was not going to be pushed around by Lee Marshall, or Jimmy, or Hettie, or even Mayor-Elect LaFlore. In fact, the more they protested, the more he was starting to think that Lizzy was right.

Maybe he should dig up those old files and see what had happened in 1968.

CHAPTER 3

Lark opened her eyes. Pale winter sunshine slanted through the curved turret windows to her right. Spanish-moss-laden branches waved beyond the windowpanes. The dance of branches and sun made a pattern across the dusky green carpet of the room where she had been sleeping and sweating out a raging fever. She didn't feel feverish anymore. Just tired. The nightmares had taken a lot out of her.

"You feeling better?" a voice asked from her left.

Lark shifted her gaze from the oak windowsills to the wizened lady sitting beside her bed.

"You remember me, don't you?" The little old lady gazed at Lark from behind a pair of upturned trifocals decorated with rhinestones. She wore her white hair parted down the middle, with twin braids pulled up over her head like a crown. Her skin was ivory, with a network of lines radiating from her eyes and the corners of her mouth. It was a good face, a kind face. The lines and wrinkles told of a life well lived. Lark wanted to capture her portrait.

This old lady had been holding Lark's hand on and off during the nightmares.

"How long have I been out of it?" Lark asked.

"Oh, a day or so. It's Sunday, December sixteenth. Christmas is almost upon us."

Lark studied her surroundings: old-lady wallpaper and Victorian furniture. "Where am I?" she asked, pushing herself up in the bed.

Lark's caregiver rested a pair of arthritic hands on an aluminum cane. Her nails were painted bright red, which clashed with her 1980s-vintage, purple plaid pantsuit. "Oh," the lady said, waving one hand, "this is Randall House. Back a hundred years ago, it used to be a hotel for the folks who traveled the railroad. We sometimes take in boarders for short periods. Doc Cooper sent you here because there was no room at the nursing home, and the hospital in Orangeburg didn't think you were sick enough to take in. We've been nursing you for a couple of days."

"Who's we?"

"The ladies of the Christ Church Auxiliary."

Oh. My. God. She was in the hands of good Christian women. Who knew the Bible Belt was really like this? She pasted a smile on her face. "Oh. Well, thank you."

"It's nothing, darlin'. Helping out poor wayfarers is a joy, especially this time of year."

The woman wasn't even being ironic or sarcastic.

"Thank you," Lark said again because it seemed appropriate.

A pang of grief hit her chest as Lark fluffed up her pillows and leaned back on them. For a little while she had forgotten that Pop was dead. Where the hell *was* Pop?

"You wouldn't happen to know where my car is?"

"Oh, don't you worry. Your car's in the lot down at Bill's Grease Pit. Your daddy's remains and your camera equipment have been removed, of course. No sense in tempting fate." The old woman gestured toward a rosewood armoire that matched the dresser and the bed. "We reckoned you'd want to keep your daddy close. And, what with all the upset forty years ago, Stony felt it might not be a good idea to leave his ashes laying around. No telling what some folks might do, even if we have, more or less, turned the page on the past."

"Stony? The chief of police?" A mental image of Carmine Falcone filled Lark's head.

"Yes, ma'am. He is." The little lady gave Lark a smile as mysterious as Mona Lisa's.

"Um...I didn't get your name," Lark said.

"Oh, darlin', I'm sorry. I'm Miriam Randall, and this is my house."

"Oh. Well. I'm sorry for imposing. I—"

"Oh, it's no imposition. You were pretty sick. I'm guessing you let yourself get worn out in the days before your daddy passed. What did he die of? He wouldn't have been very old."

"Cancer, and he was only sixty-two."

"I figured it had to be something like that. And you were at his side?"

Lark nodded. Miriam Randall might look like a harmless old lady, but she had mad skills as an interrogator.

"And your momma?" Miriam asked.

"She died a long time ago, when I was a kid." Lark looked down at herself. She was wearing a pink cotton nightgown that didn't belong to her. It looked exactly like the sort of thing a little old lady would wear. If the guys at the Baghdad Hilton ever saw her in something pink and frilly like this, she'd be laughed right out of the brotherhood of war correspondents.

"You should know that everyone in town is dying to know why your daddy wanted to have his remains scattered on the eighteenth hole," Miriam said.

Lark looked up. "And how does the entire town know of my father's last request?"

"Darlin', this is Last Chance, South Carolina," Miriam said. "News travels faster here than it does on The Facebook, or whatever you young 'uns call that thing. Of course, the speed of the gossip probably has something to do with the fact that, around here, your daddy is somewhat notorious."

"Notorious? Really? I didn't think his books were that controversial."

Miriam frowned. "Books? What books?"

"Pop's pen name was Vitto Giancola. He was the author of the Carmine Falcone mysteries."

Miriam's brown eyes lit up. "Oh, my goodness. I just love Carmine Falcone."

"Of course you do."

Miriam must have heard the sarcasm in Lark's tone. "Honey, I wasn't talking about that pretty-boy actor who plays Carmine in the TV show. I was talking about the Carmine Falcone in the books. Now, there's a man who is sexy and complicated. You know, the kind of man who doesn't say much, but manages to speak volumes with his actions."

For an old lady, Miriam was remarkably with it. "Yeah," Lark said, "but being an author didn't make Pop notorious."

"Well," Miriam replied, "when I said notorious, I meant that back in 1968 he took Nita Wills to breakfast at the Kountry Kitchen. I tell you, Lark, when Nita sat down at that lunch counter she stirred up a big heap of trouble. See, Nita is black."

"But it was 1968. Wasn't the Civil Rights Act passed in '64?"

"Well, we aren't at the cutting edge of things here," Miriam said. "By '68, Clyde Anderson, the owner of the Kountry Kitchen, had taken down his offensive 'whites only' sign. But no one really wanted to test Clyde's commitment to integration. The irony is that a year later Clyde died, and T-Bone Carter bought the place. It would probably have served us right if T-Bone had put up a sign saying 'African-Americans only.' The Kountry Kitchen is the only real café in town, unless you count the doughnut shop."

"And people here still remember that? After all this time?"

The little lady leaned forward. "You know, darlin', we probably would have forgotten all about it, but your daddy disappeared the same day he challenged our social order. And that would be the same day Zeke Rhodes died. You can imagine how people put two and two together."

"Just because he left the same day?"

"Well now, you see, your daddy was what some folks referred to as a no-good Yankee hippie. And some ignorant folks believed that Nita wouldn't have done what she did except that your daddy put her up to it. God help us when the ignoramuses band together—they go looking for someone to blame. And since Zeke had let your daddy camp out at Golfing for God, I'm thinking old Zeke might just have gotten himself in the middle of trouble that wasn't his. Of course, that's not the official story. The official story is that, within a twenty-four-hour period, the rednecks ran your daddy out of town. Nita's mother put her on the next bus heading toward Chicago, where her aunt lived. And Zeke died in an accidental fall out at Golfing for God."

"That's a lot."

"Yes, ma'am, it is. So you can imagine that there are some folks in this town, notably Elbert Rhodes, the current owner of Golfing for God, who think your daddy was responsible for Zeke's death. There is another group of folks who think maybe Zeke got into an altercation with a group of idiots. So, you see, any light you could shed on this would solve a long-standing town mystery."

"Mrs. Randall, I hate to disappoint you. I don't know a thing about Pop's stay in Last Chance. All I'm sure of is that Pop didn't murder anyone. He could be a real pain in the neck, but he wasn't mean or violent."

Just then, the door opened, and a zaftig woman with blue-gray hair stepped into the room bearing a bed table and tray. She wore a printed polyester dress splashed with blue flowers that did nothing for her larger-than-life figure.

"Ah," the woman said, stepping across the room in her old-lady flats. "I see our patient is awake."

She placed the bed table over Lark's legs. On the tray was a breakfast that would never get the American Heart Association's seal of approval: eggs, bacon, biscuits, and a bowl of something that looked like Cream of Wheat with a large pat of butter melting in it.

"I'm Lillian Bray, chair of the Christ Church Ladies' Auxiliary," polyester lady said.

"Hi, I'm Lark. Thanks for taking care of me. And, um, is that grits?"

"You've never eaten grits, have you?" Lillian asked.

"No, I haven't. I usually have a bagel and a cup of coffee. I'm not much of a breakfast eater."

"Oh," Lillian said, "I didn't think. You don't eat bacon either, do you?"

Lark looked up, right into Lillian's blue eyes. The woman's concern over Lark's dietary habits masked something else. There was just a hint of uneasiness in Lillian's gaze, as if she didn't like outsiders, or maybe she didn't care for people who weren't exactly like her.

Or maybe she was just worried that she'd made a big mistake.

Lark needed to quit projecting things onto people. It was a sure sign that she'd spent too much time knocking around places where people went to war over small, insignificant differences.

Well, at least she could put Lillian's fear about her dietary restrictions to rest. She smiled and picked up a thick slice of bacon. "That rumor about my being a vegetarian is completely untrue," Lark said between chews.

Lillian seemed a little nonplussed by Lark's snappy comeback. She cleared her throat. "I reckon that's a good thing. I mean, seeing as pork is one of the staples of our diet."

"Yes, and it's very nice to be in a place where bacon is readily available. You should try ordering a BLT in Baghdad."

Lillian dropped her bulk into an empty chair on the other side of the bed. "So you're not Jewish?"

"Nope," Lark said. It was amazing how one little word eliminated the need to explain how Pop had been born Jewish and died an atheist, or how Mom had been born Catholic and died a Buddhist. Or how, as a kid, Lark had been dragged off to Humanist Sunday School at the Ethical Culture Society. Best to enjoy the bacon and keep her mouth shut.

"Lark was just telling me that her daddy went on to become Vitto Giancola, the author of those mystery books," Miriam said into the sudden silence.

Lillian's gaze narrowed. "You don't say so. The Carmine Falcone stories? Oh, I just love that TV show. Clint Burroughs is so handsome, don't you think?"

Neither Miriam nor Lark answered Lillian's rhetorical question.

After another awkward moment, Miriam once again picked up the stalled conversation. "You've been through a lot lately, haven't you, Lark?" she said.

Lark went on alert, pausing in the middle of slathering butter on a biscuit. She didn't look up.

"So," Miriam continued in a leading tone, "those cameras look like something a professional would have. Are you a photographer?"

Lark nodded and took a bite out of the biscuit. It practically melted in her mouth, no doubt because it was made with copious quantities of lard or something. No one cooked with lard where Lark came from. She concentrated on the heavenly taste of the food and remained silent.

The conversation stalled completely until Miriam said, "You know, honey, I'm thinking that you need to find someone who understands you. Someone you can talk honestly with."

Lark looked up from her breakfast right into the glittering eyes of Miriam Randall. "What do you mean? Like a therapist?"

"Why, do you need a therapist?"

Lark's face burned, but she said nothing.

Miriam shook her head. "No, I was thinking that you need to be on the lookout for a lost friend. Someone you may have missed or overlooked. Someone who understands you and your demons."

Lillian straightened in her chair. "Demons?"

Miriam snorted. "Not demons from hell, Lillian. I was talking about the other kind."

"Are there any other kind?" Lillian gave Lark another assessing gaze, as if she were searching Lark's forehead for horns.

"Well," Miriam said. "I was talking about the demons that people create for themselves."

Lark put down the half-eaten biscuit, her appetite suddenly vanishing. "Excuse me, but I don't think I've created any demons for myself. And why do you even think I have demons?"

"Because you do," Miriam said, her deep brown eyes clear and sober.

Lark looked away. The old lady liked to meddle in other people's business, didn't she? "Any demons I have were created by the bad guys," Lark finally said.

"Bad guys?" Lillian asked.

"Yeah, like Muammar Gaddafi and the warring factions in Libya last April."

Lillian's mouth dropped open, but Miriam seemed unfazed. She leaned in and patted Lark on her blanket-covered leg. "Honey, you should be looking for someone to talk to. Someone who can help you find your balance again."

"Well, I'll be," Lillian said. "Is this one of your matches, Miriam?"

"What?" Lark asked.

"Oh, well, sometimes the Lord gives me hints about the kind of match a person should be looking for in life. And when I get a hint like that, I do my best to pass on the advice."

"You're kidding, right?" Holy crap, these nice Christian ladies were like a bunch of yentas.

"Miriam never kids, do you?" Lillian said to her friend.

"No, I don't," Miriam said.

"Uh, look, ladies, I have no interest in romance. I'm thirty-six, a respected photojournalist, and I'm completely happy with my life."

Miriam turned her gaze on Lark like a laser beam, slicing her open for the world to inspect. "Are you really happy with your life?"

"Daddy, I need the computer," Lizzy said as she walked into the little den off the front parlor.

"I'm almost finished," Stone said as he continued to stare at the screen in front of him, both amazed and humbled by the image there.

"What are you doing?" Lizzy came up behind him and stared at the screen. "I didn't know you were all that interested in the famine in Somalia."

"I'm not," he said. Riveted by the image of a young woman holding an infant who was small, starving, and obviously ill. The woman evoked the Madonna. The photo was disturbing, but he couldn't look away. There was an expression in the mother's eyes as she looked down at her infant that was so tender and so full of love and hope.

Lizzy leaned over his shoulder. "Oh, that's the photo that UNICEF used on its posters this October."

"What posters?"

"You know, at Halloween. The kids in the service club sponsored a schoolwide fast to raise awareness. Everyone was asked to donate their lunch money. It's totally a shame. You know, millions of people have died, and the famine hardly gets a mention on the evening news."

"How do you know these things? You're just a kid."

She rolled her eyes and flipped her hair and gave him that chin-up defiant stare. "I'm older than you seem to think. I read *The New York Times* every day. I edit the news and politics section of the school newspaper. I'm well informed."

Stone blinked. He was obviously not paying enough attention to Lizzy. She was growing up in front of his eyes. She looked like him, but in a lot of ways she was so much like her mother. Paying attention to starving kids in Africa was just the kind of thing Sharon did. Sharon had been his beautiful crusader.

"Why are you suddenly interested in the famine?" Lizzy asked.

"I'm not. These photos were taken by Lark Chaikin."

"What?"

He turned back toward the computer and opened another browser tab. This one showed two soldiers wearing battle gear and full camouflage. They were holding on to each other. Their eyes were closed, the emotions playing across their faces raw and arresting. Framed in the background was a rifle, bayonet impaled in the sand, with a helmet resting on the stock and a pair of boots lined up beside it.

"Wow," Lizzy said.

"Yeah." Stone didn't need to say much more than that. You couldn't possibly explain in words what those soldiers were feeling. But the photo explained it. Strong emotions churned in Stone's gut. He'd been to war. He'd lost buddies. He knew.

It wasn't an easy photo to look at. Lark had captured the spirit of brotherhood that exists in every battle-tested unit. The humanity of the soldiers sang from the image.

"Did Ms. Chaikin take this photograph, too?"

"Yeah. She did. She won a Pulitzer Prize for this one."

"Wow. I didn't know she was a photojournalist."

"Apparently one of the best. She specializes in wars and disasters. And she's been through a wringer recently. Look." He clicked on another web page. This one had a photo of Lark dressed in battle fatigues, a helmet, and a flak jacket. She was covered in blood.

"Oh, my God, was she wounded?"

"No, she was with those journalists in Libya earlier this year. You know, when the TV guy was killed. She was one of the eyewitnesses." And by the deer-in-the-headlights look on her face, she'd seen some pretty gruesome things.

"Oh," Lizzy breathed out.

"Yeah."

"You're checking up on her, aren't you?" Lizzy said.

He shrugged. "That's what I do."

"Well, that totally stinks. She rocks as a photographer. All she wants is to lay her father to rest. You and Grand-daddy should let her do it. Ashes are just dust anyway. What's the harm?

"But, oh no, instead you're in here conducting an investigation into her past, like she's carrying some kind of plague or she's a bad influence. As you can see, she's not. She's pretty brave and talented."

Lizzy shook her head. "Sometimes I hate living in this

town. People just don't seem to be able to let go of the past and move on. You know that?" Lizzy's voice cracked, and her composure slipped.

Before he could even formulate something useful to say, Lizzy turned on her heel and stalked out of the room in a huff. Damn, she was angry at him again. And that was strange because he actually agreed with her.

Sometimes he hated living in this town, too.

CHAPTER 4

David Raab opened his locker and found the note inside. The language was mean and hate-filled. He stood there with his hands shaking, feeling scared and out of place.

Maybe he should talk to Dr. Williams, the principal of Jefferson Davis High School. This new note was covered in swastikas.

Dr. Williams, an African-American, would be horrified by the notes. But that made going to him even more difficult. David had a feeling the idiots expected him to say something to the authorities. Doing that would only escalate the situation.

And besides, he didn't want Mom to know about these notes. Mom would get angry. And she'd probably blame Dad. And Dad needed the job he'd gotten here in South Carolina. David didn't want to be the reason Mom finally made good on her threats to leave Dad and take David and his brothers back to Michigan.

He didn't want to be the reason Dad gave up his job either. It was a good job, supervising the construction of a new textile machinery plant. Dad was a talented engineer, but he had been unemployed for more than a year, all because Mom had been unwilling to relocate. They had come here to South Carolina because Dad had finally put his foot down—and because this particular job paid more than Dad had ever made working for Ford Motor Company.

No, David was not about to tell Mom or Dad or Dr. Williams about the notes. He was going to do his best to fit in.

Just then, Lizzy Rhodes strode up to the locker next to his and completely distracted him. He tucked the note into the back of his locker with the other ones he'd received and grabbed his social studies notebook. He closed his locker, then snuck a look at Lizzy.

She was wearing a short skirt, a pair of black tights, and a dark sweater. The outfit was part Goth and part Emo and totally awesome and unique because Lizzy wasn't a Goth or Emo. She was just herself. Kind of weird. And opinionated. And smarter than all the other girls.

And she had a pair of awesome green eyes.

David wanted to be her friend. But Lizzy intimidated him. Just being near her made his heart pound and his mouth get all dry and cottony.

Uh-oh. She had noticed him looking at her. His face got hot. "Hi," he murmured, shifting his gaze away.

"Hey," she said in that soft, amazing drawl of hers.

He looked back. She smiled. David's day improved three hundred percent.

"You going to the editorial meeting today after school?" he asked. Jeez, what a lame question. Of course she was coming to the meeting after school. She was the assistant editor of the politics and nation section of the school newspaper. She probably thought he was a complete dork.

She banged her locker closed and looked straight at him. He had to raise his own gaze to meet hers. His whole body flushed. Why had he even looked at her? She was too good for him.

"Yeah, I'll be there," she said, oblivious to the mayhem she was creating inside him. She looked so cool and confident.

He expected her to hurry off to her first-period class. But she hesitated for a minute, leaning her hip into her locker. "Guess what?"

"What?" he said, utterly amazed that Lizzy Rhodes was actually talking to him.

"There's a Pulitzer Prize–winning photographer staying in Last Chance," she said.

"Really? Here?"

"Yeah, I know, compared to Michigan we're a little off the beaten track."

His face flamed so hot that even his ears started to burn. He shouldn't have said that. She thought he was a snob. But he wasn't. He was just surprised. Ann Arbor wasn't a big town, but it had a university. Last Chance was tiny. In the middle of nowhere.

Right, that was the sort of stuff Mom was saying all the time. Mom hated living here, and she never stopped whining about it.

"Uh, I didn't mean that the way it—"

"Yeah, you totally did. You're always talking about Michigan. But it's okay. I know what it's like to move away from home. And besides, we don't get semi-famous photographers through here very often because it's a fact that Allenberg County is totally in the boonies."

"Are you teasing me?" he asked, suddenly forlorn. Lizzy had this way of talking that was kind of snarky and wise. He never knew if she was kidding about things.

"Why would I tease you?"

He shrugged. *Because girls always do.*

She let go of a sigh that sounded totally exasperated. "No, David, I am not teasing," she said, rolling her eyes a little bit. He wanted to slink away.

That's when she reached out and patted his arm. Her touch made him freeze in place. "It's okay. I like you, David. There *is* a professional photographer in town. Her name is Lark Chaikin. I looked her up online last night. She's photographed wars and famines and stuff like that. And her father is semi-notorious."

"For what?" His arm was tingling where she had touched him.

"For taking Nita Wills to breakfast at the Kountry Kitchen in 1968. In those days, the Kitchen was owned by a white man, and Nita is African-American."

"Oh." David wasn't sure exactly how to react to that. "Why's this photographer here?"

"It's weird. Her father died, and she wants to scatter his ashes at Golfing for God."

He almost laughed before he remembered that Lizzy's grandfather owned Golfing for God. He pressed his lips together.

"It's okay, David, you can laugh. I think the situation is totally hilarious myself. The guy wants to have his ashes scattered on the hole depicting the resurrection, and according to my grandmother, Abe Chaikin has never been a Christian."

"He's a Jew?"

She leaned in a little closer. "According to the rumors around town he was. Daddy says maybe not. Granny says he probably had a conversion. I personally think there's more to this story than the grown-ups are telling me. I'm thinking we should team up, do some investigative work, maybe interview Ms. Chaikin for the paper. You could take some head shots of her, you know."

"We?" David's heart took flight in his chest. He'd been wanting to find some way to make friends with Lizzy for weeks. But she was cool, and he was kind of a geek with braces on his teeth. Why was she even talking to him?

"Don't you want to talk to a Pulitzer Prize–winning photographer?" Lizzy asked. "I just figured that you'd jump at the chance. I mean, you're always lugging around that camera of yours."

He touched the Canon SLR with the telephoto lens that his father had given him as a consolation prize when he'd announced that he was taking the job in South Carolina. David wore it around his neck almost all the time. "Yeah. Talking to a professional photojournalist would be awesome," he said.

"So, let's propose an interview for the school paper today at the editorial meeting. I'll write the story, and you take the head shots."

"Okay."

The bell rang. "Darn, I'm late for biology. We're dissecting earthworms today." She made a yucky face.

"It's not so bad. Just hold your breath when you make the first incision, otherwise the formaldehyde will get to you. Also, they don't wiggle when they're dead."

She stared at him like he was a dweeb. "Thanks for

44 *Hope Ramsay*

the advice." She started down the hallway then stopped and turned. "For the record, David, I'm not like those city girls you know. I don't mind wiggly live worms. My daddy taught me how to bait a hook when I was about four. Do you know how to bait a hook?"

Damn. He'd blown it, hadn't he? "Uh, no, my parents don't go fishing. My mother knits, though." Someone please shut his mouth before he made a complete ass of himself. "I'll see you later?" he said.

"Yeah."

She turned and strode off toward the biology classroom. He watched her go, admiring the swing of her hips, the way she kept her head up, even if she wasn't in with the popular kids. He liked her so much. There was something genuinely mysterious about a girl who knew how to ride a horse, bait a fishing hook, and was smarter than anyone else on the school paper.

His day might have gotten off to an incredibly awesome start if it hadn't been for the sudden, unwelcome appearance of Michael Bennett, wearing his Davis High letter jacket and a stupid porkpie hat tilted over his eyes. Michael was a senior, a member of the football team, and the Davis High homecoming king. Michael traveled in a social set so far above David that David probably should genuflect whenever in Michael's presence. He was school royalty.

And David was like a serf.

"You can forget about her," Michael said as he leaned against the wall, blocking David's view of Lizzy's retreating back.

David swallowed but didn't respond. There was nothing he could say to Michael that wouldn't get him into trouble.

Michael grinned. His teeth were perfect. "You heard me, didn't you?" Michael asked.

"Yeah," David said, his heart suddenly hammering in his ears.

"Good. Because she's too good for you."

On Monday morning, Lark left her sickbed and walked into town. The day was sunny and warm, like the first day of spring, not mid-December.

The unseasonable weather hadn't stopped the locals from decking out the two-block expanse of Palmetto Avenue in every manner of Christmas tinsel, lights, ribbon, and wreath. Not to mention the fiberglass sleigh with Santa and nine reindeer that hung across the main drag. The lead reindeer had a red bulb for a nose that Lark was pretty sure lit up the street from end to end. She strolled up the street toward the Kountry Kitchen, the first step of her new plan to figure out why Pop had asked to have his ashes scattered on a miniature golf course at the feet of a fiberglass Jesus.

The café had gold tinsel draped across its awning and a big red bow stuck on its door. A bell on the bow jingled as she entered the restaurant. New Yorkers would love this place. They'd think it was trendy and retro in a *Mad Men* kind of way. It certainly had a lot of stainless steel and red Formica.

Lark headed for the lunch counter and took a seat. As her *tuchis* hit the vinyl seat cover, it occurred to her that Pop might have sat at this exact spot with Nita Wills back in 1968.

Her gut burned with the thought. She was so angry at Pop—for keeping his secret. For dying before his time.

For leaving her utterly alone in the world. And for a really long list of other things that had stood between them for so many years.

"Welcome to the Kountry Kitchen. What can I getcha?"

Lark looked up into the face of a thirty-something woman with platinum blond hair that didn't look entirely natural. Her name badge said "Ricki." And she had that small-town look about her—one part curiosity and nine parts get-out-of-town. It was clear Ricki already knew everything she needed to know about Lark.

Lark wondered what kind of reaction she'd get if she ordered a bagel with cream cheese and lox. Then she thought about her encounter with Lillian yesterday morning and rejected the idea. People were uncomfortable about her being here. There was no need to flaunt her differences. She smiled up into the waitress's gray, kohl-ringed eyes. "I'll have some whole wheat toast with butter on the side, a glass of orange juice, and a cup of coffee, please."

The waitress hesitated for an instant, her gaze flicking over Lark in frank inspection. The woman cataloged everything: her old coat, her spiky hair, and her nails, chewed to the quick. The inspection made Lark feel unwelcome. That was hardly surprising seeing as Pop had come here and upset the order of things. It was to be expected.

Still, it made her feel lonely somehow.

"That's all you want?" Ricki asked.

"Well, I wouldn't mind some information."

"About what?"

"About my father's visit to Last Chance back in 1968."

Ricki's eyes went wide. "Um, uh, well, I wasn't even

born in 1968. So I can't help you with that. Let me just get your coffee." Ricki turned away and made a beeline to the coffeemaker, leaving Lark to wonder about Pop's infamy in this town. Pop would have enjoyed the notoriety, but Lark didn't. Not in the least.

Just then, the Christmas bell on the front door trilled. Lark turned. The local law strode through the door. Stone Rhodes wore his buff-colored uniform like a warrior. He was harder and more mature than the kids Lark had been embedded with in Iraq and Afghanistan, but the military bearing and haircut were absolutely the same.

His steps faltered for a moment when he saw her sitting at the counter. Then he squared his shoulders and advanced on her, taking his Stetson off as his long legs ate up the distance. The hat left a small red indentation on his forehead that Lark found oddly seductive.

His stare was as sober as the black coffee Ricki served up in crockery mugs. There wasn't anything about his bearing or gaze that spoke of weakness. He not only looked like Carmine Falcone, he had the whole he-man, alpha-male, in-charge, slow-talking, take-no-prisoners attitude going. And all that without a Jersey accent.

He dropped the hat on the counter and sat on the stool beside her. "Morning," he said in a deep voice filled with the blurred vowels of the South. "Glad to see you're feeling better."

Heat rushed through her. Chief Rhodes was handsome, and built, and reeked of testosterone and other male pheromones. And—judging by the wedding band on his third finger—he was also married.

Disappointment extinguished the fire burning in her middle.

Ricki intruded at that moment. "Hey, Stone, you want the usual?" she asked.

The chief nodded.

Not a man of many words, then. She liked him even more. A companionable silence settled over them as he drank his coffee. And she surreptitiously studied the pattern of his closely shaved beard. He looked so much like her fantasy that she had to stop herself from reaching out to touch his cheek to make sure he was real.

She picked up her toast and munched for a moment.

"That all you eating?" The chief finally spoke.

She nodded. "I'm not much of a breakfast eater."

"By the looks of it, you aren't much of an eater, eater."

Chief Rhodes sounded like Miriam Randall. Kind of motherly, despite the weaponry at his hip. She needed to back away. "So, have you told everyone in town why I'm here?"

His laugh sounded like a deep, rumbling earthquake. "Not exactly."

"No?"

"No, ma'am. But Lillian and Miriam and Annie are all members of the auxiliary. And what one of those women knows, all of them know." He paused a moment, taking another gulp of coffee. "Speaking of the ladies, I'm surprised they let you out of their sight."

"I made a jail break. Miriam wanted to force-feed me more scrambled eggs."

"Hmm." He nodded. Heat poured off his body. "So, have the ladies tried matching you up with anyone yet?"

She almost spewed her coffee all over the counter.

"Ah ha, I see they have. And what did Miriam tell you?"

Like she was going to sit there at the lunch counter and tell Carmine's doppelgänger that she needed to find someone she could talk to about the nightmares and the flashbacks. Not in this lifetime. "I think I'll keep what Miriam said to myself."

He snorted. "Good luck with that."

She rolled her eyes in his direction. He was staring straight ahead. There were sparrow tracks at the corner of his mouth and eyes. They spoke of a life lived soberly. His face was like a storybook. She could get caught up in it and forget about what was real.

She changed the subject. "I was wondering if you could tell me where I could find your father?"

A deadly spark ignited in his eyes. "Talking to Daddy wouldn't be such a good idea."

"Why not?"

"Because he isn't going to give you permission to scatter your father's ashes at Golfing for God."

At that moment, Ricki showed up with a big plate of biscuits and gravy. She put them down in front of Stone with a flirty smile and a wink. The chief was oblivious to Ricki's antics. Instead he tucked in to his breakfast like a hungry man.

"I'd still like to talk to your father about it," Lark said after a moment spent watching him eat.

He swallowed a bite of biscuit. "He's not going to change his mind. You should scatter your father's ashes to the wind somewhere. He's dead. He's not going to know the difference."

She looked away. It was true. But she'd made a promise. "I can't give up on Pop's last request. You can understand that, can't you?"

He put his coffee mug down. "I guess. You can find Daddy out at the golf course today. But if you want my advice, you'd be better off going home for the holidays. Daddy is stubborn as a mule on this subject."

"And I'm patient." Lark refrained from explaining that she didn't really have a home and never celebrated the holidays.

"Just how long are you planning to stay?" he asked.

"Until December twenty-fourth. I have a plane to catch in DC on the twenty-fifth."

"On Christmas Day?"

She shrugged. "That gives me a week to work on your father."

"Good luck."

"Any ideas on a place to stay? I don't want to impose on Miriam for a week."

"Well, I wouldn't recommend the Peach Blossom Motor Court. They rent rooms by the hour, if you know what I mean. You'll have to go to Orangeburg."

"Thanks." She stood up and threw a ten-dollar bill on the counter.

"There's one other thing," Chief Rhodes said, turning on his stool and looking up at her with a green-eyed glare. "There are folks in this town who think your daddy was some kind of hero, and others who wish he'd never come to town. Most of these folks are older than sixty. The rest of us have moved on. Last Chance has had African-American mayors since the mid-1990s, our town council looks like a rainbow. This café has been owned and operated by T-Bone Carter since 1970, and he's the great-grandson of a slave. This isn't the same place your daddy visited in the 1960s and I'm not going to stand by and let some fool Yankee come into my town and stir up trouble. Are we clear on that?"

"Fool Yankee? Really? I see that certain stereotypes are still alive and well in Last Chance." She smiled as she said it.

He frowned. "Uh, I mean..."

"It's okay. I'm not offended. But do me a favor. Don't confuse me with my father. He was a troublemaker. I'm not. I just want to scatter my father's ashes. If you let me do that, I'll get out of your hair and return north of the Mason-Dixon line as fast as I can drive."

She turned on her heel and left him to his breakfast.

CHAPTER 5

Lark arrived at Golfing for God and found it a hub of renovation activity. The parking lot was so crowded with pickup trucks and heavy equipment that she had to park on the shoulder across the highway.

She wandered through the construction site until she discovered Elbert Rhodes in a small, cluttered office located on the ground floor of the Ark. He was big-boned, with iron gray hair that he wore in a braid down his back. His goatee and black T-shirt gave him the appearance of one of those Vietnam-vet biker dudes who descended on Washington every Memorial Day. Of course, not many of those biker boys wore T-shirts that said "1 cross, 3 nails = 4given."

Maybe that meant she could appeal to his sense of forgiveness and get her grim chore taken care of.

"Mr. Rhodes, can we talk?" she asked.

He looked up from his computer screen. His eyes were the palest shade of gray, verging on silver. He looked almost wolf-like. It didn't make Lark feel any more confident.

"I'm Lark Chaikin," she said, sticking out her hand.

He stood up and took her hand. She was struck immediately by the warmth of him. Like his son, Elbert Rhodes seemed to have some kind of internal furnace that radiated heat.

"I know what you want," he said, then gestured toward a battered wooden chair that sat beside his messy desk. "Have a seat."

"I spoke with Stone this morning," Lark said. "He told me you were opposed to me scattering my father's ashes on the eighteenth hole. I came to find out why."

Elbert leaned forward. "I think you know good and well why. And I'm not going to change my mind. You should get in your big car and head back to New York or wherever you came from."

Lark gritted her teeth. What was this negative thing everyone in town had for New Yorkers and "Yankees"? Had folks treated Pop this way, too? If they had, why did he want to come back here at the end?

She smiled at Elbert and tried her best to reach him despite his prejudices. "Miriam Randall gave me her version of the story. So I gather that you think my father was responsible for Zeke Rhodes's death. But I know that can't be possible. Pop could be a difficult man, but he was not a murderer. He fought injustice all his life."

"I didn't say your daddy was a murderer. But when he decided to fight injustice here in 1968, he stepped on a hornet's nest. And his actions had unforeseen consequences—like my daddy ending up dead."

"If the consequences were unforeseen, then—"

"Why the devil did your father want to have his remains left here, anyway?" Elbert seemed visibly upset.

She backed away. "I'm sorry. I don't want to upset you.

But I don't know why he asked me to do this. It was his last request. I see that you loved your father. I loved my father, too. Even though he was not an easy man to love sometimes."

"I'm sorry. I can't help you. I never met your father. I wasn't here when Daddy died."

"How can you judge my father if you never met him and don't really know what happened?"

Elbert leaned forward, and his wolf-like gaze sent a shiver down Lark's spine. This man was filled with animosity. "All I know is that Daddy didn't slip from any ladder out here. That's just ridiculous. And your daddy was camping out here for a few days, just before Daddy died. So I figure your daddy was involved."

She let go of a sigh of frustration. "Mr. Rhodes, I made a promise to my father. And I'm going to do whatever I can to keep it, even if it means digging up stuff that you and your son don't want exposed. I really don't want to make trouble. I would really much prefer to compromise. I could just scatter Pop's ashes, say a few words, and then leave. No one has to know."

"No, that won't work. It's not my decision alone."

"What?"

He shook his head. "No. See, when the storm came through last year and damaged the golf course, I didn't have any insurance. So the town created a nonprofit committee to raise money for this renovation we've got going. The committee owns a portion of the golf course now. I can't just agree to have ashes scattered here, especially if the person is Abe Chaikin. I'd have to take your request to the chair of the Committee to Resurrect Golfing for God."

"Who's the chairman?"

"Chairwoman. Her name is Hettie Marshall."

"She's another member of the Ladies' Auxiliary, isn't she?"

"Yes, ma'am."

"Where can I find her?"

"Probably at home. Although it's Monday, isn't it?" He checked his watch. "That means she's at the Cut 'n Curl until at least noon. She has a standing appointment."

Lark left Golfing for God, drove back downtown, and parked the SUV across the street from the beauty shop. It was only eleven-thirty—half an hour before Hettie would be finished with her appointment. If Lark stormed the beauty shop, everyone would naturally assume that she was some kind of rude, snotty northerner. So she decided to wait and catch up to Hettie Marshall when she emerged from the shop.

She had a few minutes to kill, so she pulled her camera bag from the backseat. She stared at it for a solid five minutes before she picked up her Nikon.

The camera felt cold and heavy in her hands. Goose bumps attacked her arms, and the hairs on the back of her neck stiffened. Every instinct told her to drop the camera, or maybe to smash it against the ground.

The assignment in Libya had damaged her. She'd lost her fearlessness. And for some reason her camera had become a reverse talisman. She touched it, and the terrifying memories flowed.

She'd been hiding out for the last few months, using Pop's illness as an excuse not to shoot any photos. But now she had to face those fears, or give up the thing she did best. The thing that defined her as a person.

She got out of the SUV and slung the camera over her shoulder.

The day was still warm, but Lark pulled her peacoat tighter around her middle. Then she turned up Palmetto Avenue, looking for something to photograph.

The buildings on the main street were constructed of red brick and probably built a hundred years ago. In addition to the beauty salon and the Kountry Kitchen, the main drag sported a hardware store, a small post office, and a little shop called A Good Yarn. Its window displayed a variety of red and green hand-knit sweaters and was so cute, it could have been a Hallmark card.

She kept walking—past four churches, each with an elaborate and life-like crèche. On the corner of Palmetto and Chancellor, she found the hulking wreck of a theater that looked like a downsized version of one of those movie palaces from the 1920s. The architecture was Moorish, with oriel windows and a tower topped with a tarnished golden minaret. The sagging marquee, which must have lit up Palmetto Avenue in its heyday, bore the name "The Kismet."

Lark raised her camera, her hands trembling. She framed a shot of the minaret, but couldn't press the shutter. Damn it all to hell. This was not Libya. There was nothing to fear. Shooting this photo would not unleash some terrible disaster. She *knew* this in her head. But her hands seemed to have a different understanding of reality.

It was useless. Even at a high shutter speed, the shot would be blurry. So she lowered the camera and headed back up the street, trembling and defeated. And feeling terribly alone.

And then it hit her.

Pop was gone. Forever.

So was Jeb.

Her composure crumbled.

She ran up the street to the SUV, slid into the driver's seat, and rested her head on the steering wheel. She didn't cry. She sat frozen, trapped in an endlessly repeating loop of grief and guilt. She might have stayed there for hours if someone hadn't tapped on her window.

"Are you okay?"

She raised her head, momentarily uncertain of her location. A woman dressed in a brown tweed suit stared at her from outside Pop's SUV. She looked really concerned.

Lark lowered the window. "I'm okay. I was just resting."

"You're Abe Chaikin's daughter, aren't you?"

She nodded. "I'm Lark."

"I'm Hettie Marshall," the woman said as if that explained everything. Hettie gave Lark a Miss America smile, which fit her perfectly made-up face, exquisitely tailored designer outfit, and carefully coifed hair. Then Hettie opened the car door and slid her trim and shapely self into the passenger's seat.

Well, so much for trying to stake out the Cut 'n Curl. Lark's stalking skills were obviously rusty.

"I've heard that you want to scatter your father's ashes at Golfing for God," Hettie said, cutting right to the chase.

"It was Pop's last request. Elbert Rhodes suggested I talk to you about getting permission."

Hettie laughed. "Yes, I know. Elbert called Ruby earlier this morning to let her know that you were headed this way. We've been waiting for you over at the Cut 'n Curl. You disappointed Millie Polk. She was sure you were going to come barreling into the shop making loud and obnoxious demands."

Lark said nothing in rebuttal. She just thanked her lucky stars that she'd left her favorite "I Love NY" sweatshirt at home.

"So," Hettie continued, "why do you think your father sent you here?"

"I have no idea. It was the last thing he asked me to do, right before he slipped into a coma. He used to say that he found himself at Golfing for God. But no matter how many times I asked him about that, he never would explain himself. I thought he was being witty, or possibly ironic. I never took him seriously until he insisted on being buried there."

"Oh, I didn't know it was his last request. That *does* change things a little bit, doesn't it?" Hettie looked out the window, deep in thought. On the surface, she seemed placid—practically serene. And yet Lark got the feeling that still waters ran deep.

"You know," Hettie finally said, "I had my own moment of clarity out at Golfing for God. That place changed my life." She turned back, her eyes glittering with an unreadable emotion.

"Really?"

Hettie smiled indulgently. "I know. It's just a putt-putt place. But I'm serious. That place helped me to remember that every day is magic. That everything is a miracle."

Lark had no desire to engage in a conversation about miracles. Her cynicism would pop up. She didn't believe in miracles. So she pulled the conversation back on track. "Will you give me permission to scatter Pop's ashes?"

"Is that all you want? Aren't you even the slightest bit curious?"

Lark shrugged. "I guess. But I've been told a few times today that my curiosity is not welcome. I'm not the troublemaker. My father was."

Hettie pursed her lips. "Have you spoken with Nita?"

"Nita? The woman Pop took to breakfast at the Kountry Kitchen? She's still living here?"

Hettie nodded. "She's our librarian."

"If I didn't know better, I'd think you were encouraging me to stay for a few days. That would make you unique."

Hettie chuckled. "Maybe I am. Maybe you owe it to yourself to speak with Nita."

"Will you give me permission to lay Pop to rest?"

Hettie shook her head. "Honey, this is complicated. Everyone has an opinion, and we all know each other. It takes time to find a consensus, you know?"

Lark tapped her fingers on the steering wheel, her frustration mounting. "Maybe I should go to Golfing for God in the dead of night and pull off a drive-by funeral. What do you think?"

"That's always an option," Hettie said with a tiny smile. "But I think we can do better. Why don't you let me talk to Elbert and the rest of the ladies of the committee? It's always best to take everyone's temperature on a thing like this. In the meantime, you should talk to Nita. She knows the whole story, and you owe that to yourself."

"I'm sure the Rhodes family will be overjoyed to learn that I'm staying a few days. They've made me feel so welcome. Guess I need to go check out the Peach Blossom Motor Court, because I'm not going to impose on Miriam Randall for another night. She's another person who has been kind to me."

"Oh, no, you can't stay at the Peach Blossom."

"I've stayed at worse places."

Hettie gave her an assessing gaze. "That would probably surprise a lot of people. Everyone thinks you're a snob from up north."

"I got that. So maybe they'll change their tune when they see me staying at the local motel."

"No, they might think you're a floozy. I tell you what, why don't you stay out at my river house. It's very private. It's just a little ways outside of town."

"I don't want to impose on you any more than I do Miriam. I can stay at the Peach Blossom Motor—"

"No, you can't stay there. I won't allow it. Besides, the river house is empty this time of year. It won't be any imposition at all."

"You'd let me stay at your vacation home?"

"Oh, honey, it's not that grand. It's just a small place down by the river, and besides, I want to help you. To tell you the truth, I'm intrigued by your father. Something must have happened to him at Golfing for God. Something that changed him. I'd like to know what it was, because I think he and I might be kindred spirits in some way."

Kindred spirits? Ha, that was a laugh. Hettie was a sweet southern belle. Pop was a pain in the butt. They were as different as night and day.

But Lark was smart enough to keep her mouth shut. At last, someone in Last Chance was willing to help her. She was making progress.

Haley had to be a dumb ol' shepherd wearing a stupid fake beard and an itchy headdress, while Maryanne Hanks got to be the angel. All because there weren't enough boys in the Sunday School class, and Maryanne was taller than anyone else, and the angel had to be tall.

It would be okay not being the angel, except that Maryanne kept messing up her lines. Like for instance, Maryanne kept saying, "Ye shall find the babe wrapped in waddling clothes." It was pitiful. This year's Christmas pageant was going to be lame.

Maryanne had told Haley at lunchtime today that she was scared of being the angel and having to say all those lines. Maryanne wanted to be one of the sheep. The sheep just said "baa baa." But the sheep costumes were too small for her because Maryanne was kind of fat.

Well, Haley sure hoped Maryanne got over being scared because the Christmas pageant was less than a week away and this was their only real dress rehearsal. As usual, Doc and Miz Cooper, who were the Sunday School teachers for the third grade, were in charge of the pageant.

Haley stood there by the manger staring down at Bella Anderson's Bitsy Baby doll who was standing in for Baby Jesus, while Doc Cooper made Maryanne repeat her speech over and over again. And then Maryanne said waddling for the umpteenth time and started crying.

Great. All the angels in Haley's life were crybabies.

She scratched where the phony beard on the costume itched. The stupid headdress kept falling down over her eyes.

Just then, Maryanne's momma arrived at the door to the fellowship hall where they were rehearsing. Maryanne's crying got harder, and she threw herself into her momma's arms. About that time, other mommas started to arrive, too.

Of course, Haley's momma wouldn't be picking her

up from rehearsal. Haley didn't even know who would be coming for her. It could be Aunt Jane, or Granny, or even Lizzy. It probably wouldn't be Daddy.

Doc Cooper turned back toward the children in the third-grade Sunday School. "All right, y'all did really great. Keep practicing your lines, and we'll have another rehearsal on Sunday morning."

Haley didn't need any rehearsal. She knew her one line: "Let us go unto Bethlehem and see this thing which is come to pass."

In fact, Haley could recite all the words from the Gospel of Luke, and she knew the difference between waddling and swaddling. And she knew something about angels, too. She cast a glance at the Sorrowful Angel who was sitting in the corner, weeping as usual.

Haley couldn't do anything about Maryanne, but maybe she could help the Sorrowful Angel. Now was the time to put her plan into action. She straightened her shoulders and set off toward Doc Cooper, who was talking to Maryanne's mother.

"Hey, Dr. Cooper, can I talk to you about something?" Haley asked as she gave both of the grown-ups her sweetest smile. She had learned that grown-ups tended to give her what she wanted if she was polite and smiled a lot.

"Just a minute, Haley," Doc said.

He turned toward Maryanne's mother. "I'm sure if you took some time to help her learn her lines, she'd be more confident."

Maryanne's momma didn't look very happy. "Doc, I don't think it's the lines. She's terrified of speaking in front of folks."

"She'll be fine. She needs to face her fears."

Maryanne's mother nodded but didn't look all that certain. When Maryanne and her momma left, Doc Cooper knelt and brought himself down to Haley's level.

"What is it, Haley?" The doctor had reddish gray hair and freckles on his face like a kid.

"Well, I need a, um, I think they call it a consultation."

Doc Cooper smiled at her. He had wrinkles at the corners of his eyes. "Do you now? How can I help you?"

"Well, you see..." She hesitated for a moment. It was entirely possible Doc Cooper was like the rest of the grown-ups who didn't believe in angels or Santa Claus. But he was her Sunday School teacher, so it figured that he had some faith in angels.

"I was wondering if you could help Daddy."

Something changed in his eyes. "Honey, what's wrong with your daddy?"

"He needs more room in his heart. I was wondering if you could do an operation."

The doctor blinked a few times, and Haley had that horrible feeling Doc Cooper might turn out to be like Dr. Newsome or the rest of the grown-ups in town, who were always talking about angels, but not really believing in them much.

"Who told you he needed more room in his heart?" Doc Cooper asked. His forehead was all wrinkly now. That wasn't a good sign.

She thought about lying. It was sometimes easier to fib about the angel. But ever since last summer, when she discussed her angel problems with Reverend Ellis, she knew that Jesus frowned on that sort of thing.

"The Sorrowful Angel told me," she confessed. "The angel said Daddy needs to make room in his heart for love. I think that has to happen before she can get back to Heaven. I told her I would consult with you about it. Can you make his heart bigger with an operation?"

"Oh, dear. Honey, it doesn't work that way."

"It doesn't?"

"No, darlin'. I can't make a heart bigger." Doc Cooper gave Haley a serious look—the kind grown-ups always got when they were about to say something not nice. "Haley, I know you've heard folks talk about how your daddy's heart is broken. And I suppose in a way that's true, but I'm afraid I can't fix that kind of broken heart."

"Then how's he gonna get better? And how will the angel get her wings?"

"Wings?"

She nodded. "The angel needs wings. She doesn't have any wings, and I reckon that's the problem with her not being able to get back to Heaven. But she told me that if Daddy had more room in his heart, things would work out."

The doctor nodded seriously, but Haley could tell he was thinking grown-up thoughts. "Honey, usually the kind of broken heart that your daddy has gets better on its own. It just takes time."

He patted her head and stood up. Haley gazed up at him and realized that Daddy was standing right behind the doctor. He'd heard everything she'd just said.

CHAPTER 6

The next morning, Stone took a seat in Dr. Andrea Newsome's office, located in the only medical building in Allenberg. A big desk with brass fittings filled one side of the room. In the corner stood a low table and chairs, with a variety of toys scattered about.

Andrea specialized in kids with problems.

Stone sat in the middle of a couch placed before the doctor's desk. The minute he'd taken this seat, he'd regretted it. He sank deep into the cushions, and he felt like his knees were stuck in his ears.

"So," Dr. Newsome said from her place behind her desk, "you said on the phone last night that you wanted to talk about Haley's progress."

He nodded and then related what he'd overheard Haley saying to Doc Cooper the day before.

Andrea gave him a long, assessing look. "Chief Rhodes, you do realize that Haley's angel spends her nights in your bedroom." She stared down at him out of a pair of deep, dark eyes.

"I am aware of it."

"And now the angel is telling Haley that you need to grow a bigger heart."

"Doctor, there isn't any angel."

The doc folded her hands together. "Well, that may be outwardly true, but to Haley the angel is real."

"Yeah, well, it's your job to make the imaginary angel disappear."

"Haley has been traumatized. It isn't that easy."

"I reckon it's not, seeing as we have to haul her over here every week, and I haven't seen any improvement in her condition."

Dr. Newsome scowled at him. "Look, it would be very helpful if you didn't constantly challenge Haley about the angel. It's a symptom of her problems. When you tell Haley that her angel doesn't exist, it's like telling her that her problems don't exist. But for Haley, these things are quite real."

Stone found it difficult to meet the doctor's stare, so he looked down at the deep-piled beige carpet.

"Chief, have you ever thought about getting grief counseling?" Dr. Newsome said.

That had him raising his head. "Uh, I thought we were talking about Haley and her imaginary angel friend."

"We are. The fact that Haley's angel is talking to her now is significant. Up until now, the angel has been completely silent. I find it interesting that the angel's first communications are all about you. I also find it interesting that Haley imagines the angel watching over you as you sleep. She clearly sees this angel as your guardian, not hers. To Haley, the angel is a nuisance. She's made this clear on many occasions. But for some reason, she feels that you need a guardian.

"All of this makes me wonder about your feelings in relation to the death of your wife."

His muscles tensed. "That is none of your damn business."

Dr. Newsome didn't so much as blink. "I think it's relevant to Haley's issues. The angel has basically told her that you need to get over your wife's death. Why do you think Haley is thinking that?"

"Because she spends the majority of her time in the company of my mother, or the members of the Ladies' Auxiliary, or down at the Cut 'n Curl listening in on every useless bit of gossip in this county. And believe me, my daughter has a mind like a sponge."

Dr. Newsome straightened the pad on her desk, aligning it perfectly with the edge of her blotter. "Chief, I know Haley hears a lot of gossip. But sometimes what folks say around here has a lot of sense to it."

"That's saying a lot coming from a person with the number of diplomas you've got hanging on the wall."

She leaned forward. "Sometimes common sense is more important than book learning. And don't tell me you don't agree. We both know the folks around here are smart and sensible."

He nodded. "Okay. I'll grant you that. But even in this backwater filled with smart folks, seeing angels is a problem. You've got to make the angel go away."

"Have you ever thought that you're the one who has to make the angel go away?"

"What?"

"That's how I read what the angel told Haley. I've been

talking to her for a year now, and I'm convinced that she's worried about you almost as much as you are worried about her."

"So it's all my fault?"

"No, it's not all your fault. Bad things happen to good people all the time. If it's anyone's fault, blame the drunk driver who took Sharon's life. All I'm saying is that to help Haley, you should think about moving on."

"I don't want to move on. And besides, I couldn't move on even if I wanted to. Sharon was my soulmate. And if you've spent any time listening to the commonsense wisdom of Miriam Randall, then you'd know that a person only gets one of those."

"I think you could benefit from some grief counseling. I think your older daughter could benefit from it, too."

Something nasty spilled into his system. Why was it every female on the face of the earth wanted him to go and talk about how he felt? He didn't want to talk about Sharon. He just wanted to hold on to the sorrow. Somehow the sorrow kept a little bit of Sharon alive. As it was, each day it was getting harder and harder to remember her—even the way she looked sometimes.

"No," he said, rocking himself up from the too-deep couch. It felt much better to be standing there looking down at Haley's shrink. "I'm going to handle my loss the way generations of my people have handled it. In a silent and personal way. Now, do you have any other suggestions about dealing with this angel problem?"

He leaned over the desk. Dr. Newsome didn't look surprised, discomfited, or even fearful. It was damn annoying that he couldn't intimidate the good doctor the way she could intimidate him.

"Yes," she said.

"And what would that be?"

"When was the last time you had sex?"

"That's none of your business."

"I'm guessing that it's been a long time. You might think about giving up your celibacy. I know that sounds crazy, but for a lot of men, sex can be a way to let go of the pain and find a way toward new connections."

"Is that a medical opinion, because I'm pretty sure my mother would—"

"Stone, I know your mother would be horrified by what I just said, and that's beside the point. But on one thing your mother and I would agree—you need to move on. You need to date. You need a social life. And I think Haley wants that for you. She has to live with you every day, and I hear all the time that she thinks you're a grouch and a grump. Is that any way for a man to raise his daughter?"

Hettie Marshall's river house sat amid an enclave of other tin-roofed bungalows on the banks of the Edisto River, a stretch of black water overhung with arching trees and Spanish moss. Who knew that South Carolina could be so picturesque—in a vine-covered, swampy, and slightly decayed kind of way? The deep, verdant woods called to Lark almost from the moment she pulled up the gravel drive.

The light here was soft and deep and mysterious.

Lark sat on an old 1950s-style glider on the screened porch of Hettie's river house, sipping her morning coffee. It was quiet out here. Quiet and secluded. She'd actually slept well last night.

Her cell phone rang, dispelling the morning peace. She

checked the caller ID. It was Greg Chisholm, her editor at the *Washington Journal*. She had been avoiding his calls for several days. She let go of a deep breath and pushed the talk button.

"Where the hell are you? Haven't you been watching the news?" Greg yelled through the connection.

"No, as a matter of fact," she said.

Stunned silence stretched out for several awkward moments.

"I'm amazed," Greg finally answered. "You're always on Twitter. Lark, there was a 7.0 earthquake in Turkey last night. The US is sending International Urban Search and Rescue Team One out of Virginia in the morning, and I need you to catch up with them and cover the human side, like you always do."

Lark watched the mist dancing over the river. For once in her life, she felt no yearning to be where the latest news was breaking. She took a sip of good, strong coffee. She felt blissfully disconnected from the world. "I can't go."

"What do you mean you can't go?"

"I'm not in DC. I can't catch up with the Fairfax County rescue team before they leave."

"Haven't you left New York yet? I mean, your father died more than a week ago." Greg was completely lacking in human emotions.

But Greg was used to the way Lark usually behaved. She was always ready to drop everything and head into the field. She lived on the adrenaline. And, of course, she believed that recording history was a higher calling. Her photos made the world better informed and therefore safer. Nine months ago, she'd have been burning up the highway to get back to DC.

But not today.

"Where the hell are you?" Greg yelled into the phone.

"I'm in Last Chance, South Carolina. Right now I'm sitting on a porch watching a river roll by. It's beautiful here."

"Last Chance?"

"It's a tiny town hundreds of miles from anyplace where news is happening. To be honest, I feel like a fish out of water. Everyone asks if it's okay to serve me bacon."

"What are you talking about?"

"I'm here in the Bible Belt trying to take care of Pop's ashes. I'm not exactly the most popular person in town."

"In South Carolina? Really? I've never been to South Carolina. I've heard they take a dim view of Democrats down there. Which begs the question. Why would Abe want to have his ashes scattered anywhere in South Carolina?"

"It's complicated." She briefly explained the situation, and had to endure Greg snickering when she got to the part about Golfing for God.

"Lark, those people are never going to give you a green light," Greg said. "Besides, I need you right now. I'm short-staffed, and this Turkey thing is right up your alley."

Lark consciously worked at relaxing her jaw and shoulders. "Greg, I can't go to Turkey today. And I'm not sure I want to do another assignment with grieving mothers and lots of rubble. I need to—"

"Hey, you're the best we've got when it comes to grieving mothers," Greg said, completely missing what Lark was trying to tell him. The grieving mothers were heart wrenching. And she didn't have the strength or the courage anymore. She sat there watching the river run while

Greg continued arguing. After a minute of listening to his rant, she pulled the phone from her ear and flipped it to airplane mode.

She was so tired. She couldn't stand another heart-breaking assignment. Not now. Maybe not ever.

She slipped her phone into her pocket and wandered inside the bungalow to put her mug in the sink. Then she pulled her Nikon out of the canvas bag and stared hard at it for several minutes. It was just a camera, not some evil thing. She needed to get over her funk and get on with her life.

She reached for her peacoat and headed outside. As she stepped down from the front stoop, she assessed the morning light. A thick dew had fallen and clung like tiny jewels to the broad-bladed grass that spread down toward the river. The Edisto's current was strong. Pines and mossy trees jammed its banks.

She paused, savoring the small sounds—the distant rush of water, the occasional peep-peep-peep of a chicka-dee, the rustle of wind in the trees. The light was perfect. She could capture it. That's all a camera did. It didn't unleash disaster. Death did not live in her camera.

She turned up her collar and strolled down toward a tree with a long beard of dew-speckled moss and low-hanging branches. She began to think about the f-stop and shutter speed she would need for a shot that would cap-ture the light on the dewdrops. It was a luxury, really, to be able to frame a shot this way. There was never any time to think when the bombs were bursting.

Thoughts of combat and disaster crowded out every-thing as she approached the tree. By the time she raised the camera and framed the shot, her hands had gone clammy. Her heart pounded so hard that her hands shook. Any hope of holding the camera still disappeared.

She couldn't find the courage to depress the shutter button. She stood frozen for the longest time, remembering Jeb Smith's last moments in Misurata.

She might have stood there for an eternity, except that a whisper of a sound drew her attention up the river to the fishing pier.

Chief Rhodes, dressed in uniform, stood there casting a fishing line. She watched for a long moment, losing her fear in the rhythm of his casts, the play of muscles across his shoulders. He was a picture himself: athletic, brawny, and male.

She closed the distance quietly, so as not to disturb him or let him know she was there. She raised her camera and framed him. She waited for the fear, but it didn't come. Stone seemed to have an aura around him—or maybe it was just the glow of the rising sun. Whatever it was, he seemed to push the shadows aside. He lit up the field of vision. Lark squeezed the shutter. The camera made a noise.

The world did not fall apart. She snapped off half a dozen more shots. Her hands were steady. Maybe she was okay. Maybe she would get over this fear.

Stone heard footsteps on the pier before a female voice asked, "Catch anything?"

He turned and looked over his shoulder. Lark Chaikin, wearing a pair of baggy army fatigues, a black T-shirt, and hiking boots, was advancing on him. She carried a camera slung over her shoulder.

He didn't welcome the interruption. He'd been trying to figure out what to do about Dr. Newsome.

"What are you doing out here?" he asked in his best cop voice. He didn't want her to get any closer. And yet he did. It was crazy.

"I'm staying at Hettie Marshall's river house. Didn't you get that message?" she said in her slightly nasal New York accent.

"Did you leave that message?"

"No, but the news cycle in this town is so fast, I figured you would have heard by now." She gave him an open smile that seemed at odds with her slightly snarky tone.

"Since when do you even know Hettie Marshall?"

"Since yesterday. Your father suggested that I speak with her." Her eyes sparked with mischief.

"Right. But how did you end up staying at Hettie's river house?"

Lark shrugged. "I gather Hettie had some kind of experience at Golfing for God that rivaled my father's. She said she could understand why my father used to say that he 'found himself' there."

A little laugh escaped him. "I'm sure Hettie's experience was religious. I'm not sure that's what happened to your father. Not after reading that article he wrote in *The New Yorker* about how God is our nation's biggest problem."

She turned and gave him a cool gaze. "Wow, you subscribe to *The New Yorker*? Really?"

Her words were more teasing than sarcastic. And he probably deserved the jibe given that stupid thing he'd said yesterday morning about how she was a "fool Yankee." Actually, after looking at her photos, he realized she was quite a bit more than that.

"Look, I'm sorry about that stupid thing I said yesterday. I guess we all have our blind spots."

He suddenly felt guilty even though he knew he shouldn't. It was his job to check up on people. Still, he knew she wasn't a troublemaker. Her photos captured the best of people in the worst of situations. That took a real talent and an ability to know what was important.

"I saw your photographs," he said quietly. "They are amazing, and...well, moving."

"Thank you."

He turned around, feeling a little awkward and even embarrassed for reasons he couldn't explain. He cast his line again, looking to recapture his balance.

Lark leaned her back on the railing beside him and seemed to settle into the silence in a way that no woman he'd ever known had ever been able to do. She would be good as a fishing buddy, he thought. And then realized the absurdity of that thought.

Minutes passed, and he became consciously aware of her scent and her breathing and her presence. She said not one word, and it was almost ironic that he was the one to break the silence. "So, are you going to be staying until Christmas?"

"Don't know. Hettie told me she would try to talk your father into letting me fulfill Pop's last request. Hettie also encouraged me to talk with Nita Wills."

"Good luck with that."

"Is there something about Nita I should know?"

"Well, first off she's out of town until Thursday. She's at some meeting of librarians up in Columbia. And second, she doesn't like talking about what happened forty years ago."

"Well, that hardly makes her unique. But thanks for tipping me off."

He lapsed into silence again, casting his line and trying to look at her out of the corner of his eye so she wouldn't be aware of his scrutiny. What was it about this woman? She got within three feet of him and it was like his hormones woke up. And his hormones had been sleeping for a long, long time.

After at least two minutes of complete silence, she asked, "So, is fishing part of your job?"

"I come out here sometimes, when I have something I need to think about." Damn. Why had he told her that?

"It's really quiet out here. You can almost hear your thoughts."

Was she reading his mind? "Uh, something like that, yeah."

He cast his line again. He suddenly wanted to ask her what she was thinking. His thoughts had taken a strange flight of fancy. He'd come out here mad as hell at Dr. Newsome. But he wasn't mad anymore. His reaction to Lark's presence underscored the gist of Dr. Newsome's final recommendation.

Lark drew in a deep breath. "Uh, look, I'd like to apologize for being here. It wasn't exactly my choice, you know? I mean, what would you do if your father asked you to do something crazy?"

He finished reeling in the line, then leaned the fishing pole against the railing. He turned toward her and rested his hip against the railing. "I actually understand how it can be, having a parent who's a little different. I mean, my father runs a putt-putt dedicated to God."

She chuckled. "Yeah. I guess that's pretty unusual. And speaking of different, Chief Rhodes, do you always fish without bait? It's kind of a novel idea, really. You get to fish and be quiet and do your thinking without having to clean fish or throw any back."

He stood there staring at her. In a couple of sentences, she'd managed to sum up his entire philosophy of fishing without bait. And she hardly knew him. Everyone else in town worried about him when he came out here and dropped a line in the river. But this woman got it. How was that possible?

"What?" she said, cocking her head.

"You understand about the bait. I'm kind of surprised."

She shrugged. "I don't know a thing about fishing. But I've seen those fishing shows on TV. And I always thought it was kind of crazy to throw back fish you spent hours catching. But using your method, you can avoid all that and still get in your fishing time."

She tilted her head up toward the morning sun and closed her eyes. The silence grew deep and intimate.

So intimate, in fact, that he felt a sudden need to explain himself. Not because he was embarrassed, but because he suddenly wanted her to understand. "I do my best thinking out here."

"I think people need a place to think. My father was a window starer when he wanted to think."

"Window starer?"

She opened her eyes and gazed at him. "He used to stare out the window for hours on end. When he was staring, he didn't like it when I made noise. I guess that's how I learned to sneak up on people, which is a great skill to have when you're a photographer. Pop did a lot of window staring after Mom died. I was just a kid, and I learned my lesson well."

A person could get lost in those brown eyes of hers. "How old were you when your mother died?"

"About six."

Connection tugged at his chest. "My daughter, Lizzy, was nine when my wife died. Haley, my younger girl, was just two. She was actually in the car when it happened. Thank God she wasn't hurt."

"Wait a second. Your wife *died*?" She pointedly looked at his wedding band.

A jolt of surprise edged through him as he consciously touched the ring with his thumb. "You mean Miriam and the girls didn't tell you? That would be an absolute first. They've been trying to match me up with anything in skirts." He gave her fatigues a little glance.

He expected her to give him one of her snarky comeback lines, but instead she said, "I'm sorry for your loss."

"And I'm sorry for yours," he replied. "Do you mind my asking how you coped with this silent father of yours?"

"I made up an imaginary friend."

A moment of vertigo hit him. Of all the answers she might have handed him, that one was a huge surprise. It almost made him wonder if Providence had sent her there just to give him some advice. "Tell me about your friend," he said. He could hear the urgency in his own voice.

"Oh, that's easy. His name was Carmine Falcone."

Stone blinked. "But that's the name of—"

"Yeah, I know. Pop co-opted him after he realized that Carmine was strong and brave and handsome and in charge. He used to joke to his editor that I made up someone with all the qualities that Pop lacked."

He stared at her for the longest moment, wondering if there were any parallels to be drawn between himself and a weeping angel. He was not a man who liked to cry, that was for damn sure.

She laughed. It was a deep, rich sound. "Man, you've got the funniest look on your face. I know what I just said seems mean, but it was kind of true. Pop checked out for a while after Mom died, and I made up Carmine to help me feel safe. Pop figured it out, though. And once he did, he included Carmine in everything we did. He used to set a place at the table for him, not that Carmine liked Pop's cooking. And then he started writing stories about him. Pretty soon Carmine wasn't all that real anymore."

"I'm sorry for prying, but you see my younger daughter, Haley, has an imaginary angel. To be honest, I'm not inclined to set a place for the angel at the dinner table. I'd like the angel to disappear."

Her eyes softened. "I don't think wishing her away is going to work."

"You got a better idea?"

"No. I don't. But my imaginary friend disappeared the minute Pop spent a little more time with me."

"You sound like my daughter's shrink. She thinks Haley's problems are my fault. She says I need grief counseling."

"Maybe you do."

"How old were you when you got over your imaginary friend?"

She looked away for a moment before she spoke, as if she was weighing whether to tell him the truth. That worried him a little.

"Well," she said at last, "I stopped talking to him when I was about ten. But Pop never got over him because he became the hero of all Pop's books." He could sense the sorrow in her words. She was grieving for her father. He probably shouldn't have pushed her.

Or maybe she just needed someone to talk to.

To be honest, Dr. Newsome had a point. He needed to talk out some things, too. But not to some therapist. He'd much rather talk to Lark. She seemed to understand even without him explaining stuff.

They fell into a warm and comfortable silence. He turned and leaned his hands on the railing and watched the river. They stood side by each, not touching. He was aware of everything about her. Her heat, the way the sunlight turned her hair red, her smallness next to him.

Eventually, he broke the quiet. "So did your father ever remarry?"

"No. He wasn't very good at letting things go."

"Well, I guess I get that. You know, everyone keeps telling me I need to move on. Find another relationship. But I'm not good at change. I'm not even sure I know how to do a *relationship*. I got married when I was eighteen."

"Yeah, well, I'm not good at relationships either. I'm always on the move. I really don't have a home." She turned around and placed her hand over his. Her palm was warm and small. "Don't worry too much about Haley's angel. Just give your daughter some attention, and eventually she'll let the angel go. And if you want to talk about it, you know where to find me."

"Until you leave."

"Until I leave."

She gave his hand a little squeeze that practically branded his skin. Then she turned and headed back up to Hettie's house. He watched her go, surprised that a woman wearing fatigues and boots could look so desirable. And right then it occurred to him that he no longer wished to run Lark Chaikin out of town.

CHAPTER 7

Lark spent the rest of the day researching the events of 1968.

A call to the public library confirmed that Nita Wills wouldn't be back at work until the day after tomorrow.

A trip to Orangeburg to search the *Times and Democrat*'s news archives on the coverage of Ezekiel Rhodes's death proved pointless because there simply was no coverage of it. There wasn't any coverage about Pop's decision to take an African-American to a segregated diner either.

She asked a few questions around town at the post office, the yarn shop, and the hardware store, where Stone's younger brother was decidedly hostile. She got nothing.

The citizens of Last Chance either didn't remember what happened in 1968 or didn't want to talk about it. And she sure got the feeling that no one really wanted her to be there asking questions about the past.

It was after three o'clock when Lark finally stopped

in at the Kountry Kitchen for a late lunch. As usual, she'd been so focused on her research that she'd forgotten to eat and now was ravenously hungry.

She took a booth near the back, ordered a hamburger, and watched the ebb and flow of the customers. At three-forty-five, the place was overrun by teenagers, no doubt students from Davis High, based on the sweatshirts and letter jackets prominently displayed.

It might have been the 1950s, based on the number of milk shakes ordered and delivered, except for the fact that the kids at the counter were a diverse bunch. It struck Lark that in a small way, Pop had contributed to this scene playing out in front of her.

Lark found herself staring at one of the students—a coltish, dark-haired girl with green eyes. She looked vaguely familiar. And after staring at her for a few moments, it became obvious that the girl was just as curious about Lark. Eventually the girl excused herself from the group she'd been sitting with, picked up her soda, and headed in Lark's direction.

"Excuse me," the girl said. "I was wondering, are you Lark Chaikin?"

"I am."

The girl slid into the facing seat. "Hi. I'm Liz Rhodes, and I was wondering if I could talk to you for a minute."

"You're Chief Rhodes's older daughter."

The girl's cheeks colored. "Yeah. And he'd probably have a seizure or something if he knew I was talking to you."

"Really? That's interesting."

"You do know that Daddy totally wants to run you off?"

"I got that impression. I've been trying to decide if he's prejudiced against Yankees or just suspicious of anyone new in town."

Liz smiled, and it changed her face. Whoever her mother had been, she must have been some kind of beauty. "Daddy's not prejudiced against anyone in particular. He was in the marines and, unlike a lot of folks in town, he traveled the world before he ended up here. But he is kind of overprotective."

"I noticed. It's actually one of the things I like about him."

Liz cocked her head. "You don't hate him?"

"Why should I?"

"Because he's not helping you. He's totally sided with Granddaddy."

"I get the feeling that most folks in town have sided with your grandfather. It's discouraging to know that everyone thinks my father is responsible for Zeke Rhodes's death."

"Oh, but you're wrong. There are plenty of people in town who think your father was a hero."

"People like Nita Wills?"

Liz rolled her eyes. "Well, duh. Of course Nita Wills. And a lot of the African-Americans who live in town, and even some white folks, too. Granddaddy's just mad because of what happened to my great-grandfather. He needs to have someone to blame."

Lark gazed at the kids at the counter. "You know, it seems to me that Last Chance is doing an okay job of trying to get over its history. I've been sitting here thinking that it's probably wrong for me to shake things up. I'm not like my father, you know."

"Well, for what it's worth, I think it's time for someone to shake things up a little more. Like, for instance, some of us are tired of going to a school named Jefferson Davis High. I mean it's historical and all, but for some it's totally offensive."

"I see."

"And don't get me wrong, there's a group of kids who want to rename the school Obama High, but that's not going to happen either. My thought was to just call the place Last Chance High. I think it has a ring to it, don't you?"

Lark couldn't help but laugh. "I guess it does."

Liz leaned in. "Did your father tell you anything about those times? About how it felt to walk in here when Clyde Anderson used to own the place?"

"I'm afraid not. In fact, I was completely surprised when Pop asked me to have his ashes scattered here. I didn't know anything about what happened in 1968 until I got here. Can you tell me anything? I know you weren't born yet, but what stories have you heard?"

Liz shook her head. "Not many, only the ones from my grandfather, who thinks Abe was a troublemaker."

"Well, for what it's worth Pop *was* a troublemaker. He loved controversy. Maybe that's why he wanted me to bring him back here. He just wanted to stir the pot a little more."

"You think?" Liz's gaze wandered away toward her friends and a certain brown-eyed boy. Lark could almost see the wheels turning in the young girl's head.

"I'm afraid that's the most likely explanation," Lark said.

Liz turned and peered at Lark from behind her bangs. "So, uh, before my father runs you off, I was wondering if maybe I could schedule a time to interview you for the school paper?"

"You're a writer?" Lark asked.

Liz's eyes sparked with passion. "I'd like to be. I thought it might be cool to get an interview with you because, you know, we don't get Pulitzer Prize–winning photojournalists in town very often. And I think the kids in school would be totally interested to hear about what it's like to be a journalist in a war zone. And I read that you were in Libya during the revolution when that TV Journalist, Jeb Smith, was killed."

A sudden swift headache knifed through her temples. *Please, no flashbacks.* She sucked in air and forced herself to focus on Lizzy's young and innocent face. She grabbed her soda with both hands to keep them from trembling.

Man, she was screwed up.

"Uh, I don't want to talk about Jeb," she managed to say.

Lizzy nodded. "I understand. But it would still be cool if you could talk about what it's like to be embedded with our troops."

No, it would not be cool.

She wanted to grab the kid by her sweatshirt and shake some sense into her. But that wouldn't be a smart move, given that her father was chief of police. Besides, the kid was only curious, the way all kids were. At her age, Lark had been curious, too. And professional photographers had helped her along in her career. Jeb had been one of them. Jeb had been a mentor way before he became a friend and colleague.

With that thought firmly in mind, Lark nodded and said, "How about tomorrow? We can meet here, if you like."

Liz nodded and smiled. "Cool. But let's meet at the

doughnut shop across the street, next to the Cut 'n Curl.
It's quieter there."

"Okay. What time?"

"Quarter to four. And if you don't mind, I'm going to
bring one of the photographers from the paper, too. He
totally wants to meet you."

Lark nodded, not at all eager to be interviewed. But
maybe it was a good way to face her fears. She needed to
stop hiding from what had happened to her in Misurata.

Stone cruised down Palmetto Avenue late in the afternoon. The weather hadn't yet turned, the town was quiet
as a tomb, and he was thinking about this morning at the
river, talking with Lark.

And wouldn't you know it? Just as she popped into his
mind, there she was—coming out of the Kountry Kitchen
engaged in a conversation with Lizzy. Lizzy appeared to
be hanging on every blessed word the woman was saying.

Damn. What was it about that woman? He had kind of
hung on everything she'd said this morning, too.

But, even so, Lizzy was supposed to be at the Cut 'n
Curl helping Jane and Momma with Haley.

He pulled to the corner and rolled down his window.
"Lizzy," he said in his best daddy voice, "didn't I tell you
that I didn't want you hanging around the Kitchen after
school? Your granny and Aunt Jane expect your help with
Haley."

Lizzy's sharp chin got just a little more stubborn, and
she rolled her eyes.

"Besides, I don't want you bothering Ms. Chaikin."

"What you really mean is you don't want me talking
to her because you want to run her out of town." Lizzy

flipped back her mane of dark hair and gave Lark one of those wiseass-teenager looks that she'd gotten so good at lately. "You shouldn't let him push you around."

Lark gave Lizzy one of her mischievous smiles. It was hard not to like Lark when she smiled like that. "I don't ever let guys in uniform push me around."

The slight arch in Lark's brow sent a spiral of heat through Stone. Then Lizzy smirked at him as if to say, See, you've met your match. Stone knew right then that he would be in deep trouble if Lark and Lizzy ever really bonded.

"Lizzy, I told you to go check in with your grandmother. When I tell you something, I expect you to do it."

Lizzy didn't lose the smirk, and he got another eye roll. But, hallelujah, his daughter finally turned and headed down the street toward the Cut 'n Curl. She gave Lark a wave and said, "I'll see you tomorrow," as she departed.

Stone watched Lizzy for a moment as she crossed the street, walking in that loose-jointed shamble that every teenager in town seemed to have adopted. Then he turned toward Lark.

"What was that all about?"

"She wants to be a journalist. She made an appointment to interview me tomorrow."

"Well, you can just unmake that appointment."

She put her hands on her hips. "Stone, don't be an idiot. I'm not going to harm your daughter."

"No? You're going to talk to her about what you do. And I don't want you painting some glorified picture of combat for her."

"Glorified? Is that who you think I am?" Was he imagining something or did she sound disappointed in him?

He paused a moment. No, of course not. He'd seen Lark's photos. They didn't paint any kind of picture that glorified war. It was worse than that. They showed the truth.

She stepped up and leaned on the cruiser's roof. "You know, I get that you were once a warrior. So you know the truth. I know the truth. And knowing that, you can rest assured that I'm not going to make it sound like a picnic, and by the same token I'll try not to scare the crap out of her either."

He looked up into those deep and somber eyes. She'd seen too much war, he realized. And he'd just been an insensitive idiot. Again.

"Uh, look, I apologize. I just want to keep my daughter safe."

"I know," she said with a nod.

What was it about this woman? She seemed to be able to look right through him, right into his deepest self.

Just then, his radio crackled to life and saved him from saying something really stupid and embarrassing. The dispatcher's disembodied voice said, "Alpha 101 to Lima 101, we've got a signal-8 out at Hettie Marshall's place." Signal-8 meant a missing person. They got signal-8s every time old man Anderson wandered off, but never associated with anyone in the Marshall family.

"I'm not happy about Lizzy talking to you. But I guess that's not your fault," he finally said to Lark. It sounded really lame.

Lark backed away from his cruiser. "I admire the fact that you want to keep her safe. But I promised Liz I would talk to her. I'm not going to break that promise." She turned and headed up the sidewalk with a purposeful stride.

She wasn't wearing fatigues anymore, and her butt

looked cute in jeans. He really had to admire her. She was a woman who kept her promises, come hell, high water, or idiot fathers and cops.

He let go of a long sigh and toggled the radio. "I'm on my way," he told the dispatcher. He gunned the engine as he pulled out onto Palmetto Avenue. And then the adolescent urge to floor the gas pedal came over him. He flipped on his lights and hit it. The Crown Vic made a satisfying roar as he sped through town with lights ablaze. It took real fortitude not to look back to see if Lark Chaikin was watching him.

Five minutes later, he was feeling kind of foolish as he pulled into the long, circular drive that led to Jimmy and Hettie Marshall's house. The place wasn't nearly as old as Lee's mansion house. Nevertheless, it possessed an impressive number of columns and a portico.

He recognized Lee's Town Car in the drive, alongside Hettie's Audi. Jimmy's Mercedes was missing.

Well, it sure looked like Jimmy had finally decided it was time to move on to greener pastures. Between his wife and his daddy and the problems down at the chicken plant, Jimmy's life had been pretty crappy lately.

Stone bounded up the brick steps, and the front door opened even before he could ring the bell. Violet Easley answered. Violet was his deputy's mother, and she'd all but raised Jimmy Marshall, too. She'd been a housekeeper for the Marshalls nearly forever.

"Oh, Chief Rhodes, I'm so glad you're here. Miz Hettie is so upset, and Mr. Lee is about to have a fit and a half. They're in the parlor." Violet stepped back and directed Stone through the foyer and into the parlor containing antique furniture upholstered in a shiny yellow fabric.

Good Lord, how did people live in a room like this? He'd be afraid to touch anything for fear of soiling or breaking it.

He snatched the hat off his head and turned to face Lee Marshall, who had ensconced himself, with his gouty foot raised, on a gigantic couch that dominated the room. He looked just as old and unkempt as he had on Saturday.

"Have you run that woman out of town yet?" Lee asked.

"That's not why y'all called me out here. There was something about a missing person?"

Hettie sniffled from her place in a small wing chair that sat beside a thirteen-foot, impeccably decorated Christmas tree. The tree was festooned with golden ornaments and ribbons, its lights twinkling happily as the afternoon light faded from the front windows. "Jimmy's missing. He hasn't been home for two nights," Hettie said, true emotion ringing in her voice.

"Have you checked Dot's place and the country club and—"

"I've checked all his usual haunts. I wouldn't have called you if I didn't think he was missing." Hettie sounded more than merely concerned; there was a frantic note in her voice.

"I understand. I only asked because everyone knows that for the last few months he's been living down at the river and—"

"I know, but he's gotten himself sober, and he's been going to church, and he's started to address the issues at the chicken plant. He's done everything I asked so I let him come home a week ago. He had changed. I know you and Lee think I forced him to run away, but that's not true." She glowered at her father-in-law. That was a huge surprise. A year ago she would have deferred to Lee. But Hettie had changed, too.

Just like clockwork, Lee rose to Hettie's implicit challenge. "You can spout all the holy nonsense you'd like, darlin', but I'm sure Jimmy has just gone on a bender and he'll be back with his tail between his legs the minute he runs out of money."

Lee turned toward Stone. "I'm sorry," he said. "I wasn't the one who called you out here about this nonsense. I'm sure this is just another marital dispute. But since you're here, I want to know when that woman is going to leave."

"Not until she gets an answer about her father's remains." This came from Hettie, who stood up and confronted Lee. Her tears were rapidly disappearing. "In fact," she said, "I have let her use the river house."

"What? You can't do that. That house belongs to—"

"Me. That house was my daddy's. And if I want to let Lark Chaikin stay out there for a few days, while we sort out this business about her father's remains, it's nobody's business but mine. After all, I chair the—"

"Yes, I know you chair that committee. And thanks to you, my son was humiliated last summer. Have you thought about what that did to him?"

"Yes, Lee, I have. Jimmy learned his lesson last summer, and he's spent months trying to make a change in his life. And he's been doing it, bit by bit, with the help of the Lord."

Lee scowled. "The Lord helps those who help themselves. You've turned him into a pussy-whipped nothing of a loser with all that religion you're always spouting."

Hettie put her fists on her hips, glared at the nasty old man, and said, "Lee, you can get your fat behind off my couch. Go on back home because you're not being any help here."

The old man didn't budge.

Hettie turned toward Stone. "It's not like Jimmy to disappear. I know we've had our problems, but he wouldn't just walk out on me. He wouldn't. Something's happened to him."

The dumb old angel was at it again. It looked like Haley was going to need Santa's help to get the angel back to Heaven after all.

Especially since Doc Cooper couldn't fix Daddy's heart.

The angel was in her usual place tonight, hovering in the corner of Daddy's room watching him sleep and making so much noise it was a wonder, really, that Daddy could sleep through it.

But Daddy was snoring pretty loud tonight, and Haley reckoned that was better than the discussion he and Lizzy had had at the dinner table over that lady who wanted to bury her daddy at the golf course. Lizzy and Daddy were mad at each other.

And Haley hated it when they argued.

Haley tiptoed into Daddy's room. "Would you be quiet, please," she whispered to the angel.

The angel shimmered, just like the Christmas tree angel on top of the town tree. Only that angel was gold and had wings. This angel was kind of see-through and appeared to be wearing a pair of jeans and a sweatshirt.

Haley had never actually noticed that before. It was like the angel was getting more solid or something. Did angels wear sweatshirts?

Haley put her fists on her hips like Granny did sometimes when she meant business. "I mean it," she muttered. "I can't sleep."

The angel looked down at her, tears running down her face. Then the angel kind of bent down, just like Doc Cooper had done. "Your daddy needs to make some changes," the angel said.

"Changes? Like what?"

"Like everything. He's stuck in a rut."

The angel stood up again and started sniffling.

Haley was fit to be tied. She glared at the angel and said in a too-loud voice, "If I make some changes, will you stop caterwauling in the middle of the night?"

"Haley, what in the Sam Hill are you doing in here?" Daddy sat up in his bed.

"Uh, nothing," she lied. If she told Daddy she was talking to the angel, he would get mad. And he was already mad at Lizzy.

"Go back to bed. It's two in the morning."

" 'Kay."

Daddy flopped back onto his bed and started snoring again. Whew, that was a close call.

The angel continued to sniffle, only now she was giving Haley a meaningful look. Then she nodded.

"Do you really mean it?" Haley asked. "If I make some changes, will you go back to Heaven?"

"Haley, are you talking to the angel?" Daddy asked, his voice muffled by his pillow.

"Uh, no, um, well, maybe."

"Go to bed. This has got to stop."

"But, Daddy, the angel said—"

"I don't care what the—" Daddy stopped in the middle

of what he was about to say. He swung his feet over the side of the bed. "I'm sorry. What did the angel say?" he asked.

Well, that had to be a first. Daddy was never interested in what the angel had to say.

And that's when Haley realized that something had just changed. The angel realized it, too, because she stopped weeping.

Haley stared hard at Daddy's face in the darkness. "Daddy," she said, "the angel wants us to make some changes around here."

"What?"

"That's what she said. She said we were in a rut. You got any ideas of how we can get out of our rut, Daddy?"

"Honey, I'm too tired right now to talk about how we can make changes to get out of our rut. But I will think about it."

"Okay, that's good. I'll think about it, too," Haley said.

"Good. Now you go back to bed, okay? Tomorrow is a school day."

"Okay."

"We'll talk about this tomorrow."

Haley walked back to her bedroom and tried to figure out if Daddy meant that he was going to bawl her out tomorrow or if he would really talk about making some changes. She climbed back into her bed and pulled the covers up. He would probably bawl her out. That's what he usually did.

CHAPTER 8

Lark sipped her morning coffee on the bungalow's porch. She was sort of waiting for the chief of police to arrive for some dawn fishing. She had hoped they could talk some more. Or maybe just stand around being quiet.

But it didn't look like he was coming today.

Too bad. Stone Rhodes might have distracted her from real life. Instead, she found herself checking e-mails, watching the Twitter feed roll by, and wondering how the hell she was going to get herself prepared for her next assignment.

It was December nineteenth—just six days before she had to leave for Africa.

She needed to force the issue. She studied the near-jungle that grew on the opposite bank of the Edisto River. The morning light was magnificent.

She picked up the topographic map she'd purchased at Lovett's Hardware the day before and studied it. There was a swamp not too far away. According to the guys at the hardware store, the area provided habitat for all kinds of migratory birds. It was supposed to be incredibly beautiful.

She wasn't a wildlife photographer, but maybe shooting something different would get her out of her funk.

Half an hour later, she parked Pop's SUV at the end of a red clay road by a path that was supposed to lead to an abandoned hunting lodge. She pulled a telephoto lens from her camera bag and fixed it to the camera body. Then she slung the camera over her shoulder and headed down the weedy trail.

The morning was cool and dewy, but the sun, still low on the horizon, promised another unseasonably warm December day. The wood's thin canopy provided a little more light than she would get in midsummer, but still the forest was surprisingly dense and overgrown.

She followed the path for a short while, past an abandoned house, until she reached a swampy place ringed by cypresses. She stood quietly, watching a great blue heron fishing in the shallows. How cool was it to be able to watch a heron in the middle of December?

There was other wildlife, too. A snake, some turtles, and frogs. No alligators, thankfully, but she suspected they lurked someplace close by. Alligators didn't scare her. The camera around her neck was something else again.

She adjusted the camera's shutter speed and aperture, then aimed the lens at the heron, adjusting the focal length and focus. Her heart kicked as she concentrated on framing the shot.

There is nothing to fear here.

She wasn't in a war zone. There were no armed insurgents lurking in the shadows. An artillery barrage was not about to start. She didn't have to do the usual risk calculation that accompanied every trip to a dangerous destination.

None of that applied here.

So why the hell were her hands shaking? Why was sweat trickling down her back? Why was she so afraid to press the shutter?

She took a breath and held it as she squeezed off a shot. Then another. And then she pressed down on the shutter and kept it there as the heron looked up at her.

And that's when the gunfire erupted.

The bird took flight. Lark hit the muddy ground and covered her head.

And suddenly she was back in Misurata.

"You're insane, Jeb," she had called to the correspondent from International Television News as he sprinted across the street and hunkered down along a concrete wall. He was exposed.

"Yeah, but I've got the angle on the shot," he shouted back as he hoisted his video camera and trained it on a group of rebel soldiers firing rockets from a truck-mounted launcher.

Damn it. She should have beaten him across the street; she had no angle on the shot. She settled down behind a pile of rubble and trained her camera on Jeb. The afternoon sun painted his helmet in gold; his face was dirty and sported a couple of days' worth of stubble. He was completely in his element, living out there in the invincible zone.

Lark's finger hovered over the shutter. She held her breath and squeezed.

And all hell broke loose.

The incoming rocket hit a spot along the broken wall between Jeb and the rebels. The explosion was so loud

*that her world went silent. Time stopped. But her finger
stayed glued to the camera's shutter.*

*She captured the entire moment of Jeb's death. The
instant before the rocket hit, the impact, the flying shrap-
nel, and the blood. Oh, my God, there was so much
blood. She hunkered there, her finger paralyzed on the
shutter until Erick Frey from Getty Images found her.*

"Hey, you okay? I didn't hit you, did I?"

"Erick?" Lark lifted her head, momentarily confused
by the dense jungle surrounding her. She looked up at the
man towering over her. It wasn't Erick Frey. This guy was
African-American and about sixty years old. He was carrying what appeared to be a shotgun and wearing hunting
clothes.

She wasn't in Libya anymore.

"Ma'am, you should know better than to be out here
in the woods without an orange safety vest. I thought you
were a deer," the man said.

Lark pushed herself up to a sitting position. Her
fatigues and jacket were wet from the mud. Her whole
body was starting to shake.

"I didn't hit you, did I?" His dark eyes were wide with
concern.

"Uh, no, I'm okay. I just hit the deck when I heard the
gunfire."

"You're shaking."

"Uh, yeah. The mud is cold," she said, but she knew
the mud had nothing to do with the shakes that racked her
body.

Lizzy couldn't believe it. Aunt Jane had a doctor's
appointment, and Granny expected Lizzy to babysit Haley

for the afternoon. So here she sat watching the brat eat a Boston cream doughnut while she waited for Miz Chaikin and David to arrive.

The doughnut was a bribe to keep Haley quiet. She sat and watched her sister making a mess of herself and hoped that Haley wouldn't dribble chocolate or custard down her front like she usually did. Granny would definitely notice if Haley got her shirt dirty.

The little bell above the door jingled, and David came in. A flock of butterflies took flight in Lizzy's tummy. He was totally cute, from his curly brown hair to his dark, intense eyes. As usual, he had his camera slung around his neck. He slid into the facing seat.

He shifted his gaze to Haley. "Hi, kid, how's the doughnut?"

"Fine." Haley squinted up at him. "Granny says you don't have a Christmas tree at your house. I think that's sad."

Lizzy's face burned. "Haley, that wasn't a nice thing to say. We don't have a Christmas tree at our house either."

"Yeah, but we have one at Granny's house. And besides, Granny says that we used to have a Christmas tree when Momma was alive. But David hasn't ever had a Christmas tree, and I think that's just tragic." Haley said the last word on a dramatic sigh. She'd just learned the meaning of the word "tragic," and she'd been saying it over and over again.

"It's all right," David said. "I don't mind. I bet you never played dreidel or lit Hanukkah candles. Bet you never went on a matzo hunt at Passover either."

"Are those things fun?" Haley asked.

"Yeah, sure."

"Well, nothing could be funner than a Christmas tree. Or Santa Claus."

"I never had a Christmas tree either." This last comment came from Ms. Chaikin, who had arrived for her interview right on time. Lizzy wanted to choke her little sister. This was not the introduction Lizzy had wanted.

She popped up from her seat. "Oh, Ms. Chaikin, this is David Raab from the Davis High *Rebel Yell*. And this is my little sister. I'm sorry I had to bring her along. I had to babysit unexpectedly."

Ms. Chaikin sat down and gave Haley a smile. "So, you're Haley, huh?"

Haley nodded, her face a complete smear of chocolate.

"You know my sister's name?" Lizzy asked.

Ms. Chaikin nodded. "I had a conversation with your father about Haley yesterday morning."

Haley stopped chewing. "Why didn't you have a Christmas tree?" she asked.

"Because my father and I always went to Bermuda at Christmastime. He had been raised as a Jew and had no interest in putting up a tree. I vaguely remember putting up a tree when my mother was alive. She had been raised as a Catholic, but she died when I was a little kid."

"Like my mother?"

"I think I was a little younger than you are now when my mother died." Ms. Chaikin squared her shoulders and turned toward Lizzy. "You know, I don't think it would be a good idea to do this interview with Haley here."

"You've been talking to Daddy, and he told you not to talk to me, didn't he?"

She cocked her head. "Yes, he did, but I came here anyway. Don't be angry at your father because he wants to keep you safe."

"Did your father object when you decided to become a war photographer?" Lizzy flipped open her notepad.

"By that time, my father and I had a very strained relationship." Ms. Chaikin turned toward David and said, "That's a very nice camera you've got. Are you interested in photojournalism?" Wow, Ms. Chaikin had just dodged one of Lizzy's questions.

"Yeah, I guess," he said and looked down at the table in that totally bashful way of his that Lizzy thought was kind of cute.

"Tell me about your father," Lizzy asked, trying to get this interview back on track.

"There's not much to tell. When I was old enough, he recognized that I was competent to make my own decisions. Give your father some time. He'll come around eventually and realize that you can handle bad stuff."

"But bad stuff happens to little kids, too," Haley said. "I was kidnapped and in a car wreck. And now I have a dumb old angel." She propped her head on her hand and managed to look miserable.

Lizzy stifled her irritation. "You're okay, Haley. And please don't embarrass me by talking about the angel."

"No, it's all right. I'm very interested in your angel. Does she have a name?" Ms. Chaikin said.

"No. She almost never talks. She cries a lot."

"Oh, I'm sorry. Do you know what she's crying about?"

Haley shook her head. "No. But I'm starting to think she's sad about Daddy."

Ms. Chaikin stiffened. "I see."

"Can we not talk about the angel, please?" Lizzy pleaded. By the time Haley was finished wrecking this opportunity, Lark Chaikin would probably never speak to her again.

"Hey, I've got it," Haley said brightly.

"What?" Lizzy asked.

Haley turned toward David. "Hey, David, you wanna help put up a Christmas tree? Maybe if you helped us put up a tree then you could invite Lizzy over to your house to do whatever it is you do on the holidays."

"We light candles." David turned toward Lizzy and blushed. It was so cute the way he did that sometimes.

"It's okay, David, you don't have to invite me over. My sister is—"

"I'd love to invite you over," David blurted. "Hanukkah is all this week. I'll ask Mom if it's okay. I'm sure she'll love making latkes for you."

"Latkes?"

"Potato pancakes," Ms. Chaikin supplied. "They are not to be missed. You should go. Lighting Hanukkah candles is fun."

"You've lit Hanukkah candles?" Haley asked.

"I have. When my aunt Sadie was alive. She would make latkes and have us over for dinner. That was shortly after my mother died. But then Aunt Sadie passed away, too."

"You know," Haley said, rolling her eyes in Lizzy's direction, "there are all those boxes of Christmas stuff in the attic and a tree in a box and everything. We could get them down and surprise Daddy tonight by having the house all decorated. And then David and Ms. Chaikin would have a chance to be in on the fun."

Suddenly Haley didn't seem like such a pest. Maybe this was a good thing. Lizzy could invite David over and get to know him better, and Ms. Chaikin could be there as kind of like a chaperone. Then maybe Daddy wouldn't have a coronary over it.

She crossed her fingers under the table. And maybe she could kind of interview Ms. Chaikin while they were unsnarling the Christmas lights from the boxes in the attic.

"So, Ms. Chaikin, you wanna help?" Haley asked.

"Well, I don't know. I think your father might not be happy about that."

Haley sat up bolt-straight. "But the angel thinks you should help. I think this is exactly what she meant last night when she told me that Daddy needed to get out of his rut, and that we needed to make changes. The angel is smiling and nodding."

"Haley, shut up about the angel, okay?" This was so totally embarrassing.

Ms. Chaikin leaned a little toward Haley. "So she's stopped crying?"

Haley nodded. "She really wants you to help. I can tell."

Ms. Chaikin smiled. "Well, in that case how can I refuse your invitation? I wouldn't want to disappoint an angel."

Stone watched as the Allenberg County crime scene unit made a cursory inspection of Jimmy Marshall's Mercedes. The silver vehicle had been found by a couple of hunters. The car had been abandoned three miles north of town on an unpaved road that led to the old hunting lodge known as the Jonquil House. The car was locked, and as near as Stone could tell there wasn't a thing out of place. No telltale signs of a struggle, or blood, or anything else that would indicate foul play.

Still, the damn car was found in the middle of nowhere and about a mile outside of Stone's jurisdiction. Which meant that Billy Bennett had taken charge.

Allenberg's sheriff strode toward him, the late-afternoon sun glinting on his pale blond hair. Billy had always been the guy every girl had fallen ass-over-teakettle for. And he'd sure kept himself up, which probably explained why he kept winning elections despite the fact that he was a total a-hole who knew nothing about policing.

"Thanks for the tip, Stone," Billy said with one of his infernally charming smiles. "We've got it covered now. Doesn't look like much, though. I'd be willing to bet Jimmy ditched his car out here and had his girlfriend pick him up."

"Based on what?"

Bennett shrugged. "Rumor. But in this county, rumor is nearly 'bout as good as fact."

"You going to search the woods and the swamp?"

Bennett put his hands on his hips. "I don't see any tracks leading into the woods, do you?"

"I didn't look that hard. You owe it to Lee and Hettie to conduct a grid search."

Bennett looked up at the fading light in the afternoon sky and then back at Stone. "You know, unless I'm mistaken, we're standing two miles outside of the town limits of Last Chance. I don't think you have any jurisdiction here."

There wasn't any point picking a fight with Billy Bennett directly. If Stone wanted the sheriff to act, he would have to unleash Lee Marshall on him. Once Lee accepted that his son had gone missing and not run away, maybe the old man would demand action. If Lee told Billy to take a walk off the pier down at the river, Billy would do it without asking any questions.

Stone squared his hat. It was getting on to dinnertime. "Well, y'all have a nice day then. Let me know if there's anything I can do to help with your investigation. You going to let Hettie and Lee know we found Jimmy's car?"

"I got it covered."

Stone nodded and strode back toward his cruiser. Ten minutes later, he pulled his car into the driveway of the little rambler he rented. Lizzy was supposed to be babysitting Haley today because of Jane's doctor's appointment—an appointment that everyone in town already knew about.

He headed up the walk to the house, mulling over what he should do about Jimmy Marshall and Sheriff Bennett. He got halfway to the porch before the sound of the piano hit him like a Stinger missile.

He stood rooted to the ground and listened to the muffled strains of "Silent Night" and the unmistakable sound of his girls singing.

What the hell?

He rushed to the front door and practically tore it off its hinges as he opened it, his heart thumping. He stepped into the living room halfway expecting to find a woman with long honey hair and a curvaceous figure sitting at the piano, her long fingers dancing over the keys.

His disappointment knew no limits.

Lark Chaikin, with her slim body and her short spiky

hair, was playing Sharon's piano. And that wasn't all. The furniture in his living room had been rearranged to make room for the old artificial Christmas tree.

Nothing was as it should be. The tree was wrong—there weren't any red ribbons on it. The angel for the top was missing. Sharon would never have put tinsel and lights around the side window like that.

"What the hell is going on here?" he yelled, focusing right on Lizzy, who was standing beside a teenaged boy that Stone didn't recognize. "Who gave you permission to move the furniture?"

He rounded on Lark. "And I don't recall inviting you to my house. Close the piano, now...please."

Lark looked up, her mouth thinned, and her dark eyes looked wounded. "I believe this was the Sorrowful Angel's idea," she said.

Stone opened his mouth and shut it again. The words that wanted to come out were vile and profane. They weren't suitable for his daughters to hear.

He glowered at Lark and hissed. "I know your father had ways of doing things, but they aren't mine. Please leave my house." He turned on the boy. "Who are you?"

"David Raab." The boy's voice cracked, and his cheeks got red. "Uh, it's nice to meet you, Chief Rhodes. Um, Lizzy and Haley were just giving me and Ms. Chaikin a little dose of Christmas."

Stone stood there staring at the boy. Where the hell had this kid come from?

"David's new in town," Lizzy said. "His father works for Uncle Hugh. And tomorrow night, I'm going over to David's house to light some Hanukkah candles and eat potato latkes."

Hanukkah candles? Stone narrowed his gaze and pointed a finger at the boy. "Go home, David." He turned toward Lark. "You, too."

Then he turned on Haley. "Go to your room. You're in serious trouble. You know good and well that the boxes in the attic are off-limits."

Haley stared up at him with a face that was a miniature of Sharon's. "But Daddy," she said, "I told you last night that the angel said you needed to get out of your rut. We were just trying to help."

He saw red then. "Go! All of you!" He turned and stormed into the kitchen, where he picked up the water kettle and threw it with all his might against the back wall. It crashed and left a big hole in the drywall.

He stared at the hole in the wall for an eternity, struggling to breathe. For a moment, just as he'd gotten out of his car and heard that music coming from his living room, something long dead had kicked right back to life inside him.

What the hell was it? Hope?

It didn't matter. Because now all the light and air and life inside him was draining right into that stupid, stupid hole he'd just put in the wall.

CHAPTER 9

"Can we talk?" Lark asked. She stood in the doorway to the little kitchen at the back of Stone Rhodes's house.

The chief of police stood with his back to her, his tan uniform shirt stretched across his broad shoulders. He was breathing hard and staring at the hole he'd just put in his wall.

"No," he said.

"What a surprise." She stepped a little farther in the room, inexplicably drawn to him. "I understand how you feel."

He turned around, flashing angry green eyes at her. "Don't tell me you know how I feel because that's just bullshit."

"I do. I know how it feels to lose someone you love. We're more alike than you realize."

They faced off, time stretching out. He was hurting. She understood. She was hurting, too.

Maybe she could reach him and make him see. "I had a really bad day today, so when your daughters suggested putting up Christmas lights and decorations, it seemed like a good idea. They helped me forget about the dark stuff going on in my life for a little while. I'm grateful to them. Can you accept that?"

"Well, what if I didn't want a tree and decorations?" His voice sounded deep and rusty.

"Stone. Really. You just yelled at your kids for putting up a Christmas tree."

"Thanks for making me feel better," he said.

She didn't miss the sarcasm. She took that as a positive sign, so she continued. "I also thought that putting up a Christmas tree was a better thing to do with your kids than sitting at the doughnut shop talking about what it's like to be a war correspondent." She let her gaze drift away for a moment. She'd been feeling shaky all day, ever since the debacle in the swamp.

"I told Lizzy she wasn't to pester you."

She looked back at him, just in time to see muscles bunching at his jaw. "No, you told Lizzy that she wasn't to speak with me. There's a difference. And she's old enough to know it."

"And what about the boy?"

"He's a photographer for the school paper. He's smart and nice. You should let Lizzy sample his mother's latkes because, honestly, homemade latkes are to die for."

Stone gave Lark an utterly confused look.

"Potato pancakes," Lark explained. "Latkes are *the* traditional Hanukkah food."

"I see."

"Do you? Really? Yesterday I told you that my father had a hard time letting things go. I think maybe you're a lot like him. Stone, please, you should apologize to your children. And you should open up that piano and let someone play it.

It's a lovely instrument, and it shouldn't be allowed to gather that much dust. I have a feeling your wife wouldn't approve of it standing idle. And please, stop being angry at Haley because of her angel." She stared at his wedding band.

"And who made you the judge of my life?"

"No one," she said firmly.

They stood there staring at each other for a long moment that wasn't even remotely awkward. It was crazy the way the silence between them sometimes became more eloquent than words. When they spoke, they often argued. When they were quiet, there was something else. A deep current of connection.

Just then, the screen on the front door slammed, and a female voice called out. "Stone Rhodes, where in the Sam Hill are you? I need to give you a piece of my mind."

Stone closed his eyes, and the expression on his face was priceless—part annoyance and part guilty little boy. "Great," he said on a gust of breath, "just what I need to make my day complete. You and my mother ganging up on me."

An instant later, an older woman with dark curly hair bustled into the kitchen. It didn't require a photographer's eye to conclude that this newcomer was related to Stone. They had the same green eyes and bone structure.

The woman's gaze swept the scene, lingered for a moment on the chief, and then turned in Lark's direction.

"Well, I declare," she drawled, "you're Abe Chaikin's daughter."

"Yes, I am."

"I'm Ruby Rhodes, Stone's momma." She reached her hand out, and Lark shook it. She had small, warm hands and a twinkle in her eyes.

"So, I hear you've been helping Haley with her angel."

"Momma, don't—" Stone's words were a warning, but the tone was all wrong. Obviously, Ruby had her son exactly where she wanted him.

"Uh, maybe I should go," Lark said. She'd already said too much.

"No, honey, there's no need for that. Lizzy just called me up and told me the whole thing, and I have to say, it's so nice to see Stone's front room decorated for the holidays." She turned toward her son and scowled. "The last few years he's been something of a Grinch, haven't you, son?"

"Momma, please."

Ruby shook her head and rolled her eyes. "Well, he has. He's been a grumpy Grinch."

"Lizzy called you?" Stone asked.

"Yes, she did. She's in her bedroom bawling her eyes out. She's sure you're not going to let her go to David's house tomorrow, and that you'll make her take all the decorations down, and that you were so nasty to Lark, here, that Lark will never speak to her again. All in all, son, I'd say you did yourself proud today in the alienating-your-teenaged-daughter department."

"Right." He looked away from both of them and studied the hole he'd just put in his wall.

Ruby turned toward Lark. "Honey, we're having a big family dinner tonight, and I thought it might be nice if you'd come and join us. It would make Lizzy and Haley feel so much better if you did. They seem to have taken to you like ducks to water."

"You want me to come to dinner, really?"

"Yes, I do. And if you want, you can play my piano all you want. It might be fun to have a little sing-along after dinner. It being the season for caroling and all."

Stone let go of a deep, mournful sigh that might actually have been classified as a groan.

Lark studied his back for a long moment, aware of the attraction she didn't want to feel. She should decline this invitation. Then again, Ruby was Elbert's wife, and Elbert was the man standing in the way of her fulfilling Pop's last request.

"I'd be delighted."

Stone felt like he'd been trapped inside one of those stupid girlie shows on *Masterpiece Theatre* where the hostess holds a dinner party and makes sure that the two unmarried guests are seated next to each other. It was an interesting move on Momma's part seeing as Lark was unlikely to be staying for a long time.

Plus it kind of pissed him off that Lark was worming her way into Momma's confidence. Lizzy was already awed by her. And Lark seemed to have completely beguiled Haley, because she simply accepted the angel as a fact of life. His little girl had babbled all night about how the Angel liked Lark and how Lark liked the Angel.

It was annoying in some way he couldn't quite articulate. And then there was the fact that Lark was...

Way too attractive.

The family had come together to help Momma decorate the big tree she always put in her front room. His brothers and sister had brought their new spouses, and Momma's house practically burst at the seams. He felt like the odd man out this year. Everyone was so happy, and so settled, and so married.

He stood in the corner by Momma's breakfront, sipping a longneck Bud and staring at the interloper in the parlor. Lark was reaching up to hang an angel on a branch above her head and her T-shirt rode up, exposing a wedge of creamy skin above the waistline of her jeans.

Unwanted heat flowed through him.

Haley pranced at Lark's side, her golden hair escaping her ponytail. His little girl seemed to come alive in Lark's presence. And to her credit, Lark was listening carefully and patiently as Haley directed the placement of every one of Momma's angels.

Clay and Jane, Stone's brother and sister-in-law, watched Haley's antics with the sappy look of expectant parents. Jane had made her big announcement at the dinner table. Not that anyone was really surprised that Jane was expecting a baby, since the whole town knew she'd had a doctor's appointment today.

Stone was going to be an uncle. It was a weird feeling. He was used to being the only married one.

He left his spot by the dining room arch and strolled into the living room. Then he picked up a glass ball and hung it on a branch next to where Lark was standing.

She was so tiny. And yet she was unbelievably strong. And like a firefly or something, she had this internal glow about her. He stood there for a long, embarrassing moment wondering what he should do next. Decorating Christmas trees wasn't one of his talents. Neither was talking to women he found attractive.

"So," she said as if she understood his sudden awkwardness, "you're going to be an uncle."

"Yeah, Uncle Grumpy," Stone's younger brother, Tulane, said. Stone wanted to drop-kick Tulane across the living room like he'd done when they were kids.

"He's trying," Lark said with a little smile. "It's not

always easy for warriors, you know." Her voice was soft, and she glanced up at him. Once again he got the uncanny feeling that she really understood. He'd never been Mr. Christmas even when Sharon was alive.

"Hey, y'all, I've got all the photo albums," Momma said from across the room. She came into the parlor weighed down with half a dozen books. "Come on, girls, I know you want to see all those naked pictures of Tulane. He had such a cute butt when he was a baby."

Tulane groaned. "Momma, please."

"Oooh, lemme see," Sarah, Tulane's bride, said as she elbowed her way across the crowded room.

In about five seconds Momma was reigning on the living room couch with Sarah, Jane, and Stone's sister, Rocky, beside her, peering at every embarrassing photo ever taken. Lark took a seat on the rolled arm of the sofa while Hugh, Rocky's husband, leaned nonchalantly over its back, no doubt looking for photos of Rocky when she was little.

"Momma has a real talent for preserving the worst photos ever taken," Clay said.

"You know," Lark said, "I did a project in college about that very thing."

"A project on dodgy photos? You don't say?" Hugh gave her one of his raised eyebrows.

"Well, not exactly. I did this project where I scanned hundreds of photos from family albums. I was looking for the art in plain sight. But I discovered that every family album has the same photos," she said.

"What are you talking about?" Stone asked.

She looked down at the album in Momma's hands. "See this one?" She pointed to a photo of Stone on his first birthday. He was crying, and the single candle on his birthday cake was burning brightly.

"Not one of my better portraits," Stone commented.

"But so you," Momma replied.

Lark laughed. The sound carried him away.

"But how is this photo in someone else's album?" Momma asked.

"Well, this particular photo isn't, but every family album has a picture of the crying baby and the cake with one candle."

"That's kind of creepy," Stone said just to be argumentative.

"Honestly, son," Momma said, "if you want to be a negative person, you can just take your negativity out on the porch or something. I think it's kind of sweet that every family has a photo of a baby on his first birthday. It connects us one to the other, you know? What other photos fall into that category, Lark?"

"Well, the naked baby, the first haircut, the first day of school, the graduation, the picture of the kids without their front teeth." Lark looked up and smiled at Haley when she said that.

And Haley smiled back. Her front teeth were starting to grow in, and she was beginning to get that Bucky Beaver look to her that all kids got at one point or another.

"I think that's a very comforting thing to know," Momma said.

Clay chuckled. "Just don't get any ideas and start posting those naked baby photos on Facebook and tagging me, okay?"

"Just you wait, Clay, your baby will have a naked butt picture, too," Momma said.

Jane giggled, and Clay shook his head. "Never in a million years," he said.

Stone headed back to the kitchen with Tulane for another beer while the oohs and aahs and embarrassing moments continued unabated in the living room.

"Lark's not so bad, you know," Tulane said, popping the top on another beer.

"Don't. She's here because Momma invited her and because she wants to scatter her father's ashes on the eighteenth hole. Daddy's not going to relent on that topic, but Momma is waging one of her little wars. And as usual, I'm stuck right in the middle."

Tulane slapped him on the back. "Cheer up, Stony, the holidays will be over before you know it, and you won't have to put up with all this merrymaking." His brother sauntered back into the living room and leaned over the back of the sofa while he gave his wife's shoulder a little squeeze.

Stone watched from the doorway for the next thirty minutes as older albums were brought out and thumbed through, until the family was looking at photos of Momma and Daddy when they were young.

"Holy sh—" Lark said, cutting off the profanity before she embarrassed herself. "It's Pop. How could that be?" She leaned over the photo album, a frown folding between her eyebrows.

"Oh, my, I forgot about that picture," Momma said. "That's Zeke, Bert's daddy, right there." Momma pointed to the photograph, and Stone took a few steps into the room so he could look at the photo over Momma's shoulder.

"Is that Nita Wills with them?" Rocky asked. "She looks so young and happy."

"They all look happy," Lark whispered.

"They're on the eighteenth hole," Sarah said. "Look, there, right behind them, it's the statue of Jesus. I wonder who took the picture?"

Momma lifted the corner of the photo out of its little tabs and looked on the back. "I remember now. This was one of the pictures in Zeke's camera when he died."

"Did Daddy take that picture?" Tulane asked.

Momma shook her head. "No, Bert and I weren't here when Zeke died. Bert was up in Washington in Walter Reed hospital, and I was up there with him. He'd just gotten back from Vietnam. That was before any of you were born." Momma looked across the room at Daddy. Daddy was in a broody mood. He wasn't happy about Lark being there either.

"Honestly, Bert, how long are you going to hang on to your theory that Lark's daddy was responsible for Zeke's death?" Momma asked

Lark visibly tensed, looking from Momma to Daddy and back again.

"Well, he meddled in things, and that made trouble. And my daddy always managed to get himself in the middle of trouble," Daddy said. It was clear that Momma was winning this particular battle. Momma was a hell of a campaigner.

"Honestly, Bert," Momma said, moving in for the kill, "it's time to let go. It all happened a long time ago. And looking down at this picture, I'm pretty sure that your daddy wouldn't want you blaming Abe Chaikin. They look like they're friends. Why would anyone have even taken this picture if they weren't friends?"

Daddy got up and walked out into the backyard. Stone

knew exactly what was going on in Daddy's mind. Zeke had died too young. And when he died, Daddy's life changed forever.

None of them ever discussed this out loud, but everyone in the family feared there was a kernel of truth to the tale that the Rhodes craziness was handed down from father to oldest son.

It had happened that way with Daddy. One day he was recovering from physical wounds, and the next he was seeing angels. They said it was PTSD, but Daddy never believed that. And the only thing that had changed was that Granddaddy had passed.

There had been a time when Ezekiel Rhodes had been a respected war veteran himself and a lawyer living up in Atlanta. But when his own daddy passed, something snapped inside his head. He left his life in Atlanta and came back to Last Chance to build the golf course on some family land.

Stone didn't believe in angels. Except down in the places of his psyche where he was afraid to go.

"You know," Momma said into the silence that settled in the wake of Daddy's departure, "I'll bet Zeke took that picture himself. He was always messing around with his camera. I didn't know it was your daddy in the picture when I put it in this album, but I saved it because it was the last picture ever made of Zeke."

Lark gave Momma a weak smile. "I'm glad you had it developed. Seeing Pop standing on the eighteenth hole makes it real somehow. I really need to talk to Nita Wills about what happened. She's supposed to be back in town tomorrow."

Momma patted her hand. "It's all right, honey. Whether

we like it or not, fate brought your family and our family together forty years ago."

"Yes, but it's more than that. Pop wants to be laid to rest in the spot where that photograph was taken. And I suddenly have more questions than answers. I don't think I ever saw my father smile like he's smiling in that photo. He was happy here."

She sounded shaken.

"Well, I think we need to find you some answers," Momma said, casting her motherly gaze at Stone and beyond him where Daddy was brooding and smoking a cigar out on the back porch. "And maybe when we do, Bert will let go of the past and give you his permission to lay your daddy to rest. Looking at this picture, I can understand why a person might want to go back to a place and time where they were happy. But life moves forward, not backward."

Momma's gaze riveted Stone to the floorboards. She was sending messages. And he wanted to hear them for once. But he had no clue how to get going.

Lark gave Momma the tiniest of smiles. It didn't last very long, and before it faded from her face, she was pushing up from the couch. "Thanks, Mrs. Rhodes. I really appreciate you inviting me for dinner tonight. It's hard when you lose a loved one, and you made me feel right at home. But I need to get going."

Stone put his beer down on the coffee table. "I'll walk you to your car."

Lark gave him a funny look. "It's just a couple of blocks away, in front of the Kountry Kitchen."

"I know where it is, and I'd feel better escorting you."

By the bunching of muscles along her jaw, he could tell she didn't think she needed an escort. But he didn't care.

"Take your time," Rocky called as he followed Lark through the front door, "we've pretty much eaten all the pie."

"I grew up in New York. I think I can find my car without help," Lark said as she raised the collar of her coat against the evening chill.

"Looks like winter may make an appearance, after all," Stone said in his deep, rumbling drawl, obviously ignoring the bait she'd just tossed in his direction.

"Are you making small talk?"

"Uh-huh." His words turned to steam in the cold air.

Damn him. He was so even-keeled now. So strong and manly and Carmine-like. Carmine would never have let a lady walk to her car in the dark either. It was infuriating.

They walked in silence down the block for a few moments before he spoke again. "I take it, from some of the things you've said, that your last couple of assignments have been tough."

Her feet faltered on an uneven bit of pavement. Stone grabbed her upper arm. "Steady there," he said, his warm breath spilling over her cool cheek.

She shrugged off his hand. "I'm okay."

"Are you? Really?"

"Look, I'm sorry I got all holier-than-thou on you earlier. You really ticked me off when you started yelling at your kids. Like I told you, helping Haley and Liz put up a Christmas tree made me happy. Your daughters gave me something to laugh about. And I haven't had much to laugh about recently."

He stopped.

She stopped.

The feeble light from a streetlamp lit up the threads

of gray in his hair and sparkled in his eyes. "I'm sorry I lost my temper." He took a deep breath. "I seem to have to apologize every time we talk, huh?"

She shrugged. "It's okay. I'm tough."

He jammed his fingers into the pockets of his jeans. "Yeah, I get that. It was just that, see, I was surprised is all. I heard the piano..." His voice trailed off, and then he coughed to cover whatever weakness might have been exposed by his words. "Anyway, I'm glad the kids cheered you up. I can see how Haley adores you. And Lizzy thinks you walk on water. And, well, I get this feeling that maybe you understand stuff about me. Stuff no one does."

"You were a marine, weren't you?" she asked. "I've known a lot of marines over the years. Maybe that's why. What division were you in?"

"Sixth Marine Regiment," he said. "We breached the Saddam Line in 1991. It was a pretty big firefight. I was barely nineteen."

Stone spoke in short sentences, but his words packed a wallop. He'd seen things in 1991 he wanted to forget.

She suddenly wanted to tell him all about what had happened this morning out in the swamp. She wanted to talk about how she was scared of her camera.

What was it about Stone Rhodes that made her feel so brave? It was probably his uncanny resemblance to Carmine Falcone.

Man, she needed to get away from him. Now.

She turned without saying another word and headed toward her father's big SUV.

"You okay living at the river?" he asked. "It's kind of remote out there."

"I'm really okay. And I'm sorry about what happened."

She got into her father's car, slammed the door, and peeled away from the curb. She allowed herself one glance in the rearview mirror. Stone stood under a streetlight, wearing a pair of jeans and a sweater. He looked like her deepest fantasy.

Which meant that he wasn't for real.

The Sorrowful Angel came into Haley's room and sat on the bed. The bed kind of sank on one side when she sat down, just like when Granny or Daddy sat on the edge.

Haley opened her eyes and looked up at the angel. She wasn't weeping or wailing.

"I tried to make changes," Haley whispered, "but Daddy got really, really mad. And then that lady made him even angrier. I'm sorry. I stink at this."

"No, you don't. You made changes. You certainly got your Daddy out of his rut. Now your daddy needs to learn how to laugh again," the angel said.

Haley stared at the shimmering angel. "You really think my changes were good?"

The angel nodded.

"How am I supposed to make Daddy laugh? Daddy never laughs," Haley whispered.

"Tell him jokes." The angel stood up and drifted through the wall that separated Haley's room from Daddy's.

Boy, Daddy was too mad about the changes she'd made in the living room furniture to laugh at any of the jokes that Haley already knew.

She was going to have to get some much better jokes.

CHAPTER 10

Sharon's grave was near a towering magnolia that perfumed the Christ Church cemetery in the summertime. But today the place smelled of winter. Someone had put a Christmas wreath by her headstone.

Stone squatted down, studying the yellowing evergreen decorated with pipe cleaner ornaments and fading glitter. He swallowed hard.

Clearly Haley's handiwork, probably with the help of Stone's sister-in-law Jane. A folded piece of fading construction paper with a crayon picture of a Christmas tree was tucked into the wreath. He opened it to find a single piece of double-lined paper with Haley's carefully printed words:

Dear Mother,
How are things in Heaven? I am OK. Can you ask Jesus to help the angel get back to Heaven? I think she is homesick. That is all I want for Christmas.
Love,
Haley

Stone choked on his emotions, and he had to squeeze his eyes shut and pinch the bridge of his nose to keep from breaking down.

"You want to talk about it?"

Stone turned and stood in one motion, chagrined that someone had snuck up on him. Aunt Arlene was standing there with a gotcha look on her face.

"Uh, hi, Aunt Arlene. I, uh, I gotta go." Stone pocketed Haley's note, then strode down the path toward the church parking lot.

"Stone, wait," Arlene called after him. "Come sit with me for a minute. I think you need to talk about Haley's note."

"I don't want to talk."

"Okay, then, why don't we talk about Roy Burdett's new bass boat. I saw it yesterday. It's pretty cool. It's all composite, has a package of fishing electronics to die for, and it's a pretty shade of blue. Laura-Beth picked the color."

Stone turned around and stared at his aunt. Before Uncle Pete died, Arlene and Pete used to spend half the summer fishing up at Lake Marion. The walls of Arlene's den were covered with fishing trophies, mounted fish, and photos taken over the years. "Don't you let Roy Burdett turn your head with that boat."

She giggled. "Honey, I know how to fend off married men. I wrote the book on that a long time ago." She strolled forward, took him by the arm, and half led, half dragged him over to a small concrete bench not far from Pete's grave site.

"So," Aunt Arlene said, "what brings you out here on a nice morning like this?"

Stone took Arlene's hand in his. "How're you doing, Arlene?"

"I'm fine. I play bridge every week. I go to the book club meetings every other Wednesday. I have my hair done on Thursday. And I have church on Sunday. I work every day at the store. I have friends. I get lonely, sometimes, but it makes me feel nice when Roy Burdett comes in and flirts with me. When was the last time you flirted with anyone?"

"It's been a long time." Of course, last night he'd wanted to flirt, but had messed it up entirely by talking about combat and Sharon's piano. Too bad he had yelled at Lark before he decided that flirting with her was what he wanted to do.

Boy, he was confused.

"Catch any fish lately?" Arlene asked. "I hear you do a lot of fishing down at the pier on the river."

"Arlene, you know good and well that I don't use bait or a lure."

"Why is that? I can't think of anything more boring than fishing without bait. It's mighty peculiar, if you want my honest opinion."

He laughed. It felt good to laugh. "Yeah, it is."

"So why do you do it?"

Stone thought about it for a moment. He thought about his behavior last night, yelling at the girls. He thought about Lark Chaikin with her dark eyes fired up with indignation. Even a city girl like her knew it was crazy to fish without bait.

He gulped down air and spoke. "After Sharon died, when I was offered the job here, one of the perks was knowing that the chief of police was welcome to fish from the pier anytime. So naturally, my first week on the job—this was about six weeks after Sharon's accident—I went down there with a can of worms and my fishing rod.

"I baited my hook, and I threw the line in. And durned if I didn't get a hit right away. It was a little panfish, about yea big." He measured out about five inches between his index fingers.

"Not big enough to keep," Arlene said.

"Yeah. But the damn fish had swallowed the hook." His voice wavered. "I worked for five minutes to get the hook out, but by then the fish was dead."

"It happens."

"Yeah, I know. And I never had any problems with it before. But I couldn't deal with that dead fish. I didn't want to be responsible for it. If I were a stronger man, it wouldn't have bothered me. Or maybe, I would have just given up fishing altogether. But I couldn't do either."

"So you fish without bait."

"It's not bad. The best part of fishing isn't catching fish. It's the casting and the reeling in."

"Ain't that right. Pete used to say that a man could hear himself think out in a bass boat. Once, your uncle told me that it was amazing what he could hear in the silence."

Stone patted Arlene's hand. "Well, it's been nice talking fishing with you, Aunt Arlene, but I gotta go."

"Stone, they have a grief counseling group that meets on Thursday night. I've found that it's very help—"

"You're the third person this week who's suggested that I need grief counseling. But I'm not much for talking in a group setting, and certainly not to the people I'm supposed to be serving and protecting. I don't need people gossiping about my feelings. They already gossip enough in this town."

"I suppose that's fair. But you should talk to someone. Maybe—"

"I gotta go."

Arlene grabbed his hand with a fierce grip. "You listen to me, son, and you listen good. I didn't understand what you're going through until recently. But I've learned something by losing Pete. We all have a hole inside us. Every single person on the face of the earth."

That stopped him. He turned. "A hole?"

"Yeah. You can't be angry at God for making you that way. You have that empty place for a reason."

Stone could feel his brow lowering in a scowl. "Aunt Arlene, I didn't take you for one of those holy rollers."

"I'm not. I'm not trying to get you to come back to church on Sundays. I'm just trying to point out that you're hoarding yourself and pouring your love into something that can't give you anything back. Sharon is gone. Uncle Pete is gone. We loved them both when they were here, and they loved us back. But I sure know that your uncle would be disappointed in me if I went out on Roy's bass boat and fished without any intention of catching a fish. That's living half a life."

Arlene shook her head in disgust. "Fact is, Pete would be horrified. Son, you're holding on so hard to Sharon that the empty place inside is about to swallow you whole. Only love can fill that empty place inside. You have to let go. I think the Buddhists would say that you have to transcend."

"Right." Stone had no idea what Arlene was talking about. *Buddhists? In Last Chance? No way.* "I gotta go."

But Arlene wouldn't let go of his hand. "Have you thought about consulting Miriam Randall?"

"What?"

"You heard me. If you won't talk about your grief to

the minister or a psychologist, at least let Miriam help you find someone else to talk to."

"Miriam already found me my soulmate. I don't believe in much, but I do believe that. And my soulmate is buried right over there, by the big magnolia."

"You're right, I know that." Arlene's voice was so calm and quiet.

"Then what in the Sam Hill are you talking about?"

Arlene gave him a pointed look. "Has it occurred to you that believing in Miriam Randall's abilities has boxed you into a corner? I happen not to believe that God is so mean-spirited that He would give you a soulmate, take her away, and then insist that you spend the rest of your life battling the empty place inside. Love is God's greatest gift."

"So, let me get this right. You want me to ask Miriam to find me another soulmate?"

Arlene's over-made-up eyes lit up with amusement. "Yes, I do. Miriam knows about love. And I'm pretty sure that she doesn't, for one minute, believe that the Lord wants you to live the life you've been living the last few years."

"I don't want another soulmate."

"Of course you don't. That's part of the problem right there."

"Thanks for the advice, Aunt Arlene." She finally let go of his hand, and he stood up.

"Honey," she said as he was about to turn away, "the only thing that matters in this life is love and kindness. If you turn away from love, you're just consigning yourself to misery. Go find yourself a girlfriend."

Stone had no idea what to say in response to that, so he said good-bye. He turned and strode through the graveyard and out to the parking lot. When he reached the sanctuary of the Crown Vic, he sat for a good fifteen minutes reading and re-reading Haley's letter to her mother.

Maybe Haley's angel was right. He needed to make some changes. For Haley's sake, if for no one else.

The nightmare awakened Lark at about two in the morning. The dream was always the same.

She was on a street filled with rubble and smoke, and she was framing a perfect shot of warriors at work. And then she pressed the shutter, and the world went to hell. No matter how hard she tried to stop it, she couldn't take her finger off the shutter.

She got out of bed and paced the small bedroom for hours. Dawn was lighting up the sky when she finally managed to fall back to sleep. And then she slept until after noon and woke up groggy and out of sorts.

She'd wasted most of the day. It was well into the afternoon before she finally headed out to find Nita Wills. Lark left her camera behind.

The Allenberg County Public Library was a 1970s-style building that shared space with the Last Chance Police Department. Her stomach knotted as she entered the glass double doors. She didn't want to run into Chief Rhodes... much. And of course, she wanted her talk with Nita to solve all of the mysteries her father had left her.

The library wasn't very large. Its cinder-block walls were painted a bright yellow that glowed under the fluorescent lights. A few long tables occupied the front of the room adjacent to the only windows. The stacks occupied the back of the room.

The main patrons this afternoon were schoolkids.

"Hope you weren't expecting a real quiet place to read," the woman behind the reception desk said in a hushed voice.

The woman smiled, and Lark's heart turned over in her chest. Nita's hair was longer and her figure fuller, but she was the same woman in the photograph Lark had seen last night. Nita had an open face and a pair of dark, intelligent eyes. One look at her face, and Lark understood why Pop had befriended Nita all those years ago.

"We have a study hour every Thursday for grade-school kids, but it's hard to keep the library quiet," Nita whispered.

"I can see that."

"So, you're new. Are you one of the people who've come to build the factory? If you are, I have some information right here on our book club. It meets every other Wednesday evening." She stood up from her chair and pulled a flyer from a stack on the counter. "It's a great way to meet new folks. I have to tell you that the membership is all women, though."

"Uh, thanks, but I'm not here with the factory, and I'm not planning on staying long. I'm so glad to meet you. I'm Lark Chaikin, Abe's daughter."

Nita's face changed. The smile vanished, and her dark eyes narrowed. "I heard you were in town," Nita said.

"I know this might not be a good time..." Lark cast her gaze toward the kids lining the long tables. She recognized Haley Rhodes among them, kneeling on a chair and bent over a book, her hair falling out of a pair of pigtails.

"You want me to talk about your father, don't you? I heard that he recently died," Nita said, pulling Lark's attention away from Haley.

"Yeah. It's been a little more than a week. He wanted to have his—"

"I know what he wanted. It's all over town."

"Can you tell me why?"

Nita blinked. "You don't know why?"

Lark shook her head. "Pop used to talk about the trip he took in 1968. He always made a big joke out of Golfing for God. But then he'd get this funny look in his eye and tell people that he found himself on the eighteenth hole. He never mentioned it was a hole with a larger-than-life statue of Jesus. That alone should have been worth some kind of comment or explanation, given Pop's view on religion. Ever since I arrived here in Last Chance, the father I thought I knew has become a complete stranger."

"I'm sorry. I can't shed any light."

"But you and he broke the rules."

"Yes, we did. And we stirred up a hornet's nest. All in all, I wish I had never done such a thing," Nita said.

"Why?"

"Well, someone had to sit down at the lunch counter and get things moving here in Last Chance, but I wish I hadn't been the one. I'm not a brave woman. Somehow your daddy talked me into it, and I'll never understand how he did that."

This wasn't exactly what Lark expected to hear. "I see." Lark reached into her purse and pulled out the photograph.

"I was at Ruby Rhodes's house for dinner last night, and the family was looking through an old photo album and came across this one. Ruby said it was probably the last photo ever taken of Zeke. You all looked so happy. Why?"

Nita shrugged. "I have no idea. We were young and

foolish. Oh, not Zeke, of course. Zeke was just plain crazy."

"Really?"

Nita nodded. "Elbert is peculiar, but Zeke was crazy. He used to stand on the corner of Palmetto and Julia on Sunday morning and preach so loud that folks attending church at Christ Episcopalian, the First Methodist, and the Last Chance AME could hear him." She giggled. "Used to annoy my uncle, Reverend Robinson, something fierce."

"You knew Zeke well?"

"I did a little bookkeeping for him. Back in 1968, I was a student at Voorhees College. I left school here and restarted at the University of Chicago in 1970. I left Last Chance for a long time. I came back when my husband died. I thought this town would be a better place to raise my daughter, Kamaria. I was right. She's done well for herself. She was just elected mayor."

"So you can't explain why Pop sent me on this wild goose chase?"

Nita shook her head. "No, I'm sorry. Your daddy was here in Last Chance for a grand total of ten days. I didn't know him at all. We just did a silly, foolish thing that changed my life in ways I can't even fully explain. And not all those changes were for the good."

Nita was holding something back. Lark had spent enough time with journalists to know when someone was lying. So she pushed a little harder.

"Do you think my father was responsible for Zeke Rhodes's death?"

Nita's eyes sparked with anger. "No. And don't you go listening to that story."

"Stone's father seems to believe it."

"The truth is what I told everyone forty years ago: Your daddy had nothing to do with Zeke's death. I can't help it if there are crazy people living here who believe in conspiracies." Nita's voice had dropped down to a hoarse whisper, and by the vehemence of her words, Lark knew that she had pushed one of the librarian's hot buttons.

"So Zeke's death was an accident?"

"I didn't say that. But your daddy had nothing to do with it. I was there when Abe said good-bye to Zeke. I watched him drive off in that VW bus of his. And that's where the matter should be left." Nita gave Lark a sharp and meaningful look. She wasn't going to say anything more, but it was clear that Nita thought Zeke's death was not accidental.

"So, if that's true, then why does Elbert dislike me so much?"

"It's not my place to explain that. You might want to ask the chief of police. Now, if you don't mind, I have work to do."

Nita turned away and headed toward a group of kids who had forgotten to use their library voices. Lark was about to leave, utterly defeated, when she saw movement out of the corner of her eye. She shifted her gaze just in time to see an older boy give Haley's pigtails a hard and malicious tug. Haley let out a yowl of protest, but by the time Nita looked up, the culprit had scooted to the water fountain where he made a show of loudly slurping water.

Nita gave Haley her stern-librarian look, and the little girl's eyes filled with tears.

The look on Haley's face cut Lark right to the quick, and she found herself crossing the library instead of leaving it. Just then, the brat at the water fountain straightened up and headed back toward his chair. As he passed Haley, he called the little girl a name that shocked Lark to her core. No way Haley knew what that word meant. Lark was surprised the boy did.

The little girl was stoic. She knew she had been insulted in some way, but she pretended to read her book. She tried to ignore the insult with a valor that ought to have won her a medal.

"Hey you," Lark said to the bully. "What's your name?"

The kid looked up, a blush coloring his cheeks.

By now Nita was heading in their direction. "Is there a problem?" the librarian asked.

"Yeah, there is. You want to tell the librarian what you just did?" Lark stared at the kid.

"Drew?" Nita turned her deadly librarian look on him.

"I was just getting water from the fountain."

"Uh-huh," Nita said. "And while you were at it, you pulled Haley's hair. I saw you."

"You did?" Drew and Lark said in unison.

Nita glared at the kid. "I'm a librarian. I have eyes in the back of my head."

"I bet you didn't hear the filthy name he called Haley," Lark said.

Haley turned in her seat and gazed up at Lark with a grateful expression on her precious little face. Warmth flooded through Lark.

"What did he call her?" Nita asked.

"I'm not going to repeat the word, but it was inappropriate and if I were his mother, I would go get a bar of soap." Lark tried to give Drew a scary-lady look. Evi-

dently her death-ray vision was not nearly as effective as
Nita's. Drew seemed unimpressed.

He wasn't even impressed a moment later when Stone
Rhodes sauntered into the library all spit and polish in his
uniform and looking like a warrior. Lark's body flushed,
and her stomach dropped three inches. Man, she was
behaving just like a sixteen-year-old girl with a crush on
an older man she could never have.

Haley took that minute to leave her chair and rush
right toward her father. She wrapped her arms around his
legs in a hug so fierce it made Lark's heart ache. He squatted down. "What's up, sugar beet?" he asked.

And that's when Haley repeated the word that Drew
Bennett said, in a voice that was very far removed from
a real library voice. "Miss Lark told him that he needed
to have his mouth washed out with soap. And the angel
clapped when she said that. Daddy, I think the angel really,
really likes Miss Lark."

The chief looked up at Lark. She expected to see anger
in his gaze. Anger for the bully who'd used such a filthy
word for such a sweet child. Anger that Haley had mentioned her imaginary friend. Anger that Lark had gotten
involved at all.

But there wasn't a shred of anger in Stone Rhodes's
gaze. No, his gaze was hot. His green eyes sparked with a
longing that made Lark's middle burn with desire.

Man. Her wayward and confused heart melted right in
her chest.

"You called Haley Rhodes that filthy word?" Nita
hissed at Drew. She grabbed the boy by the arm and forc-
ibly dragged him toward the chief.

"Stone, would you please take custody of this young

man and let his daddy know that I do not tolerate bullies in my library."

Stone straightened up and turned toward the kid, who had yet to show even the slightest bit of remorse. "C'mon, Drew," he said. "You and me need to have a little talk."

"I don't have to go with you. It's a free country. And my daddy is sheriff, which means he outranks you."

Stone's fist closed around the kid's upper arm. "Not when you use language like that in *my town's* library. C'mon, I'm getting Deputy Easley to watch you until your daddy comes to bail you out. And I wouldn't put it past the deputy to actually wash out your mouth."

"You can't do that. Besides, my daddy uses that word all the time."

By the flex in the muscles along Stone's jaw, Lark got the distinct impression that the chief of police was holding his tongue as he half dragged the kid out of the library, across the entrance foyer, and into the offices of the Last Chance police department.

Lark turned toward Haley. The little girl was staring after her father, and she looked so alone. Lark put her arm around her shoulder. "So, what were you reading?" she asked.

"A joke book."

"A joke book? Really?"

Haley nodded, but she seemed subdued.

Lark snagged the little girl's hand and drew her back toward the place where she'd been sitting. "C'mon, you can read it to me."

"Okay, but you're not the person who needs to laugh. Maybe I can practice on you and then maybe you can come with me and Daddy on our date."

"Date?"

Haley nodded and whispered in her library voice. "Yeah, see Lizzy is on a date tonight with David, so Daddy is taking me to the mall in Orangeburg for dinner and then we're going to visit Santa."

"Oh, well, I'm sure your father doesn't want me tagging along."

Haley looked up just as Stone reentered the room. "Hey, Daddy," she said, forgetting all about her library voice again. "You don't mind if Miss Lark comes on our date with us, do you?"

And to Lark's utter astonishment Stone Rhodes put his finger to his lips, gave his daughter a meaningful but utterly loving look, and then gazed at Lark.

"Are you free?" he asked.

CHAPTER 11

Haley clutched the book she'd checked out of the library and read out loud, "Why did the robber wash his clothes before he ran away with the stolen money?"

"Easy," Daddy said, "because he wanted to make a clean getaway."

Miss Lark laughed. But Daddy didn't. Daddy was spoiling everything again, because he knew all the jokes in that dumb old book. Daddy had no sense of humor.

"Where did you learn all these jokes?" Miss Lark asked Daddy. They were sitting at a table at the fried chicken place near the mall, and Miss Lark hadn't eaten any chicken at all. She'd ordered a salad.

"I think Lizzy had that book when she was little."

"That's no fair," Haley grumped.

"Okay, try me again," Daddy said.

Haley flipped through the pages and picked out a joke. "Okay, here's one. What does a snowman eat for breakfast?"

Daddy frowned. He leaned his head on his hand and

tapped his cheek with his fingers. He looked at Miss Lark. He kind of smiled. Miss Lark definitely returned his smile. "You got any ideas?" he asked.

She shook her head. "Nope."

"Okay," Daddy said, "I don't know that one."

Haley struggled not to smile. "Frosted Flakes," she said.

Miss Lark laughed, again. This time Daddy kind of smiled, maybe, just a little bit.

The Sorrowful Angel cried.

Haley closed the book, defeated. "Okay, can we go see Santa now?" she asked.

"What, no more jokes?" Daddy asked.

She shook her head. What was the point? Daddy hadn't laughed, not even once.

And the Sorrowful Angel was crying harder than ever. It was time to ask for some real help. Santa would probably know what to do.

But half an hour later, after she'd told Santa what she wanted for Christmas, Haley knew she was going to have to figure it out on her own. It turned out that Maryanne Hanks was right. She'd told Haley yesterday that Santa was just a story that grown-ups made up. Haley hadn't believed Maryanne yesterday. But now she knew the truth. Santa had been wearing a fake beard.

You'd have to be blind or stupid not to realize it.

And even if Santa's beard had been real, the Santa she'd just consulted was just like every other grown-up. Once Haley tried to explain about the angel, Santa had gotten that look in his eyes. It seemed to Haley that if anyone believed in angels, it would be Santa.

She held on to Daddy's hand as they walked out into the parking lot. She wanted to cry as hard as the angel.

"Santa isn't real, is he?" she said.

Daddy stopped and so did Miss Lark. Miss Lark bended down and took Haley by the shoulders. "Santa is just as real as your angel," she said.

Haley looked into Miss Lark's big, brown eyes. She was telling the truth. And now that Haley thought about it, Miss Lark was one of only a few grown-ups who didn't get that funny look on her face when the subject of the angel came up.

"You're sure? Because Maryanne said that Santa was just a made-up story."

"I'm sure. You have to have faith in him, Haley. There are lots of things in this world that people can't always see. And Santa Claus is one of them," Miss Lark said. "But Santa is one of the best things in this world—like angels. And don't you ever forget it."

Stone walked Lark to the door of Hettie Marshall's river house. The porch light was on, and the yellow glow put a spark in her dark eyes. She was so tiny and so fierce. He'd thoroughly enjoyed her company, even if she and Haley had spent an inordinate amount of time talking to and about the angel.

"I don't know whether to be thankful or furious about the way you compared Haley's angel to Santa," Stone said.

"I thought I handled that brilliantly."

He did, too. But he didn't want to admit it. "You didn't tell her the truth," he said. His protest sounded lame.

"The truth is depressing." Lark cocked her head and looked up at him like a lost puppy dog.

"But she's going to figure it out pretty soon," Stone

said. "She's eight. It's the age when kids start figuring things out. What do I do then?"

She laughed. It was a bright sound. "Coward. It's easy. You pay attention to her and let her know that Santa is still real."

"But—"

"Look, Stone, I had a father who relished every opportunity to explain the truth to me. Every miracle, every scrap of magic. He explained it all. I hated being seven. I made up Carmine Falcone when I was seven."

"He isn't real either. He's just a character in your father's books."

A little crooked smile touched her lips. "Let your daughter believe in what she wants to. Didn't you believe in Santa once? Although I'm having a hard time seeing it. Right now you look kind of like the Grinch with a shiny badge."

A sudden, unexpected laugh burbled up from his chest. It was a short thing, but it almost felt as if something inside had broken away.

"Ah ha," she said, her dark eyes filled with a devilish gleam, "the big strong warrior knows how to laugh. Too bad you didn't laugh at Haley's jokes. Next time, you should fake it, even if you've heard the joke before. She was trying to cheer you up."

"You've called me that twice. Why?"

"What? Warrior?"

He nodded. "I'm a cop, not a warrior."

She shrugged. "The two are not mutually exclusive. You're a warrior even if your war is over."

"But yours isn't, is it?"

She looked away and the spark left her eyes. What was

going on with her? Something. He wanted to press the point and get to the bottom of it. But he didn't know how.

An utterly unwanted urge to protect her swelled up in him. She was so tiny, a whisper of wind might blow her away. But he'd seen her photographs. She was the warrior, not him.

Maybe that was why he wanted to stay and talk with her. He'd never known a woman who had been to war before. But Haley was waiting in the truck, and he had to pick up Lizzy at David's house. And besides, he had a feeling she didn't really want to swap war stories. He had a feeling her stories were pretty grim.

So he did the only thing he could think of on short notice. He leaned forward and gave Lark a quick kiss on the cheek. "Thank you. For saving Haley's faith in Santa. And because I had a nice time on our date," he whispered, and then turned on his heel and hightailed it back to his truck.

Haley had witnessed the entire encounter. She would tell Momma about that little kiss. And everyone in town would know about it tomorrow.

But he wasn't sorry.

"Barukh atta adonay eloheynu melekh ha-olam she-asa nissim la-avoteynu ba-yyamim ha-hem ba-zzman ha-zze."

Lizzy had no idea what the Hebrew words meant, but they had an interesting lilt to them as David and his family spoke them aloud.

David, wearing a small white skullcap, lit the candle that sat in the tallest place on a nine-armed candelabra. Only four candles had been placed in the candleholders.

The candles were all different colors and looked totally festive.

David's father leaned over and said quietly, "The English translation is: Blessed art thou, Lord our God, King of the universe, who wrought miracles for our fathers in the days of old at this season."

David finished lighting the first candle. He blew out his match, then picked up the lit candle and handed it off to his younger brother Jonathan. Robbie, another brother who was only five, looked on with a solemn face.

"Why are there eight places on the menorah, Robbie?" Mrs. Raab asked the little boy as his older brother lit the remaining three candles from right to left.

"Because the oil lasted eight days instead of one. Because a great miracle happened here," Robbie said with the same kind of fervor that Haley sometimes used when she was repeating a lesson from Sunday School.

Mr. Raab stepped in and explained. "Hanukkah is a celebration of a miracle that happened right after Judah the Maccabee reclaimed a temple from the Syrian king. The temple was cleaned and rededicated, but there wasn't enough oil for the light in the tabernacle to burn for more than a day. By some miracle, though, the oil lasted for eight days, until more purified oil could be found."

"Yeah, but the best story is the one about Judith," David said. He looked up, a gleam in his eye. "She's the one who—"

"I know the story of Judith," Lizzy said. "We studied it in Bible camp this summer. She's the one who got the evil general totally drunk and then beheaded him, right?"

"Bravo," Mr. Raab said. "Not many people around here read their Old Testament."

"Oh, but the best stories are in the Old Testament. My grandfather says that—" Lizzy stopped midsentence before she repeated Granddaddy's colorful thoughts on the Old Testament.

"What does your grandfather say?" Mr. Raab asked.

Lizzy gave a totally lame shrug and said, "Oh, he always says that he likes the Old Testament better. And I suppose he has a point. I mean, out at Granddaddy's golf course, the Old Testament holes are way more fun than the New Testament ones. Y'all are in for a treat when they get the old place fixed up. The plague of frogs is the best one."

Mrs. Raab didn't look amused by what Lizzy had just said. "Is there truly a hole at that golf course that depicts the plague of frogs?"

"Yes, ma'am."

"How?"

Heat crawled up Lizzy's face. Why had she even brought Granddaddy up? "Uh, well, see, there are these frogs on either side of the fairway and they spit water."

"C'mon, Mom, it sounds fun," David said.

"Making fun of the Passover story isn't right," she said, then turned and stalked into the kitchen.

David moved away from the window where the menorah had been placed. "We let the candles burn until they go out." He stepped a little closer, invading Lizzy's space. Her stomach fluttered.

He whispered, "What does your grandfather really say about the Old Testament?"

She looked up into David's dark, clever eyes. "Uh, well, he says it beats television for excitement."

David smirked. "That's not the complete truth, is it?"

She shook her head. "No. He says that if you're looking

for sex and violence, you'll find it in the Old Testament."
Heat crawled up her body from her toes to her forehead.

Amusement lit up David's eyes. "Awesome. He's got a
point. Have you read the Song of Solomon?"

Lizzy felt like she might go right up in a column of
flame. "Yeah, in Bible class this summer."

They might have stood there looking into each other's eyes if it weren't for Robbie. He tugged on the edge
of Lizzy's sweater. "Hey, you wanna learn how to play
dreidel?" he asked.

"Sure," Lizzy said. Robbie was a mini copy of David,
with the same dark curly hair and dark eyes.

"Cool." Robbie turned and ran toward the family room.

David muttered as he and Lizzy followed, "You may
regret learning this game. How many pennies are you
prepared to lose? Because Robbie may look young and
innocent, but inside him, there lives a gambler with awesome luck."

"Gambler?"

"Yeah, dreidel is all about gambling."

Lizzy sat on the floor in the family room with David
and his brothers. The boys quickly explained the object of
the game, played with a four-sided top, each side printed
with a Hebrew letter that provided instructions on what
to do with the pennies in the pot. One letter meant do
nothing, another meant take half, a third meant take all,
and the fourth meant put a penny in the pot. Every player
antied up a penny, and the gambling started.

Robbie might have been only five, but he totally rocked
at this game.

Dinner was served about the time Lizzy had lost all
her pennies and pocket change to little Robbie.

She sat with the Raabs at their dinner table, surprised that they didn't say grace. They had prayed earlier, but not now. The food consisted of potato and onion pancakes served with sour cream and applesauce. It wasn't exactly what Lizzy would have expected for a dinner. Latkes were kind of like breakfast hash browns. But she could understand why David and his brothers loved latkes. They were totally delicious.

She also appreciated why David and his brothers loved their holiday, even though the Raabs didn't give elaborate or expensive gifts.

They didn't seem to miss the gifts. And it struck her that even though David was missing out on Christmas, he had things that Lizzy didn't have.

Like a mother.

Of course Lizzy wanted Mrs. Raab to approve of her, but she also totally understood why David's mother was uncomfortable. Probably, if Momma was still alive, she would be uncomfortable with David. Lizzy didn't remember Momma very well, but all the folks in Last Chance sure did. They were always saying that Momma had been a real dedicated churchwoman who volunteered for every cause and who had lived her life like a true Christian.

These accolades about her mother were almost always accompanied by negative comments about how Daddy never set foot inside a church.

Yeah. Momma would probably have disapproved of David, just like Mrs. Raab disapproved of Lizzy. Not that Mrs. Raab was mean. She went out of her way to be polite, but it was the kind of politeness that sets a person apart.

Despite the awkwardness, Lizzy still had a great time, and she wasn't ready to leave when Daddy finally came to pick her up around nine o'clock. Thank goodness her father showed up at the door wearing something other than his policeman's uniform. Mr. Raab was some kind of brainy structural engineer, and Mrs. Raab made it clear that she kind of looked down on people who never went to college, like her father.

"Come in, Chief Rhodes," Mrs. Raab said. "Can I get you a cup of coffee? Some cookies?"

"No, ma'am. Haley's out in the truck waiting." Daddy turned toward Lizzy, who was getting her coat out of the hall closet. "You ready to go?"

"Uh, Chief Rhodes," Mrs. Raab said as she put her hand on Daddy's arm. "My husband and I would like just a short word with you."

And with that, Mrs. Raab practically dragged Daddy back to the kitchen.

"Oh, boy," David said. "Mom's going to give him an earful."

"An earful of what?"

David looked slightly guilty. "Mom isn't too wild about us being friends."

"Because I'm Christian and you're Jewish?"

He nodded. "It's totally stupid. The real problem is she's not happy about being here. She liked living in Michigan. My aunts and uncles are there. The only reason we're here is because Dad had so much trouble finding a job back home. Mom is always complaining about how we have to schlep all the way to Orangeburg to find a synagogue. And the synagogue there isn't as conservative as she'd like. She also has to drive Jonathan there three times a week for Hebrew School or he's not going to be ready for his bar mitzvah next year."

"That's a total bummer, but I don't see why any of that means we shouldn't be friends."

"Yeah, if you were a guy, maybe. But Mom isn't happy about me having a *shikse* girlfriend."

Lizzy's heart kicked against her ribs. "What's that mean?"

"It means a girl who isn't Jewish."

"I'm not your girlfriend."

David took her hand in his. His palm was a whole lot bigger than hers, even if he was about the same height. "You're my friend and you're a girl. In fact, you're the best friend I've got in Last Chance. You may be my only friend."

"No, that's not—"

"Yeah, it's true. I don't fit in here. But you don't ever make me feel unwelcome." He grinned. "You even know the story of Judith. You scored a few points with Dad on that one. And probably with Mom, too, but she doesn't want to admit it. I think they both expected you to come in here trying to sign me up for Jesus, or talking about how great Christmas is in comparison with Hanukkah. She was mad about me getting home late yesterday because we put up a Christmas tree."

"Well, that makes your mother and my father *both* angry about that."

"Yeah. I'm sorry."

"It's okay. My dad is a total grump this time of year. But here's the thing, I've decided not to let grumpy people ruin my holiday. I think the lighting ceremony was totally awesome. I enjoyed the latkes. I'm glad I came."

"So am I." And before she could stop him, David leaned down and gave her a quick kiss on the cheek that made her insides go a little crazy.

Just then, the door to the kitchen opened, and David took a big step away from her.

"C'mon, Lizzy, let's go. Haley's waiting." Daddy sounded angry again.

It was annoying. Between Daddy and Mrs. Raab, it sure did look like the adults in Lizzy's life had lost the meaning of the words "holiday spirit."

CNN was filled with political news, and Stone wondered why he even bothered to watch it. But he didn't turn the TV off. He liked to sleep with the television on. The voices made him feel less alone when he climbed into bed at night. His bed was just about the loneliest place on earth.

He leaned back against his pillow and tried to find his way to sleep.

But he couldn't.

He was angry at the Raabs for suggesting that he break up Lizzy's friendship with David. He was worried to distraction about Haley and her angel and mortified by his stupid failure to realize that his daughter was trying to cheer him up tonight. He had a raft of daily worries, not the least of which was Jimmy Marshall and the lack of action on the part of the Allenberg Sheriff's Department.

And on top of all that, he was having trouble keeping Lark Chaikin from invading his thoughts. He settled his hands behind his head and studied the ceiling in the blue TV light. He should have been bolder tonight. He should have kissed her on the lips.

Regret assailed him. Followed by a prickling sense of guilt.

He rolled out of bed and paced the floor, antsy as a

teenager. Why did he feel like he was cheating on Sharon? It was stupid.

He sat on the edge of his bed and heaved a big sigh.

Haley was right. Lark was right, too. He needed to make some changes. He needed to quit feeling guilty about Lark. He needed to quit being a Grinch.

He smiled at the thought. Lark had called him a Grinch with a badge. Yeah, it kind of fit, didn't it?

He looked down at his hands. His wedding band winked at him in the flickering light.

"I miss you so much," he whispered as he caressed the gold with his finger. He stared at the wedding band for a long time. In his heart, he still felt married. He wanted to remain faithful to that love. But yesterday at Momma's house, he'd also felt so single and alone. His brothers and sister were all hitched up now, and he was the odd man out.

A married man shouldn't feel so lonely. Wearing the ring wouldn't ever bring Sharon back.

It took more energy than he thought it would, just to slide the damn thing off his finger. And then, once it finally came off, he was left with an indentation and a white line where the ring had rested for twenty years.

He put the ring on his bedside table. Then he turned off the television and climbed back into his lonely bed. But he didn't sleep.

He kept thinking about Lark Chaikin.

CHAPTER
12

Lark studied the photograph with a critical eye. She'd taken the shot with a large f-stop, thereby controlling the depth of field. Stone Rhodes, caught in the act of casting a fishing line, stood out sharply against an unfocused background of muted green. She'd managed to frame the photo with a small wisp of Spanish moss in the foreground, and she'd caught the tiniest of half grins on the chief's mouth.

It was amazing she had been able to shoot him at all. What was it about Stone Rhodes? His image—the first real photograph Lark had taken in months—lit up the LCD screen on her laptop in a preternatural way.

In fact, for a photograph taken in winter, this one practically teemed with life. The vitality of the man came through in the play of muscles, the tendons in his neck and jaw, the tension in his beautiful big hands. The background held the green of living things.

It was like Stone Rhodes had pushed all the shadows out of the field of vision. It was a crazy thought.

This image seemed to capture everything Carmine

Falcone represented. And that was a little frightening, too. She was thirty-six years old. She didn't need an imaginary friend and protector.

She indulged herself for longer than was absolutely necessary to Photoshop some of the small imperfections. She reveled in the photo. She knew that, even after she left Last Chance, a copy of this photograph would perpetually live on her hard drive. She would drag it out and look at it when she needed courage, or reassurance, or hope.

And she would always remember that little awkward kiss he'd laid on her cheek last night. What was that all about? She'd been so busy the last few days picking fights with him. And why had she been doing that?

Maybe because she hated the idea of needing a big strong shoulder to lean on.

She pushed up from the small kitchen table and disconnected her camera from the computer. She wasn't going to let fear get the best of her. If she could shoot a photo of Stone Rhodes, she could shoot a photo of anything. And she would get herself back to normal today, if it was the last thing she did. On December twenty-fifth, she would be on that airplane headed for Africa. She would be ready to do her job again.

She headed outside.

Wispy curls of steam rose from the river into the chilly morning air. Winter seemed to be making a reappearance. She headed toward the river. She got halfway down the riverbank before she saw Stone, standing on the pier, casting a fishing line.

Holy crap, he was up early. It was barely dawn. She raised her camera and poised her finger on the shutter.

She ground her teeth together and squeezed off a shot. Nothing disastrous happened.

She watched him for about five minutes before she realized that something had changed. There was a small Styrofoam cup sitting on the planking by his foot, and a tackle box, too. He was using bait.

She stifled the urge to sneak up on him. Her ability to quietly trail people came in handy when she was trying to get truly candid shots. But she didn't want to startle him, so she cleared her throat and made sure her boots made noise as she walked out onto the pier. He twisted and gazed over his shoulder. One glimpse of those deep green eyes, shaded by his uniform Stetson, had her heart pumping hard in her chest.

"So you've got bait," she said.

"Yeah. I brought it for you."

"For me?" She peered into the Styrofoam coffee cup filled with wiggling dirt. "Oh, gee, I don't think anyone has ever given me worms before."

He chuckled. It was a deep rumbling sound. He should laugh more often. It was incredibly sexy.

"Come here. I'm going to give you a fishing lesson."

"What makes you think I want to learn how to fish?"

He peered at her from under the brim of his hat, and the look on his face was priceless. Stone Rhodes was an experienced warrior, but he was also vulnerable on the inside, like a green kid fresh from boot camp. He seemed just a little nervous.

That made two of them.

"Well," he said after a long moment, "I reckon you could benefit from fishing."

"Really? What makes you say that?"

One of his shoulders lifted a little. "You have a tough job, Lark."

A shiver started at the base of her spine. He had been to war. He knew.

When she didn't reply to his comment, he continued, "See, fishing is Zen. You cast a line, you reel it in, and you repeat the process. And all that kind of frees your mind."

"Really?"

"Yeah. The Zen works better without bait, but I think I'm in the minority on that, so I'm trying to conform." The tiniest of smiles touched his lips.

"So, this is like fishing therapy or something?" She let her voice go just a little bit flirty.

And he responded right on cue. His eyes darkened just a little, and his smile deepened enough to show a row of expression lines bracketing his mouth. He was gorgeous.

"You wanna try?" he asked in his deep southern drawl. Carmine didn't have a drawl like that, but maybe her imagination had been lacking when she'd first invented him. She would make amendments. In the future, when she imagined Carmine, he would have a drawl. Definitely.

She stepped forward. "So what do I do?"

"I'll show you." He put the reel in her hands and then stepped behind her. He wasn't close enough to touch her, but her skin reacted just the same. He radiated warmth, and she wanted to pull that warmth around her like a comfy sweater.

She hefted the rod in her right hand. "Okay, what do I do with this thing?"

He placed his hand over hers, where she held the rod. His hands were rough and warm…and he'd taken off his wedding ring. He was also fishing with bait. Not to mention the fact that he'd kissed her last night. Her mouth went dry.

"See this button?" he said, pulling her distracted thoughts back to the moment. He pointed with his thumb to a little push button on the top of the reel.

"Yeah."

"Put your thumb there."

She did as he directed, and he placed his much, much larger thumb on top of hers.

A minute ago, she'd wanted to draw his warmth around her shoulders, and now it was almost as if he were draped there. She could hardly breathe from the awareness.

"So," he continued, his voice strong and steady and seemingly unaffected. "There's a rhythm to a cast. You press that button down, and you reach back, and when you cast, you release your thumb. If you don't release, the line gets tangled up."

"Okay," she said.

"Ready to try?"

"Uh-huh." She would have said anything to him at this point. Her heart was pounding, and her brain chemistry had gone wild. She had to fight against the urge to drop the damn rod, turn in his arms, and lay a big wet kiss on him—right on his mouth this time.

But if she did that, he might run away. And she didn't want Stone to run. She was enjoying his company—more than she should, more than was wise. So she tried to keep it all together. To hold him there by going along with all his fishing nonsense.

"Ready?" he asked.

"Uh, yeah." Her voice sounded unsteady. Surely he was aware of what he was doing to her insides.

He raised the rod, and her right hand went along for the ride. He did exactly as he'd explained, pressing the button on the reel until he threw the line.

The line flew out in an arc, the reel hissing as it ran. The hook and the little red and white thingie on the end hit the water with a little plop.

"Now," he said, releasing his hand, but continuing to lean against the railing on either side of her. "You watch the bobber."

"Bobber?"

"The red and white thing."

"Ah."

"If it goes under, you've hooked something."

The current took her line and tugged at it, the bobber dipping below the surface. "It's already going under. How can you tell if a fish bites?"

"Don't worry, you'll know."

"How do I reel it in?"

"Just turn the crank."

She experimented and got the feel of reeling it in. Eventually she had reeled the hook, line, and bobber all the way in.

"Okay, you try casting by yourself."

He stepped away, and the cold seeped right up her back. Suddenly fishing didn't seem nearly as much fun.

She attempted to cast her line and almost strangled herself with the camera around her neck.

"Here, give me your camera. It will make it easier," he said.

She took off the camera, but hesitated for the smallest instant before handing it to him. He sensed her reluctance to let go because he said, "Don't worry, honey, I'll guard it with my life." He pushed off the railing beside her and plopped down onto one of the long benches that lined the pier. He stretched out his long legs and crossed his ankles.

He was suddenly too far away and looking way too relaxed. Damn.

"Go on, cast the line," he said.

"Uh-huh." The man didn't seem to understand that she was not precisely looking for the Zen of fishing.

"It's all in the rhythm, honey," he added with a little glint in his eye.

Holy crap, was he actually flirting back?

"I'll keep that in mind," Lark said as she turned away and concentrated on casting the line.

She practiced, and after a while, she had to admit that there was something kind of serene about casting a fishing line into the river.

Although true serenity was completely impossible with Stone Rhodes sitting there silently watching her. The man had a way of disturbing the atmosphere just by breathing. He didn't say a thing, yet she became increasingly aware of him as the silence deepened.

And then something hit her fishing line and pulled hard. The bobber went under, and her fishing rod bent almost double. "Oh, shit, I think I just caught something. Help, what do I do now?"

Stone unfolded himself from the bench and stood beside her. "Just let the fish take the line for a minute."

His gentle voice continued to give her directions on when to reel and when to let the fish have line. The fish pulled and tugged and swam one way and then another. Eventually, she brought it up to the surface, where its back flashed silver against the dark water. She handed the rod over to Stone at the last. He walked over to the gap in the railing where a ladder stepped down into the current. He'd grabbed a fishing net, and dipped it into the water and hauled up the fish.

"Holy crap, he's really big," she said.

Stone chuckled. "No, not so big."

"No?" The fish looked to be about eighteen inches long.

"It's a channel catfish. This is a baby compared with the big 'uns that you can catch. Hardly worth the work of cleaning it."

The fish was flopping and struggling in the net, and suddenly Lark wasn't nearly as excited about fishing as she'd been when she was battling the fish on the line. "So, we're going to throw it back?"

Stone had the fish in his hands now and was carefully taking out the hook, even though the fish was flipping its tail wildly. There was something unbelievably gentle about the way he managed the fish. And he didn't just toss it back in the water. He submerged it and gently let it go.

Lark breathed a sigh of relief as the fish swam a little way off and disappeared into the murky depths of the river.

He stepped back up onto the pier, grabbed a towel that lay across his tackle box, and dried his hands. "So," he said, pinning her with his green-eyed stare, "now you know why I usually don't bother with bait."

"Yeah, I guess I do."

He sat down on the bench and picked up her camera. "You've been out taking photos of our fair town, huh?" he asked.

The unease crept up her back. She remained silent, and he looked up at her, his eyes sharp and questioning.

"Sometimes I feel like maybe I should shoot photos without a memory card," she finally whispered.

"Is that so?" He looked down at the camera and found the on button. And without any permission, he began to flip through the paltry collection of photos she'd shot the last couple of days.

He grunted as he flipped through the photos of himself. "You snuck up on me," he muttered.

"Yeah. I have a talent for that," she said.

He didn't react to her snark. Instead he kept flipping through the photos without comment for half a minute until something stopped him.

A frown rumpled his brow, and he squinted at the screen. "What the hell is that?"

"What is what?" She sat beside him on the bench.

He angled the camera in her direction, so she could see the small screen. It was one of the photos she'd taken of the heron, right before the gunfire had thrown her into the flashback.

"It's a heron."

"That's not what I'm talking about." He pointed at a small red speck in the background. She had used a big depth of field so the background was in focus. "What's that?"

"I have no idea. I wasn't photographing that."

"It's red."

"Yeah, so?"

"You might see some red berries out in the swamp this time of year, but that is not berry red. You see orange safety vests out there all the time. But not red ones."

"It could be a bird. A cardinal?"

"No way. You got a way of blowing this up?"

"Sure. I've got my computer up at the house, why?"

"Because I have a bad feeling about that photograph. Jimmy Marshall was wearing a red golf shirt the day he disappeared."

She stared at Stone while a familiar chill crept through her body from her head right down to her boots.

Stone shouldn't have said anything. He should have simply asked for a copy of the photo. But no, he'd had to open his mouth. And the minute he told Lark about Jimmy Marshall, her face drained of color. She suddenly transformed into the sick and troubled woman he'd found out at the golf course a week ago.

When had he stopped thinking about her as a problem and started thinking about her as one of his own? One of the people he was sworn to defend and protect.

He couldn't say. But the frightened look in her doe eyes put a kink in his gut. Damn. What was wrong with him?

He should never have looked at her photos. He should have stood behind her and helped her with the rod. He should have made a move while they were standing together that way. He should have...

Well, it was water under the pier now. He stood up. "C'mon, let's go look at that picture. I'm sure it's nothing."

She took her camera back and gave him a stiff-shouldered shrug. "No, I've got a feeling it's something."

"Why would you say that?"

She put the camera around her neck. "Because I have a talent for capturing shadows."

She turned and hurried up the riverbank. It took him a minute to snag his pole and tackle box. Giving her a head start.

He'd seen her photos. They captured light, not shadow. He ran after her. "Wait, Lark."

She didn't wait. She marched up to Hettie's house and through the door. By the time he caught up, she had already fired up her laptop.

"What did you mean back there? About the shadows?"

"It's like I said before, sometimes I wish I shot images without a memory card." She looked up at him, her brown eyes bright.

"The photo of the heron in flight was a beautiful thing, Lark."

"Not if it's also a photo of a dead body."

"But you don't know that."

"No, but that's the way it always works. The shadows are there in the background. Always."

Her voice grew rough, and the brightness in her eyes turned into tears. She fought them bravely and turned her focus on the computer and her camera, despite the fact that her hands were shaking.

Stone stood there, not certain what to do. He wasn't a very smooth guy. He had virtually no experience with women. He'd already blown his chance for flirting down at the river.

Now Lark was on the verge of a meltdown, and it was partially his fault. Sharon rarely had crying jags, but then Sharon had never been to war, had never seen the things Lark had seen.

"Here. Here's your damn photo," Lark practically choked on the words and then she stood up and walked into the kitchen.

Stone forgot all about the photograph and followed her. She was standing by the sink, staring out the window at the river, but Stone had a feeling she was a million miles away. He had a lot of buddies who came back from the Gulf War with post-traumatic anxiety. He knew the signs. She was deep in its grip.

For some reason, war had never affected Stone that way. He'd seen terrible things, lost buddies, done things that he didn't want to remember. But all of those things had made him stronger somehow—more determined to keep the people he loved safe. He hadn't done a good job of that with Sharon, and in some ways, that failure just ticked him off.

Well, here was someone who needed him right now. And he wasn't going to stand there and do nothing.

So he walked up behind her and put his hands on her shoulders. "It's going to be okay," he said.

He halfway expected her to argue with him, but instead she surprised the crap out of him by turning around and wrapping her arms around his middle.

She fought against that first sob. And he admired her for it, but he knew somehow that she needed to lose that battle. He didn't say a word. He just stood there being strong for her.

She fell apart in his arms. And it was all right. For the first time in a long, long time he felt useful. Like he understood why God had put him here. He was here to hold Lark while she confessed her fears, fell apart, and put herself back together again.

And he discovered that Aunt Arlene was right. Pouring yourself into something that wasn't alive anymore made the hole inside seem deep and vast and endless. But giving himself to the living made him feel complete. It was almost as if he could feel his heart beating again for the first time in years.

• • •

Lark sat in the passenger's seat of Stone's police cruiser, a blanket tossed over her shoulders and a Styrofoam cup of coffee clutched in her hands. A weather front had come through an hour ago, and a cold, miserable rain had started to fall.

She shivered.

After she'd embarrassed herself by getting tears and snot all over Stone's crisply pressed uniform shirt, she had insisted on leading Stone into the swamp and showing him where she'd shot the heron in flight. It hadn't taken them more than ten minutes to find the dead body. By that time, she had completely resigned herself to the fact that the little speck of red in the background of the photograph was the late James Marshall.

Not that anyone could have recognized the dead man after he'd spent a few days in the swamp. But Stone said it was Mr. Marshall, and she was ready to defer to his judgment.

The Allenberg County Sheriff's Department arrived on the scene pretty quickly, and within half an hour of the body's discovery the swamp was filled with flashlight-toting deputy sheriffs wearing bright orange rain slickers.

They left Lark alone. And despite her fear, she found herself framing and shooting photos. Each photo was a battle with her nerves. But she managed to find the shutter and press it. Again and again.

She captured the scene: The cop cars with their lights ablaze. The trickle of water down a windshield. Drops of water on a bright yellow body bag. But these photos were different. Stone Rhodes appeared in every single shot. He seemed to be the only human being she was brave enough to frame in her lens. With him in the photo, she could find the courage to press the shutter.

Without him there, however, she would have been a shivering wreck.

If she were good at lying to herself, she would have come away encouraged by her progress. But she was a terrible liar. She couldn't fool herself. Her flight to Africa left in just a few days, and she wasn't ready. She was going to have to call Greg and let him know.

And if she wasn't ready to go back to Africa, where the hell did she belong? That was a truly terrifying question. Because wherever she went, she was going to be utterly alone. Aside from her war correspondent friends, she didn't have much of a life, and with Pop dead, she didn't have any family either.

Stone opened the cruiser's back door, pulling her from the dark thoughts that assailed her. He tossed his wet hat on the backseat, then took his place behind the wheel.

He wore a big, heavy raincoat, and he was drenched. Despite his Stetson, his hair clumped damply along the back of his skull; even his eyelashes looked waterlogged. She studied every detail of him, cataloging his face. *This is how Stone Rhodes looks when his hair gets wet. This is how Stone's whiskers look after a long day. This is how the light from the overcast sky makes his eyes go a little gray.*

She thought it might take a lifetime to learn everything there was to know about his face.

He turned toward her. "I guess I should thank you. Sheriff Bennett refused to do a grid search of the swamp when we found Jimmy's car a few days ago. If you hadn't taken that photograph, we might never have found him, and his wife would have been left to wonder."

"Was he murdered?"

"Not clear. He was shot in the head, but it could be self-inflicted. Jimmy was having some problems. We'll have to wait for the coroner's report."

She nodded and took a sip of her lukewarm coffee.

"Just in case this wasn't a suicide, I want you to move back to town."

She turned. "Why?"

"Because until just recently, Jimmy was living in the river house where you're staying. And while there is good reason to think he might have committed suicide, there's also good reason to think that he might have been murdered. Jimmy was kind of a screwup. And he was into something—there were irregularities down at the chicken plant, and he was the CEO. Hettie was making him clean up his act, but it wouldn't surprise me if we were dealing with something nasty. And as long as that's the case, I want you where I can keep an eye on you."

"I'm a big girl, you know."

He turned his gaze on her like a truth-seeking missile. "I know that, but I'd feel better if you were living someplace neutral. So I called Momma, and she's getting the apartment above the Cut 'n Curl ready for you."

"But—"

"I know you love to argue, but I'm not going to argue about this. And the next time you want to take a long walk in the swamp, I would appreciate it if you would let me know first. It's just stupid for anyone to go off into the swamp on their own. We have gators and poisonous snakes out there."

"And other living things," she said. Like hunters.

Stone held her stare, and to her surprise the corner of

his mouth lifted just a little. "You know, I admire you. Most any other woman would be shocked and horrified by what we found out there today. You stood around and took photos."

She turned and watched the water droplets on the windshield. It was easier when she didn't have to look at his face. His face made her brain short-circuit.

"Sheriff Bennett has claimed jurisdiction over the case, you know," he said. "This swamp is outside the town limits. Which is why I'd appreciate it if you would let me see the photos you took today."

She turned, her heart pounding. "I'm not a crime scene photographer."

His eyes gentled, and she found herself drawn up into the heat and the kindness she found there. He knew some of her secrets. "I know that," he said, "but I'd like to see them anyway. You never know what small thing, like a speck of red in the background, can break a case wide open."

She shivered. "You won't like the photos I took today. You won't find anything remarkable in them," she whispered.

"You can't be sure of that."

She closed her eyes and sagged back against the seat. "I'm pretty sure."

"Why?"

"Because you're in every one of them," she confessed in a hoarse whisper.

She heard him exhale, but she didn't dare open her eyes to look at him. She'd just confessed that she was infatuated with him. And she wasn't about to explain how he looked like Carmine Falcone, or how framing him in her lens made the shadows disappear. If she was going crazy, then she'd try to go crazy in a dignified way.

Thankfully, he didn't respond to her confession. Instead, the engine of the Crown Vic roared to life. He pulled the cruiser onto the road, the windshield wipers thumping and the tires hissing over the wet pavement.

Ten minutes later, he pulled the cruiser up in front of Hettie's river house. "I'll help you get your things," he said.

She hazarded a glance in his direction. It unsettled her right down to her core. He was so handsome and so steady. She couldn't let herself fall for him. That would be stupid. "I'm okay on my own."

"No, you're not." This was not an argument. It was a statement of fact.

"You come out here on patrol every night. I feel perfectly safe out here."

"I know. But with you in the apartment above the Cut 'n Curl, I'll have Momma looking after you, too. And don't underestimate the abilities of my mother." He gave her one of his rare smiles, complete with all those sexy lines at his mouth and eyes.

"And," he said, reaching out to run his finger through her damp, shaggy hair, "Momma's going to want to give you a makeover. I take that as a real positive sign all the way around, and I'm not normally a positive thinker."

She cocked her head. "A makeover?" Her voice kind of squeaked, but mostly because of the electricity Stone's touch had created all across her scalp and down her spine and right into her middle.

He grinned like a wicked co-conspirator. "Yeah. I personally don't think you need a makeover. I think you're okay the way you are, kind of like a firefly, tiny but bright and fierce. Momma, on the other hand, ascribes to the notion that natural beauty can always be improved upon, and she's going to try to improve you."

"And you're telling me this, why?"

"Because if you play along with Momma, she's going to help you get your daddy's ashes scattered at Golfing for God. She likes you. She's been telling everyone in town all about your photo album theory. I wouldn't be surprised if Reverend Ellis figured out a way to use this idea of us all being one big family of man in his sermon on Sunday—it's the sort of Christmassy thing that he would probably do."

"You're kidding."

"Honey, I don't kid about this. Your photo album comments have gone viral in Last Chance. And that means Momma is going to watch over you like an angel. And that makes me feel good. So you're just going to have to get with the program, because I'm not arguing about this."

"But—"

"Lark, I'm a small-town policeman. And policing in a place like Last Chance requires the ability to manipulate churchwomen and hairdressers without them knowing that they've been manipulated. So, see, the makeover is going to be entirely Momma's idea. And I'm asking you to play along with it."

Laughter snuck up on her. It started as a little giggle, but grew into a full-blown guffaw that made tears leak out of the corner of her eyes. Laughing pushed back the shadows. It was a gift from some wonderful, clean, safe place that she had forgotten about.

"So," he said, once she had stopped giggling, "you'll move into the apartment above the Cut 'n Curl, and you'll let Momma do this thing. For me?"

"I'm afraid," she said.

"I know," he whispered back, his eyes so sober and honest.

"I'm not talking about my camera. I'm just saying that I'm not a big-hair, lots-of-hair-spray kind of girl."

He ran his hand through her hair, like he was tousling a child's hair, but it was so much sexier. "Yeah. I like that about you. I'll grump and tell Momma that I don't want you to be changed too much. That should help."

Time seemed to hang suspended for a moment as his hand stalled in her hair, and then he pulled her gently forward. She came willingly, knowing that this was what she'd wanted since last night. This time he didn't kiss her cheek.

The kiss was softer than she expected—almost shy and tentative, but incredibly warm and unbelievably erotic. She had never been kissed like this before.

And in a corner of her mind she knew, without question, that she had more experience in kissing than Stone Rhodes did. But somehow that didn't matter. This kiss was not about recreational sex, or passing the time, or having fun.

No, Stone Rhodes was not a guy like that. And when he decided to kiss someone, he moved in like a marine, with clear intent. His kiss was deliberate, as if he'd been thinking about it for some time.

But there was nothing deliberate about the groan that escaped him when she deepened the kiss. There was nothing planned about the way his hand pressed the back of her head, or the way her own palm found the side of his face and explored the texture of his beard.

And it wasn't surprising that, by the time they managed to pull away from one another, the inside windows of the cruiser had gone all steamy.

They stared at each other for a moment, but neither of them was ready to discuss what had just happened. One thing was certain, though: If Stone Rhodes wanted to keep her safe, even from phantoms, she was going to let him.

Hadn't she been fantasizing about a man like this since she was seven?

"I don't have a lot of luggage, but you can help me pack Pop's car," she said. Her voice was surprisingly strong and clear considering the way her heart was pounding in her chest.

"Good." He turned and snagged his Stetson from the backseat, then opened the cruiser's door to a cold, hard rain.

CHAPTER 13

David looked up from his lunch to find Lizzy Rhodes standing over him smiling. His face grew hot.

He'd been trying to avoid Lizzy all day. Not so much because Mom disapproved of her, but because of the crazy way he'd felt last night when he'd kissed her good night. He still hadn't quite come to terms with the fact that Lizzy seemed to like him back.

He stared up at her, feeling confused and conflicted. "My mother thinks it's a bad idea for us to be friends."

David was kind of pissed off at his mother. But at the same time, he understood that Mom was going through a harder time adjusting to the move from Michigan than anyone else in the family.

And it had all come to a head last night. Mom created a big scene and threatened to take David and his brothers back home to the Midwest. This morning Mom and Dad were not talking to each other.

David kind of wanted to go back to Michigan, too. But

he also kind of wanted to stay here and get to know Lizzy better.

Lizzy pulled out a chair and threw herself into it. "Are you going to let your parents push you around like that?"

"Mom's kind of mental right at the moment. It's not easy living here, you know?"

"Yeah, I guess. So are you not going to be my friend now?"

"Are we friends?" Why couldn't he let himself believe that Lizzy liked him?

She cocked her head. "Of course we are. I came to your house last night, and..." Her voice faded out, and when David looked up, her face was kind of red.

A smile tugged at his lips. "You're blushing."

"You are, too."

"What were you about to say?"

"I was just about to say that I didn't mind you kissing me last night."

His whole body got hot. "That's good." His voice cracked. He was such a dork.

"I don't want our parents to tell us we can't be friends. That would be like what happened when Abe Chaikin came to town and tried to have lunch with Nita Wills at the Kountry Kitchen. I think all of us have moved on from those times."

He glanced at her Obama T-shirt. "Yeah, I think we have."

"I totally enjoyed the latkes." She reached into her book bag and pulled out a note. "This is for your mother. It's a thank-you note."

"Awesome. Maybe Mom will—"

Before he could finish the sentence, someone hit him

on the back of the head with an open hand. It didn't hurt, but it was a complete surprise and a violation of his space.

"Hey, you," a disembodied voice drawled from behind, "I thought you and I had an understanding."

Lizzy was up on her feet, hands on her hips, before David could find the courage to move. "Michael Bennett, who do you think you are, coming up on someone and hitting them that way?"

David turned around to find his highness, the homecoming king, smirking at the two of them. For once, Michael wasn't wearing his stupid porkpie hat.

"I was just reminding him of a conversation we had a few days ago. You remember that conversation, don't you?"

David remembered. But things had changed. "Look, Michael, Lizzy and I work on the paper together. We're friends."

"Wait a second, did you and Michael have a conversation about me?" Lizzy demanded, looking from one to the other of them.

David's face burned. How was he supposed to tell Lizzy that he'd almost, sort of, agreed that he should stay away from her?

"Yeah, we did. I told this Jew boy to stay away from you. And you should have enough sense to stay away from him."

Outrage ignited within Lizzy Rhodes, and it shone like a beacon that even David could see.

"You're a total idiot and a bigot, Michael. Go away," Lizzy said. "And if you violate David's space again, I'm going to tell Dr. Williams, and I'm pretty sure he frowns on anyone spewing hate in this school."

Michael turned and glared at David. "You and I will settle this another day, when you don't have a girl around to fight for you." He turned and sauntered off.

David's heart was pounding, partially from fear and partially from Lizzy's awesome display of courage. She was going to think he was a loser now. He should have been the one brave enough to turn and face Michael and tell him to screw off. On the other hand, telling Michael Bennett to screw off was probably a good way to get himself killed.

"You shouldn't have spoken to him that way," David said looking down at the Formica tabletop.

Lizzy reached across the table and touched his hand. Her palm was soft and delicate. "He's a bully, David. Someone has to stand up to him."

"Walking away is usually the best policy."

Lizzy chuckled. "You sound like my grandfather. He's always talking about walking away from fights. But last summer when Lillian Bray said something ugly to my little sister, Granddaddy kind of lost it and tore up Miz Bray's flower bed. I gotta tell you, the kids in Sunday School were totally impressed with my granddaddy for putting Miz Bray in her place like that. So, I figure there's a time for walking away and a time for standing up. And Michael is a jerk in addition to being stupid."

"Hey, y'all." Cassie Nelson came hurrying across the lunchroom and slipped into the chair next to Lizzy. "Did you hear the news?"

"What news?" Lizzy asked. Lizzy and Cassie were BFFs. It was amazing that Cassie knew something that Lizzy didn't. David was sure the two girls had ESP or something. Cassie was the editor of *Rebel Yell*'s sports section.

"Jimmy Marshall's dead," Cassie announced dramatically. "Mother called me just now and said his body was found in the swamp near the Jonquil House. He was shot. Everyone in town thinks he killed himself, but Mother heard that your daddy thinks it's murder."

David and Lizzy looked across the table at one another. "You thinking what I'm thinking?" Lizzy asked.

David wasn't sure what Lizzy was thinking. She was always just a few steps ahead of him. But being with her was like being stuck in an adventure. "Uh, I guess."

Lizzy hunched over the table and spoke in an urgent voice, "We should go out to the swamp and take some photos of the crime scene. Maybe interview some of the people who were involved in the investigation. We haven't had a murder in Allenberg County since I've been living here."

"But most folks say he killed himself," Cassie said. "And everyone in town is all worried because if Mr. Marshall is dead, then what's going to happen at the chicken plant? Things haven't been going too good there for a while."

Lizzy turned and gave Cassie a hug. "Don't you worry, now, things are going to be okay at the plant. Even if Mr. Marshall has passed, his father is still alive, and Hettie won't let the plant go under."

Cassie nodded. "Yeah. But Mother's a mess. You know how she gets about things. She's all worried that Daddy will lose his job." Cassie gave a long-suffering sigh.

Across the room, someone dropped a tray. They all

turned. It was Michael Bennett. "I'd laugh at him, if he wasn't so pathetic," Lizzy said.

David watched as Michael quickly picked up the mess he'd made, pitched it in a trash can, and went running from the room like it was on fire. All around them, the lunchroom was growing kind of quiet as the news of Jimmy Marshall's demise made its way through the student body.

"I wonder what got into Michael?" Cassie asked. "It's not like his folks depend on the chicken plant."

"Who cares about Michael? He's a jerk," Lizzy said. She turned toward David. "Are you with me? If we want to be journalists, we should try to write about this story. Especially since Last Chance doesn't have a real newspaper—except for the *Rebel Yell*. School is out for the holidays next week. We could start working on this tomorrow."

David wasn't at all sure about a couple of high-school kids writing about a murder or suicide. But if Lizzy wanted to do it, then he was going to do it with her. His mother and Michael Bennett could just go mental if they wanted to.

"Okay," he said, "where do we start?"

"In the swamps, of course," Lizzy said.

Lark wearily climbed the stairs to the small apartment above the Cut 'n Curl. Stone followed her up the stairs, but Lark could tell his mind was turning over the events of the morning. He was in full-out cop mode.

She opened the door and found Stone's mother waiting for them. Ruby took one look at Lark, shook her head, and said, "Oh, you poor thing." She took both of Lark's hands in hers.

Lark was shocked by the warmth of Ruby's palms. She hadn't realized she was freezing cold. For an instant she felt not merely warmed by Ruby's touch, but enveloped in the kindness of her spirit. Genuine concern filled Ruby's eyes, and Lark had a strong feeling that it would be safe to take Ruby's portrait, too.

Ruby enveloped her in a tight, warm, motherly hug. "I've heard all about what happened this morning." Ruby released Lark and turned toward Stone. "I declare, you should have your head examined for taking Lark out there to find that body."

"It wasn't his fault. I wanted to go," Lark said.

Stone didn't react to his mother's scolding. He just tipped his Stetson, mumbled something about needing to get back to work, and left.

Ruby put her arm around Lark. "Why don't you come on down to the shop? We've got hot coffee and good company down there."

"I was wondering," Lark asked as Ruby guided her toward a flight of stairs at the back of the apartment, "if there's someplace where I could get a food platter or something for Hettie? I feel so bad for her. I know when Pop was sick, it would have been nice if someone had sent me food. I kind of forgot to eat toward the end."

Something changed in Ruby's demeanor. "Honey, do you mean to tell me that you were dealing with your daddy's illness and no one was looking after you?"

Lark shrugged. "There wasn't anyone to look after me."

"Didn't your father have friends?"

"Yeah, a few—mostly online friends, to be honest. He was a solitary man."

"What about you?"

"Well, most of my friends are war correspondents. They're scattered to the four winds. Anyway, I was thinking it might be nice if—"

Ruby patted her shoulder. "Honey, the food situation has been taken care of. Lessie is making squash casserole, Thelma is cooking a roast, Millie is working on some bean casserole and mac and cheese, Jenny's bringing pies, of course." Ruby took a big breath and continued, "Annie's bringing a salad, and Rachel is bringing cookies. Miriam and Lillian are already over there sitting with Hettie and Lee. I'm sure Violet has the coffee going and probably some of her okra and stewed tomatoes already on the stove. Hettie's in good hands for the moment. If you like, once I close up shop, you can come with me to pay your respects."

Lark didn't say a word as Ruby escorted her down the back stairway into the beauty shop. All she could think about was how nice it would have been if Ruby and Miriam and Lillian and the rest of them had been there the last couple of weeks of Pop's life. Those weeks had been spent in the hospice by Pop's bedside. Lark had snatched most of her meals at the McDonald's across the way.

Being alone was the price she had to pay for living out beyond the edge.

"Here you are, honey," Ruby said, gesturing to an empty pink chair by an old-fashioned hair dryer. "I had Ricki deliver a sandwich and some chicken soup when I heard what had happened." She snatched a paper bag from her work area and handed it to Lark. "You go ahead and eat that soup; it'll warm you right up. The weatherman says we might get ice tonight. I sure hope not. I was enjoying the Indian summer, and tomorrow is going to be a busy day, it being my last Saturday before Christmas."

The little bell at the front of the shop jingled, and a patron named Louise came in. Ruby set to work while Lark ate a very late lunch, surprised to discover that she was ravenously hungry.

About ten minutes later, Jane arrived with Lizzy and Haley in tow. The girls looked pink-cheeked from the cold.

Lizzy made a beeline toward her. "Is it true, what I heard at school? Did you find Jimmy Marshall's body?"

"Lizzy," Ruby said, "that's not—"

"No, it's all right," Lark said. "To be honest, it was your dad. He found the body in a photograph that I'd shot a couple of days ago."

"What?" Ruby and Louise both turned to stare at Lark just as Haley came over and climbed right into Lark's lap like she had a reason to sit there.

Lark wasn't sure what to do with the kid. But it felt nice when Haley snaked her little arms around Lark's neck and gave her a hug as big and warm as Ruby's. "The angel is worried about you," Haley whispered, then she gave Lark the sweetest kiss on the cheek. "But she says Daddy will take care of you."

"So?" Lizzy pressed. "What's this about Daddy and a photograph?"

Lark took a deep breath and explained what had happened in as calm a voice as she could muster.

"Oh, how horrible," Louise said, "to take a photo of something so beautiful and have it also contain something like that. You didn't see it when you took the picture?"

"No." Lark didn't explain about the hunter, the gunfire,

or her flashback. And she sure didn't say anything about the shadows lurking at the edges of the frame until after the photo was shot. She usually didn't notice the shadows. But they were always there, like Jimmy Marshall's body.

Instead, she gave Haley a little hug and breathed in her little-girl scent. She smelled like cinnamon. "Mmmm, you smell like something good to eat," Lark said.

"Oh, we made clove and orange pomanders in—" She slapped her hands across her face, and her eyes grew round. "Oops."

"It's okay, sugar, I didn't hear what you said," Ruby commented without missing a beat.

Haley rolled her eyes and leaned in. "I was making it for Granny for Christmas," she whispered.

"So," Lizzy interrupted, "do you think it was murder?"

"Lizzy!" Ruby scolded from across the room.

"I don't know," Lark replied. "Stone said Mr. Marshall had a gunshot wound to the head."

"Yeah, but if it was suicide wouldn't they have found the gun?" Lizzy asked.

Lark blinked at Liz. "I hadn't thought about that. I guess so, but it was swampy. The gun could have fallen into the water."

"So they didn't find a gun?" Louise asked.

"I don't think so."

"All right, y'all, that's enough," Ruby said. "I expect Stone will get to the bottom of things."

"Ha! You know good and well that Billy will be doing the investigating," Louise said. "And I don't think that boy could investigate his way out of a paper sack. When are you going to convince that son of yours to run for sheriff?"

"I'm not going to," Ruby replied. "Stone has to decide that's what he wants. And he's still making up his mind." Ruby looked up into the mirror and stared right at Lark. "He's been stuck in his life for a long time."

"Well, I can understand that," Louise said, "what with him losing his soulmate and all. But life goes on. My Henry's been gone fifteen years, and I've gone on without him."

"Granny," Haley said from her perch on Lark's lap, "if Daddy found his soulmate and she went to be with Jesus up in Heaven, can he ever get another one?"

"That's a good question," Ruby said.

"I wish he could find another one," Haley said, resting her head on Lark's shoulder. "I think Daddy is lonesome."

Lark's girl parts chose that moment to recall Stone's recent kiss. Maybe he wasn't as lonesome as people thought, because that kiss had been hot. She was pretty sure that Stone wouldn't be averse to taking things to a more intimate place. Thinking about sex and Stone in the same thought set Lark's heart to racing.

"Well," Ruby said as she finished blow-drying Louise's short hairdo. "I want to believe that a person can love twice in a lifetime. But Miz Miriam gave your father advice a long time ago, and he followed it. I can't say I ever heard of Miriam giving anyone advice twice."

"Hey," Lizzy said, "what kind of advice did Miz Miriam give Daddy anyway? I don't think anyone has ever told me that."

Louise frowned for a moment. "Oh, I think it was something about how he needed to go out and tame a crusader."

"What?" Lizzy looked confused.

"Well," Ruby said, "I think Miriam told your daddy that the woman he should be looking for was a person who wanted to change the world. And that his job was to make sure she remembered that the world starts at home."

"And Momma was always getting involved in projects, wasn't she?"

"She was the most dedicated churchwoman I ever met," Louise said. "I know that she would be disappointed in Stone, the way he's turned away from church these last few years."

Lizzy rolled her eyes and gave Lark one of those teenager looks. She leaned in and whispered, "That's what they all say about Momma." Then, in a louder voice, Lizzy proclaimed, "I wish I remembered Momma better because it's tough being the spawn of a saint."

"Elizabeth Ames Rhodes, that's a terrible thing to say," Louise said. Ruby scowled at her granddaughter in the mirror.

Haley cocked her head and gave her sister a long look. After an awkward silence, Haley said, "I feel the same way."

Lizzy turned toward her sister. "No, you don't. You don't even understand what I said."

Haley shrugged. "Maybe not, but whatever it means, you made the angel happy. She just stopped crying and smiled. So if it made her happy, then I want it, too."

All activity in the shop came to a stop. Everyone stared at Haley.

Lark felt a little sorry for the kid. She understood what it was like to talk about a person who wasn't really there.

It was Jane who broke the tension with a little laugh

that didn't sound strained or put on. "Well, isn't that nice. It sounds like the Sorrowful Angel has a sense of humor."

Ruby gave Jane a skeptical look and handed Louise a hand mirror so she could see the back of her head.

A moment later Jane spoke again, firmly and deftly changing the subject. "You know, Lark, you'd look so much better with a few highlights, and maybe not so many layers."

"I was thinking the very same thing," Ruby said.

Lark held her breath. Here it came. Just like Stone had predicted.

The last thing she wanted were highlights that would grow out in Africa, leaving her roots exposed. And she had always worn her thick hair like this, because the layers made it easy to dry and kept it from frizzing when she was sent off to the tropics.

But how could she make them understand? They were kind. They were good people. They didn't know her life.

And then it occurred to her that she didn't *want* to go back to Africa. And once she let that thought blossom in her head, she started to realize that maybe, just maybe, she needed more than a new haircut and some highlights.

She needed to make over her life.

"I'll speak to him if I damn well please." Lee Marshall's voice sounded through the door to Stone's office. An instant later the old man came barreling through the door looking as mean as nine miles of rusty barbed wire.

"My son did not kill himself," Lee proclaimed. The old man stood there, his frame drawn up as straight as it would go. He carried a cane, but he wasn't leaning on it. His eyes looked red-rimmed, his jowls grizzled with unshaved beard.

"I never said Jimmy killed himself," Stone replied as he gestured toward the hard metal chair beside his desk. Lee eyed the chair for a moment, and a little of the starch went out of him.

"Billy told Hettie it was a clear case of suicide," Lee said. "Stone, that just makes no sense. Jimmy didn't have the balls to kill himself. Besides, he was under the thumb of that holy-roller wife of his, and she would have disapproved of something like that."

"Sit down, Lee. You and I both know Billy's an idiot. We won't know what happened until we get the coroner's report. And that won't happen for a while, what with the holidays coming up and all."

"How long is a while?"

"Not until after Christmas."

"You've got to be kidding. They're going to keep my boy's body for that long?"

"I gather Doc Humphrey has gone to Aspen for the skiing and won't be back until late next week."

Lee collapsed into the chair. His hands were just the tiniest bit shaky as he clutched his cane. "I should give Billy Bennett a piece of my mind."

"Yes, you should. He might listen to you. He sure as shooting doesn't listen to me. By the time Doc Humphrey figures out the cause of death and Billy actually starts investigating, the crime scene will be useless. Of course, the rain didn't help anything."

"Damn it, Stone, Jimmy did *not* kill himself."

"I'm sorry for your loss, Lee." Stone invested his voice

with as much compassion as he could muster for the old coot. It had to be hard burying your only child. And Hettie and Jimmy didn't have any kids, so Lee would never have grandchildren. The Marshall line was coming to an end. It was sort of ironic, considering how many Rhodeses there were in Allenberg. A hundred and fifty years after Diamond Jim Marshall beat Chancellor Rhodes in a poker game, Chance Rhodes's descendants appeared to have won.

Lee cast his gaze over the blown-up printouts of Lark's photographs that Stone had been examining when Lee had interrupted him.

"What are these?"

"Photos of the crime scene taken a couple of days ago."

"A couple of days ago, but—"

"Lark Chaikin was out taking photos of wildlife. She photographed more than she intended to. That's how I found Jimmy's body. You should be thankful I didn't run her out of town. If we'd left it up to Billy, we might never have found your son."

Lee leaned forward and grabbed the photos off Stone's desk. He pulled out a pair of reading glasses and studied them, flipping through them, one by one. Stone didn't say a thing. Jimmy's body was clearly identified in the one blowup of the heron in flight.

"These were taken on that old road that leads to the Jonquil House, weren't they?" Lee asked.

"Yes, sir."

"That's mighty strange."

"How so?"

"Jimmy never went out that way—not alone, anyways— not into that swampy woods. He was terrified of snakes."

As Lee spoke, his hands started to tremble, and his jowly cheeks went red. It was a strange reaction, more anger than anything else.

"Thank you, Stone," the man said as he pushed himself out of the chair. "Clearly I need to talk to the sheriff."

No sooner had Lee departed than Kamaria LaFlore, the mayor-elect of Last Chance, arrived. She didn't knock either.

"The town is in an uproar. Is Jimmy Marshall really dead?" she asked as she sat herself down in his chair. Kamaria must have come from her day job at Voorhees College, where she taught African studies. She wore a suit and a take-charge attitude.

Stone folded his hands on his desk. "Yes, ma'am."

"How did he die?"

"The cause of death has not been officially determined."

"I heard he was shot in the head." Kamaria's gaze narrowed.

"Well, that's true, but how the bullet hole got there, what caliber the gun was, and the rest of the important details remain unclear."

"Are you saying he was murdered?" Kamaria didn't look very pleased.

"No, I'm saying I don't know how he died. But you can relax because Jimmy didn't die in Last Chance."

He picked up one of the wide-angle shots of the crime scene. "It happened out in the swamp on the old game trail that runs from Bluff Road to the Jonquil House. It's Billy Bennett's jurisdiction. Billy says it was suicide, but he hasn't yet consulted with the coroner. Lee is on the warpath, though, so the situation is likely to get more complicated."

"Did you find the gun?"

"No, ma'am. Billy called off the search before the dive teams could come out."

"Why would he do a thing like that?"

Stone gave the mayor-elect a direct stare. "I've got two theories. The first is that he's an idiot. The second is not as flattering."

"Are you saying that the sheriff is trying to cover something up?" She leaned forward.

Stone reached into his bottom desk drawer and pulled out the old paper files that he'd copied from the county archives a few days ago. He handed them to Kamaria. "It wouldn't be the first time the Allenberg sheriff covered something up."

She frowned. "What is this?"

"It's the investigation into the death of Zeke Rhodes. I have to be honest with you, Kamaria, I never bothered to look at these files before, because all this happened before I was born. It seemed irrelevant until Lark Chaikin arrived in town."

Kamaria's eyes grew round. "Stone, I realize that I have not yet been sworn in as mayor of this town, but I'm going to ask you to please put these files back where you found them. I don't want you digging up the past. In fact, I wish you had run that woman out of town the minute she arrived. She's been after my momma asking a lot of questions. She's got Momma all upset."

"I'm sorry about that. But Lark has a right to be here. And besides, if I had run her out of town, I wouldn't have found Jimmy's body."

"What?"

Stone explained the situation.

"What is it about the Chaikins?" Kamaria asked rhetorically when he'd finished. "They show up in this town, and people start dying."

"Lark Chaikin didn't kill Jimmy Marshall. And after reading that report of what happened in 1968, I don't think my grandfather died by falling off a ladder either. I think someone beat him to death. And I don't think it was Abe Chaikin."

"Stone, drop this. My mother could get hurt."

"I know that. But don't you want to get to the truth?"

"Are you asking me to stop the Bennetts from doing whatever they want in their jurisdiction?"

"No. I don't know that we can. But we can investigate the cold case. Zeke's so-called accident happened inside the town limits."

"Listen to yourself, Stone. You sound crazy, like your daddy. Who wanted to kill Jimmy Marshall? And why would the sheriff be so determined to cover something like this up?"

"Jimmy was no saint. I'm pretty sure he bribed an inspector to keep the chicken plant open. And he might have borrowed money from the wrong sort of person. That sort of thing can get a person into some real hot water."

"So you think this was blackmail?" Kamaria asked.

"No. Blackmailers usually don't commit murder. And neither do loan sharks. You can't collect from a dead man. To be honest, I'm more concerned because Billy Bennett has been kind of dragging his feet on this case."

"Stone, please, this isn't a good time to pick a fight with the Allenberg Sheriff's Department. I want you to forget about those old files and I want you to let Billy Bennett do his job the way he sees fit. I like you. I don't want to get ugly over this. So I'll just remind you that your contract with the town is up for review next month, and it's customary for an incoming mayor to clean house."

CHAPTER 14

Ruby called them the casserole brigade, and Lark had to admit that Ruby's friends had an understanding of logistics that rivaled U.S. CENTCOM in Afghanistan. The women fed a veritable army of people who stopped by Hettie's house that evening. They put Lark to work in the kitchen because she hadn't brought anything to eat and because the dishes were piling up fast.

Hettie seemed to be holding herself together. She was a brave woman, and Lark was happy to help in any way she could. In fact, standing in Hettie's kitchen with her hands in soapy water, Lark had found a kind of fellowship with the ladies of the auxiliary. Her mother had died when she was young. Lark didn't have girlfriends. This community of women was new to her.

The only community she knew about was the brotherhood that existed among soldiers in the field. But in a way, *Semper Fi* applied as much to the ladies of the auxiliary as it did to the marines she knew. These women were always faithful. And when bad things happened, they closed ranks and took care of their own.

By the time Ruby drove Lark back to the beauty shop, the rain had turned to sleet, and the forecast was for ice through much of the night. Ruby was in a hurry to get home before the roads became impassable.

"Now, honey, if the power goes off, and it probably will, you just give Stone a holler. That apartment's going to get cold if the baseboard heating goes out. So don't you be stoic, you hear?"

"I won't. Thank you for everything."

"Oh, it's nothing, honey. Thanks for coming out and helping in the kitchen. You didn't have to do that, you know?"

"I wanted to. It really made me feel better about everything." She didn't explain how, for just an instant this evening, she felt as if she belonged here.

Ruby smiled, the dash lights limning her face in green. "I know. In fact, everyone knows. I'd say you went a long way toward changing some minds today. Not that people should have judged you, but people do sometimes. Don't you worry, now, I'm working on Elbert, and we'll figure something out for your daddy."

"Thank you."

"You have a good night. And you call if the lights go out. Don't be shy."

"I won't."

Lark hurried through the sleet to the stairway. The steps were slick already, and she suspected they would become treacherous before the night was out.

So much for Indian summer.

She had just hung up her wet pea jacket and was

searching the kitchen for a kettle and some tea when someone tapped at the front door. The knock startled her, but when she saw the silhouette of a man wearing a Stetson through the window curtains, all her fears vanished.

And the temperature in the apartment rose a good ten degrees.

She hurried to the door and opened it. Stone stood there looking tall and strong and sober as black coffee. She had to fight the urge to walk right out there and wrap him up in her arms. He looked huggable, even if he was wearing a rain slicker, a holster, a bulletproof vest, and twenty pounds of communication equipment.

She didn't act on her desires. Instead she stood there taking him in. The corner of his mouth lifted just a fraction, and Lark felt oxygen-starved.

"I see Momma had her way with you," he said.

Lark self-consciously touched the short bob that Ruby had given her. "Your mother has a gift. I was so sure she was going to give me something that required a ton of hair spray, and instead she gave me this. It's probably the best haircut I've ever had."

His smile deepened. "Thanks for playing along with her. I also heard you spent the evening over at Hettie's place. People are surprised." He paused for a moment. "But I'm not."

He reached into his trouser pocket. "I came to return this." He handed her the memory card containing the photos she'd shot that morning out in the swamp.

She took the card, their fingers brushing in the exchange. "Did you look at all the photos?"

"Yeah." His voice was low. A plume of steam escaped

his lips. It was amazing how much meaning the man could put into a single word.

"Come in," she said. "I was just making some tea. You look like you could use something warm."

He hesitated for a moment, then pushed off the door frame. "I can't stay long. The weather's turning and it's only a matter of time before someone slides into something. We'll probably have downed tree limbs and power lines, too."

He hung up his raincoat and Stetson next to her wool coat, then divested himself of the utility belt and holster. The tiny kitchen shrank the moment he stepped into it.

"I think there's some tea up here." He pulled open one of the cabinet doors just as she was heading in the same direction. They bumped hips. And like charged electrons, the motion sent them both spinning off to opposite sides of the kitchen.

He found the tea. She reached for the kettle. Somehow they managed to get water going and find a teapot and mugs without running afoul of each other again.

The sudden lack of words between them left her with no choice but to focus on the ping of sleet against the window above the sink. Lark stopped herself from saying something inane about the weather.

She had something she wanted to say, but it wasn't inane, and it would probably shock him.

He took a seat at the small kitchen table. She turned and leaned back against the counter. "Haley said something very interesting this afternoon," Lark said.

Stone cocked his head. A flame burned in his eyes. "Haley is always coming up with zingers."

"She said she thought you were lonesome."

"That's hardly a startling observation."

"You don't have to be," Lark blurted.

He stared at her unblinking. "Are you making me an offer?"

"Life is short. Just ask Jimmy Marshall."

The kettle whistled to life, saving Lark from further embarrassment. Why the hell was she having such a hard time telling Stone that she wouldn't mind warming his bed for a few nights? She'd never had a problem doing that before.

She turned away, filling the teapot with hot water.

The silence was thick and tense until he asked, "So is this some kind of holiday gift?"

She picked up the teapot and put it on the table. She sat down. "Okay, forget I said what I just said. I have a different moral code than you do. I find you attractive. I got the impression from the kiss you laid on me earlier today that the feeling was mutual. But I get that this is a small town and you're kind of, well, old-fashioned."

His lips quirked. "That wasn't a compliment, was it?"

"No, yes. I don't know," she murmured.

"No?"

She poured the tea and wrapped her hands around her mug. The warm cup was a contrast to the storm raging outside the window. Stone *was* old-fashioned. Last Chance was old-fashioned. They took care of their own here. They embraced tradition. It was crazy to think that Stone would be willing to bed down with her, just because he was lonely.

Just because she was lonely.

She pushed that thought away. Maybe instead of jumping into the sack with him, she should talk with him.

Maybe she should listen to the advice Miriam Randall had given her. Stone was so much like Carmine, and she'd always told Carmine everything.

She screwed up her courage. "About this morning, when I fell apart. See, I had a bad experience in Libya last April." It seemed like such a relief to say it out loud like that.

He reached across the Formica tabletop and snagged her hand. There was more warmth in his hand than in the mug of tea. "I figured as much. Libya, huh?"

"I was in Misurata and ..." Her throat closed up.

"I know. You were there when that TV guy was killed."

"You know about that?"

He shrugged. "I checked up on you when you first got here. I saw your photos, and I read that you were a witness to the incident in Libya."

She didn't know whether to be flattered or ticked off. "You checked up on me?"

"It's what I do. I always check up on strangers. You want to tell me what went down in Libya? I'm a pretty good listener."

She already knew that about Stone. If there was anyone who would actually hear what she had to say, Stone would. She took a big breath and started. "His name was Jeb Smith. He was my friend. Well, actually more of a mentor. And if I hadn't been such a coward that day, I would have been sitting right beside him when the rocket hit. But I chose not to cross the street."

"Shit." He squeezed her hand.

"But I shot the whole thing. All of it."

"What? His death?"

She nodded. "I captured it all. During the rocket

attack, I got stuck in some weird way, and I couldn't move my finger off the shutter. And now, I'm kind of scared of my camera."

He didn't say anything for a long time. He just held her hand and managed to communicate a world of comfort with his fingers. When the silence had grown long and deep, he finally said, "I lost a buddy the same way. He was next to me, then suddenly his head exploded. A sniper took him out. It shook me up for days. But that stuff is just random. You can't blame yourself for surviving."

She looked up into his eyes. He really did know. He really could understand.

"I have to get on a plane to Somalia in four days." She left the thought hanging. It was too hard to admit that she really didn't want to go. She'd never been a coward. But she didn't want to return to the field.

"Is that why you want to sleep with me? You figure I'm safe because you're only going to be here for the next few days?"

The vehemence in his tone surprised her. He'd misunderstood. "No, I—"

"See, that's the reason I'm going to ignore your offer. I know how that goes."

"How what goes?"

"How easy it is to take comfort in someone and then get on a plane." He let go of her hand.

"Is that what happened with you and Sharon? Did you love her and then leave her?"

She had been shooting in the dark, but when his jaw flexed, she knew she'd hit the mark. She expected him to get up and walk out. Instead, he took a big breath and started talking. The words came slowly. "We were kids when we got married. Both of us barely eighteen. We were hot for each other, but Sharon was determined to marry a college boy. She broke up with me when I joined the Marines."

"So how did you end up married?"

"Miriam Randall gave me a forecast that fit. And I talked her into marrying me. Man you should have seen me down on one knee running my mouth. I don't think I ever talked so fast in all my life."

She gave him a smile that he didn't return. "I'm sure your speech was very moving."

"I wanted to marry her. I loved her. She loved me. But I think she regretted her decision."

It was hard to think about any woman who might regret marrying Stone.

He stared down at his untouched tea for a moment, then he spoke again, "We thought we had a plan for the future. She was going to go to college while I did boot camp. And then Iraq invaded Kuwait, and I ended up smack dab in the middle of the Gulf War. And Sharon ended up pregnant."

Lark counted the years. "That was in 1990. Lizzy's not that old."

Stone took a deep draught of the tea and put the cup back on the table. "My son's name was Tyler. He was born three months early with a congenital heart defect. In 1991, when I was off breaching the Saddam Line, my wife was dealing with the mess I left behind. She gave up on getting that college degree."

He finally looked up at her, his eyes haunted. "She threw herself into caring for Tyler the way she threw herself into everything. Tyler lived for four years. And for most of that time, I was on deployment. I saw the world on Uncle Sam's dime, but I hardly knew my son."

"Why weren't there any photos of him in the album?" Lark blurted. This was shocking. And heartbreaking.

He blinked. "Momma knows better."

"Really? That doesn't sound like your mother."

"Sharon and I decided to put the past in the past when I left the service. And by then Lizzy was here. We had a pretty good life, I thought. But on the day Sharon died, she told me she wanted to sign up to take courses at the community college."

He paused for a moment, clearly battling his emotions. "And I had the balls to question whether she could manage classes and the kids at the same time. I knew damn well that she wanted a college education. I'll never forgive myself for what I said that day.

"I also wonder what might have happened if we hadn't argued. Would she still have ended up at that intersection when that drunken asshole ran the light?"

He got up violently and stalked out of the room. Lark remained behind in stunned silence. For days now, she'd been hearing about the beautiful love between Stone and Sharon, how their marriage had been predicted by the infallible Miriam Randall, how they were soulmates, how he'd run off with Sharon when they were young. The picture everyone painted was the picture of a storybook love.

No one had said a word about a little boy with a broken heart named Tyler. No one had said anything about Sharon giving up her dreams.

And now the truth was lost forever in the story that was left behind.

Damn it. People needed to quit hiding the truth. Stone

and Sharon hadn't been a fairy tale. They had been a loving couple who'd faced the worst life could hand them and still stuck together. Why was a fairy tale better than a story like that?

Stone stood at the windows and stared down at the sleet accumulating on Palmetto Avenue.

Damn it. Why the hell had he opened his mouth? He'd come to talk to Lark about her problems and ended up confessing his. He ought to turn around and force her to tell him all the gory details about what happened in Libya. It would only be fair, now that he'd spilled his guts about Tyler and Sharon.

He heard her stand up and take a few steps. Stone turned around to find her standing in the kitchen doorway looking both fragile and brave. He couldn't imagine a woman so tiny in the middle of the Libyan civil war. But she'd been there. And she was battling her way back. Boy, she was some kind of strong woman.

"Things will be better tomorrow," Lark said. "It's the winter solstice—the longest night of the year. And it's a fact that tomorrow there will be more daylight than there was today."

Two strides had him standing right in front of her. "That's a comforting thought," he murmured. He cupped her cheek in his hand.

She leaned into the touch. "Yeah. And if you looked at the photos I shot today, you understand why I see you as a light in the darkness. I don't really understand how or why. But when I frame you in my camera, all the shadows disappear, and I'm not afraid to squeeze the shutter. Ironically, that scares the crap out of me."

She reached out and touched his face, her finger tracing fire across his skin.

He trailed his thumb over her lips and then leaned down and gave her a kiss. He lingered there, barely touching her. Her lips ignited a flame inside him.

"I want you," he whispered. He pulled back a fraction.

She ran her hand up over his scalp, her fingers sending ripples of reaction down his back. "And I told you what I wanted. But I'm still leaving in a few days. Are you okay with that?"

"Are you?"

She nodded. "I'm always getting on airplanes. That's what I do. It's who I am."

She got up on tiptoes and kissed him. Her breasts pressed up against his vest. Damn it all, why the hell hadn't he taken the fool thing off? She was way too far away.

She opened her mouth.

Boy, she was sure making this easy for him. He moved in. He lost his mind for a while in the heat of her mouth. He cupped the back of her head to get a little more leverage.

She let him. Then she let go of a little sexy noise that told him she was having a good time. And he ran his hands down to her back and pulled her a little closer.

His hands found her hips. She had a cute little shape, didn't she? Damn.

She was sure accommodating. His heart beat in his ears, and he felt just like the eighteen-year-old who had lost his virginity on his wedding night. The errant thought wrapped itself around his brain in a toxic way. He pushed at it. Why the hell was he thinking about that right now?

This was now. That was then.

But it was too late.

She backed up a little. "You have second thoughts, don't you?" She gave him a little smile like she knew what was going on in his head. Then she moved off to the other side of the room.

He stood there breathing hard, trying to figure out just what the hell had happened.

He might have had a chance to figure it out if his damn radio hadn't chosen that moment to crackle back to life with the news that there had been a three-car wreck at the intersections of Route 70 and the Charleston–Augusta Road.

Lark gave him a weary smile. "Well that's kind of ironic. Without the ice, you might have slipped." She sighed. "It's probably for the best. I wouldn't want to leave you with regrets."

He didn't know how to respond to that, so he answered the dispatcher. Then put on his belt and his holster and raincoat. But right before he headed out her door, he turned toward Lark and studied her.

She was stubborn and hardheaded and different from any woman he'd ever known. She was willing to give herself to him—with no strings attached.

It was just plain stupidity to cling to old-fashioned ideas. He wanted her. He wanted her bad. He was willing to live with his regrets. Hell, he already had a million of them.

So he crossed the room and pulled her right up into a big, fat, wet, sloppy kiss. And boy, it felt real good, and he let her know it, even if he didn't have any words to explain it.

And then he turned, put on his Stetson, and stepped out into the ice storm. But it sure was interesting the way Lark's kiss managed to keep him warm the rest of the night.

And it was a long night, too. The longest night of the year.

CHAPTER 15

Haley cracked an eye. The light from outside her bedroom window looked unusually bright. Lizzy, fully clothed in jeans and her big red Christmas sweater, was standing in front of the window looking annoyed.

"What's that light?" Haley asked.

"It's the ice. It's everywhere," Lizzy said.

Haley crawled out of bed, aware that the angel was standing in the corner studying Lizzy very carefully. The angel looked more worried than sorrowful.

Haley hurried to the window and looked out. Ice covered every branch and twig of the peach tree that grew in the backyard. The morning sun sparkled like diamonds in the branches.

"Oh, it's pretty."

"Yeah, it's pretty, but it's a pain," Lizzy said. She turned away from the window. "I'm going to have to walk up to the stables. I was going to ride my bike."

"Why were you going to ride your bike? Granny will drive you."

"I didn't want to bother Granny." Lizzy pulled the knitted hat that matched her sweater down over her hair. "Tell everyone where I am, okay? I promised Mr. Randall I would help him clean the stables over Christmas break."

"You did?"

"Yeah, I did. And don't forget to tell Daddy or he'll burst a blood vessel or something."

"If you're working for Mr. Randall, why would Daddy be mad?"

"Because he's mad all the time." Lizzy pulled her gloves out of the dresser.

"You aren't really going to Mr. Randall's stables, are you?"

Lizzy gave her the stink eye, and Haley knew for a fact that Lizzy was lying. Also, it helped that the angel was shaking her head.

"Look, you tell Daddy I'm at the stables, or I'm going to let Granny know that you are the one who broke that teacup she loves so much. I know you buried it out in the backyard."

Fear prickled Haley's backbone. "You know about that?"

"Yeah, I do. So just mind your own business," Lizzy said. "Tell Daddy and Granny that I'm at the stables, and I'll be back for dinner."

Haley hated lying for Lizzy. But if Granny ever found out about that teacup, Haley's backside was going to get paddled. Not that Haley had ever in her life been spanked, but breaking the teacup and then lying about it was probably enough to get a real spanking. That teacup had belonged to Haley's great-great-grandmother.

Haley turned back to look at the ice outside her window. It was real pretty, but it left her feeling bad in some strange way. Ice wasn't exactly snow.

She sighed.

"Your father needs to forgive," the angel said.

Haley turned. She was tired of hearing stuff like this. The things the angel wanted Haley to do were too hard. Haley couldn't make Daddy's heart bigger. And Daddy wasn't ever going to laugh again, 'specially not at the dumb old jokes in that book she'd taken out of the library.

She made a face at the angel. "Is this like the time I had to forgive Maryanne when she messed up the hair of my Ghoulia Yelps Monster High doll?"

The angel didn't answer.

"Well, because if that's what Daddy has to do, then you're asking for a lot. I mean, Maryanne ruined my doll, and I had to tell her not to feel bad about it 'cause it was an accident, but I know it wasn't any such thing."

Haley pressed her head against the cold window and let her resentment of Maryanne fill her up with misery. Maryanne was such a pest and a pain. Why did she have to forgive Maryanne for messing up Ghoulia? And why did Maryanne get to be the angel in the Christmas play?

Her breath fogged the window while she thought about her problems.

"Who does Daddy have to forgive?" she asked after a long moment.

The angel didn't answer.

"You think he needs to forgive me and Lizzy?" she asked, thinking about the broken teacup. She probably needed to apologize to Granny for that and pray that Granny would forgive her. But she didn't think Daddy would care all that much about a broken teacup.

She thought on this for a long time, and then she realized that Daddy didn't need to forgive her for breaking that teacup, because the cup didn't belong to Daddy. It belonged to Granny. So really, the angel was saying that Haley had to apologize for something even bigger than that.

She turned and looked at the angel and thought about all the problems the angel had caused since last Christmas. Maybe Daddy had to forgive Haley about the things her angel had done.

The angel stared right back at Haley but didn't give her any sign. And wasn't that sort of like a sign in itself?

So that meant that Haley had to be like Maryanne and apologize for the angel. Which didn't seem very fair, since Haley hadn't exactly asked to be burdened with a Sorrowful Angel.

But it was clear that she would have to do it anyway.

She made up her mind. She would be brave. Because she needed to find a way to get that angel back to Heaven if it was the last thing she did.

By the time David met Lizzy out on Bluff Road, it was almost ten o'clock, and the ice had pretty much melted away in the bright sun. Riding his bike on the icy road had been a challenge.

Lying to his mother about having a sore throat so he could get out of going to *schul* had been insane. He was going to get into trouble.

But it didn't matter. If Mom didn't want him to be friends with Lizzy, then she gave him no choice but to turn into a sneak. And besides, the chance to have an adventure with Lizzy was something that didn't come along every day.

She was wearing a floppy red sweater and a matching wool hat. Her jeans were tucked into a pair of big rubber boots with yellow duckies on them. She was beautiful.

They pulled their bikes into the underbrush beside the road and found a trail leading into the woods. The trail skirted the edge of a cypress swamp that was still frosty from last night's storm.

David followed Lizzy, her red sweater a startling flash of color against the browns and greens of the trees and the swampy water. The place smelled of decay, and David kept an eye trained to the path, making sure they weren't blundering into snake nests or worse. He kept telling himself that it was a cool day, and reptiles were cold-blooded.

Also, he wasn't about to tell Lizzy he was scared of snakes. She seemed to be afraid of nothing.

They reached an area of muddy ground that had been pretty badly trampled. "This must be the place," Lizzy said as she boldly strode into the mud, her boots squishing with each step.

"Okay, you should take some photos, and I'm going to search for the gun."

"What?"

"You know, the gun. It's missing. If we find it, it will be a scoop."

David refrained from pointing out that they were unlikely to find the gun here, since the police had obviously been all over the area pretty thoroughly. Instead he took the lens cap off his Canon and started shooting photos. He took a few boring shots of the swamp and trampled earth, and then he focused on Lizzy as she wandered around, poking under logs and peering into the shallow water.

She was magnificent. The cold touched her cheeks with red, and the sun glinted in her green eyes. He watched with admiration and amusement as she picked up a stick and started poking it into the dark water right at the edge of the swamp. She was leaning over a fallen log, frowning in concentration.

"Hey, I found something," she called.

He was astonished. He picked his way over the sodden ground. "Is it the gun?"

She levered the stick up and out of the water. Snagged on its end was...

He stared at the muddy, sodden thing a long moment, trying to decide what it was.

"Well, that's interesting," Lizzy said, pulling a plastic bag out of her jean pocket and dumping the dripping thing into it.

"What the hell is that?"

"A porkpie hat, like the one Michael wears."

"You're kidding."

She shook her head. "What do you think it means?"

"I think it means that half the school has beat us out here."

"Yeah, but Michael wasn't wearing his hat yesterday. And he dropped his tray when he heard about Jimmy Marshall being dead. You think he lost his hat out here at the same time Jimmy Marshall killed himself? That would explain why his father is dragging his feet on the investigation."

"Jeez, Lizzy, you have a real active imagination."

She stood up and brought the bag over to him. She opened it and looked down. "Well, lookie there, it's even got his name in the band."

David looked down at the waterlogged hat, and sure enough the name "Michael Bennett" had been scrawled into the inner hatband.

Lizzy snorted. "Like he totally had to put his name in it because there's more than one guy at school who wears a stupid hat like this."

"It's not exactly the smoking gun you were looking for."

"No, it's not. But I sure could use it to embarrass the crap out of him." She chortled evilly.

"How? By turning it in to your father and trying to pin Mr. Marshall's murder on the Davis High homecoming king?"

She snickered. "Yeah, something like that."

"Well, there are a couple of problems with that. First of all, you'll have to explain to your dad why you were out here in the swamp with me. And second, I don't think you've got much of a motive for Michael. And third, while Michael is a jerk and a bigot, I don't see him being brave enough to actually kill anyone."

Lizzy cocked her head. "See, that's the problem with you. You're always so rational."

"Lizzy, we aren't going to find a gun out here, you do know that? And finding Michael's hat doesn't mean anything."

She put her hands on her hips and studied the area for a moment. "Yeah, you're probably right. We'd need to have diving suits and all that to find the gun. But it was fun to come looking."

"Yeah, it was." He tried to stop grinning at her—it was such a pain having braces. And she probably thought he was dorky looking because of them.

"Hey, you want to see something?" Lizzy asked.

"Of course." Anything to prolong the adventure.

She stashed the plastic bag in her backpack and took off in the opposite direction, following an old trail that led away from the swamp toward Bluff Road. "Where are we going?"

"To the Jonquil House," she said, as if that explained everything.

They walked for about ten minutes and finally came to a clearing where an abandoned house stood. It looked kind of like one of those movie haunted houses where some scary old person lived. The paint had peeled off, leaving the wooden siding a silvery gray. Most of the windows were broken, the porch sagged, and the railing looked like a skeleton with missing teeth. The yard was littered with beer and pop cans.

"Why do they call it the Jonquil House? Did the Jonquils live here once?"

She turned, her emerald eyes dancing with amusement. "No, silly, a jonquil is another name for a daffodil. In the springtime, this field is totally covered with them. When they bloom, they cover up the beer cans."

"Oh." A flower, God, who knew? "Uh, so do they do haunted houses out here at Halloween?"

"Not the kind the grown-ups organize. I remember some teenagers taking me out here to go snipe hunting once, when I was like twelve."

"Snipe?"

She gave him a wicked smile and skipped over toward the sagging porch steps. She sat down and looked up at him. "David, I'm going to give you a very useful piece of advice. If Michael Bennett or some other bully tries to take you out snipe hunting, you just tell them no, okay?"

"What's a snipe?"

She giggled. "There is no such thing as a snipe. That's the point."

"Oh."

He crossed the weedy grass and sat next to her. "You think I'm a dork, don't you?"

She turned. "No. I think you're smart and interesting. You're just from the city is all, and city folks don't know about snipe hunting. I'm just helping you out, you know—What's that?" Lizzy interrupted herself and turned toward the path that led out of the clearing.

An instant later, a group of boys—most of them seniors—came striding out of the woods. Michael Bennett was in the lead, with Justin Polk, Jon Nelson, and Ben Everett following behind. The boys were carrying a twenty-four-pack of beer. Clearly they intended to add to the litter already scattered everywhere around the derelict house.

It was time to go.

David stood up. "C'mon, Lizzy, let's get out of here."

"Well, well, well, look what we found," Michael said as he strode into the clearing. "Lizzy's got herself a little Jew boyfriend."

Lizzy stood up and put her hands on her hips. "Shut it, Michael. No one wants to hear your stupid opinion. David is my friend and his religion doesn't matter."

"Let's go," David said again.

"What's the matter, are you scared?" Michael strode up to David and looked down at him in a totally challenging way. The idiot wanted a fight.

"I'm not scared of you," David lied. "I'm just not interested in spending time with a bunch of guys who want to drink beer and leave litter lying around." He kicked at one of the pop cans on the ground at his feet.

"Are you calling me a litterer?"

David had the sudden urge to laugh. Michael was kidding, right?

The next thing David knew, Michael had snatched David's jacket in his fist and started shaking him back and forth. "Don't you smirk at me. I'm better than you are, you hear?"

"Hey, Michael, what are you doing?" one of the other boys said. "Let him go home to his mother."

Michael let David go with a jerk, and David fell back into a pile of old cans. "You can go," he said, "but not with Lizzy."

"What?" Lizzy said. "I go where I please."

"Not with him, you don't." Michael took a step toward Lizzy, and that was all it took for David to find his courage.

Or maybe to lose his good sense.

He sprang up from the ground and tackled Michael around the ankles. The big kid went down with a crash. That was great, but what happened next was not.

Michael regained his footing and landed a withering, right-handed, closed-fisted punch to David's nose. David fell backward and ended up staring up at the sky with his ears ringing and blood gushing.

He braced for another assault, but it didn't come. He lay there breathing through his mouth because his nose didn't work anymore.

He sat up, trying to stanch the flow of blood from his nose. A couple of the other boys were holding Michael back. The homecoming king was ranting and cursing and spouting a lot of hate.

Justin Polk turned toward Michael. "Shut your trap."

Michael stopped yelling.

"You know, you're a moron, Bennett," Justin said. "You have to be crazy to dis Chief Rhodes's daughter. And, to be honest, what just came out of your mouth disgusts me."

Justin turned away and came over to David. "We're not all like him," he said, offering a hand. David didn't take Justin's hand. He climbed to his feet on his own.

Lizzy came over and put her arm around David. His nose was hurting, but somehow it felt a lot better with Lizzy's arm around his shoulder.

Then Lizzy burst his bubble when she said, "Oh, my God, I think he broke your nose. You're going to have black eyes. We need to get you some ice."

Justin handed her a cold beer. "Put this on the bridge of his nose. It'll stop the bleeding."

"Thank you, Justin," Lizzy said. "You've just restored my faith in the Davis High football team." She turned toward David. "C'mon, we need to get back to town."

They got halfway to the path before Lizzy stopped and turned. "Hey, Michael," she said. "We found your hat. We know where you've been and what you've done. So you watch your step."

She turned and took David's hand and led him from the woods.

"Why'd you taunt Michael like that? I mean, we won the fight."

"We?"

He shrugged. "So, okay, Justin stopped the fight."

"I just decided I should use my leverage. Those boys are terrified that I'm going to snitch on them. Daddy doesn't tolerate underage drinking."

"Oh. But you aren't going to tell on them, are you?"

"I don't know. I haven't made up my mind. I mean, what if Michael's hat is an important clue? And besides, Michael is a bigot. I really wish I were bigger. If I were, I would have tried to tackle Michael like you did. That was pretty brave of you."

David didn't feel very brave. Mostly he felt stupid.

Stone wrapped his hands around his mug of coffee and gazed through the Kountry Kitchen's tinsel-draped windows. He could just see the Cut 'n Curl across the street. He'd patrolled through the center of town five times this morning hoping that he might catch just a glimpse of Lark. But she must be sleeping in this morning. Her car was still in the parking lot out back. He'd checked.

Five times.

He stared into his coffee as his mind turned back to the feel of Lark's lips against his. He got that feeling in the pit of his stomach—like he was free-falling.

He wanted to take Lark up on her offer, even if she was planning to leave town in a few days. He didn't want to be sitting here a year from now wondering about a chance not taken.

He flattened his hand on the Formica and studied the faded skin on his ring finger. He suddenly wished he'd taken his wedding band off last summer. The white line was an unwanted reminder that he'd been with only one woman his entire life.

How the hell was he supposed to get what he wanted when he was so inexperienced at this kind of thing? He'd never had any casual relationships with women before.

He felt like a complete and utter fool. He wasn't used to feeling so humbled and so unsure and so incompetent.

"Hey." Someone gave him a quick pat on the shoulder.

He looked up to find his sister-in-law Jane sliding into the seat next to him. "Ruby sent me over here to get something to eat. I was feeling sick."

She gave him one of her goofy-sweet smiles and then hailed Ricki, the waitress. Jane ordered a bowl of oatmeal, even though it was almost lunchtime.

"So, are you spying on Lizzy?" Jane asked.

"What?"

"She's sitting in the back booth with that boyfriend of hers. She's hiding behind a menu, and he's trying to look nonchalant. Which is kind of difficult because he's holding a bag of ice on his nose. My theory is that the kid decided to ride his bike on an icy road and paid the price."

Stone blinked and refocused his gaze toward the back of the room. Sure enough, his teenaged daughter was back there not very successfully hiding.

"Aaaah, teenaged love," Jane said dramatically.

Stone returned his gaze to his coffee as the wild and errant thought crossed his mind that David Raab was having more luck with Lizzy than he was having with Lark. Then he remembered that he didn't want David to get too lucky with his daughter.

"Hey, it's okay," Jane said when he balled up his fist. "I've already given Lizzy the girl talk, you know?"

He straightened and glared. "You did not."

She nodded. "Yes, I did. It was easier for me to do it. Less embarrassing for everyone involved, since I'm just her aunt by marriage. You can thank me later. Lizzy has a good head on her shoulders. You've done a good job with her. She's not going to make any stupid mistakes like I did."

Jane's oatmeal arrived, and she turned her attention to it.

"That's comforting."

"She'll be fine." Jane paused for a long moment. "I'm not so sure about you, though."

He grunted. "I thought you were always optimistic."

"I try to be. But I'm starting to wonder about you."

"How so?"

"Because you're sitting here sipping coffee instead of knocking on the door of the apartment above the Cut 'n Curl."

He almost spewed his coffee.

She giggled. "You're as obvious as a three-dollar bill. If you're interested in Lark, then you need to go talk to her."

"Thanks for the advice."

"I realize that talking is not your strong suit. But you're going to have to try."

"Did you come over here for the purpose of embarrassing me? Because, to be honest, you don't look very morning sick."

She leaned in and whispered, "I faked it. I saw you come in here, and I figured someone needed to rescue Lizzy before you made her cry again. And also, you've run the circuit of town five times this morning, which is three times more than you normally do. And you never cruise through the parking lot at the Cut 'n Curl."

"How did you know that?"

"I was taking out the trash, and I noticed. As for the rest, well, Thelma saw you on her way in, and Millie saw you on your way out, and then Louisa saw you when she stopped at the dry cleaners, and Annie saw you when she stopped to pick up some doughnuts for the book club holiday get-together. Ruby's cell phone has been ringing up a storm today."

"Great." He propped his chin on his fist.

"Just go on up those stairs and ask her out on a date. The world will not come to an end if you do that."

"I've never been on a date."

"I'm sure you and Sharon went out," Jane said gently.

"Yeah, but it wasn't a date. Not like that. I knew Sharon when I was in the third grade." His whole face heated up. This was pitifully embarrassing.

"Well, she's over there waiting for you."

"How do you know that?"

"Because she keeps watching you cruise through town. We've heard it now from Millie, Thelma, Louise, and Annie. Not to mention Lessie Anderson."

He squeezed his eyes shut. "You know, I think I know why Andy Griffith never remarried, if the folks in Mayberry were anything like they are in Last Chance."

"Look, Stone, I can just imagine what's going through Lark's mind. She's up there, alone, trying to figure out what to do with the rest of her life now that her father has passed. She's watching you, and she's trying to figure out if she should wander over here and pretend to be hungry. But she's holding back."

"Uh-huh, and why's that?"

"Because of Sharon."

Stone glared at his sister-in-law. It was truly annoying the way Jane could put her finger right on the heart of the matter. "You've been taking lessons from the church ladies."

His glare bounced right off her. "I have tricks I could teach them. I saw the way you watched her the other night when we were looking at the photo albums. You're interested in her, and that's like the most amazing thing that's happened in this town in a long time."

He had no reply to give her. And there was no point trying to intimidate Jane, he had tried and failed on numerous occasions. Seeing how happy Jane had made his younger brother, Stone had finally given up and decided to love Jane just like everyone else in town did.

She reached over and touched his left hand, turning it over so that she could see his naked finger. "Stone, everyone in town knows you took off your wedding band. You don't do a thing like that without people noticing. It's been the single biggest topic of discussion at the beauty shop for days now. It's even outpacing speculation about Jimmy's mysterious death, which is saying something."

"But I don't even know how to ask a woman out on a date. And where would I take her?" he asked, his voice sounding suddenly panicky in his own ears. "I used to take Sharon to the picture show at The Kismet. But The Kismet is closed now."

"Why don't you take her up to old man Nelson's cornfield and stroll through the Christmas lights."

"But people go up there to…"

"Right. That's what they do." A slow, naughty smile lit Jane's face.

She patted his hand. "It's about time. Ask her out. And when you get to one of the dark places, don't be shy."

Jane got up and put a five down on the counter. She leaned down and whispered in his ear. "Please don't let Lizzy know that you know she's back there with David.

Let her have her date. The whole town is watching them, too. And no one is going to let Lizzy or David get into trouble."

She straightened up. "On the other hand, I think the Christ Church choir might break into a rousing rendition of the 'Hallelujah Chorus' if you managed to get into trouble with Lark Chaikin."

Jane squeezed his shoulder again and swept out of the café.

Stone sat there for thirty seconds, screwing up his courage, then he pushed up from the table and strolled across the street, aware that every woman in the Cut 'n Curl was watching him.

He paused for a moment at the stairs to the apartment, then he took a bracing breath, reminding himself that he was a warrior who had coolly faced down the enemy.

He climbed the steps two at a time.

CHAPTER 16

Daddy was taking an incredibly long time in the shower. Lizzy heard the water running as she sat on her bed staring down at Michael Bennett's soggy hat.

The events of the morning had been rattling around in her head all day. She knew she shouldn't tattle on the boys who hung out at the Jonquil House. But what if they knew something about Jimmy Marshall's death?

The sound of water stopped. Lizzy gave Daddy ten minutes to get dressed, then she knocked on his bedroom door.

He opened it directly. "What's up?"

"Uh, Daddy, before you go, I need to speak with you about something important."

Daddy gave her his serious look. "Is this about David, and how you weren't exactly at Mr. Randall's stables this noontime?"

Heat crawled up Lizzy's face. "So you *did* see me at the Kountry Kitchen."

"Not until Aunt Jane pointed you out. How did David get the bloody nose?"

"He got into a fight with Michael Bennett."

"Great. Where did this happen?"

"We went out to the swamp this morning."

"Why?"

She shrugged. "I thought we could look for the missing gun, you know?"

Daddy leaned against the door frame. He looked totally badass when he did that, even dressed in jeans and a plaid flannel shirt. "I'm pretty sure you'd need a wet suit and some dive gear to find that weapon."

"Yeah, I know. But I tried anyway. And while I was messing around in the water, I came up with this." She held up the plastic bag.

"What is it?"

"It's Michael Bennett's porkpie hat."

"And this is why David got into a fight with Michael?"

She shook her head, then explained what had happened that morning.

"Well, I have to say I'm impressed with Justin Polk," Daddy said when she'd finished her explanations.

"About the hat, Daddy?"

"Yeah? What about it?" He glanced at his watch. He was preoccupied. Daddy hadn't even given her grief for going into the swamp without telling anyone.

Lizzy took a deep breath. "Michael always wears his hat. But he didn't have it yesterday at school. So he must have lost it before yesterday. That means he was in the swamp, maybe even at the same time as Mr. Marshall died. He might have seen something. Or maybe he's even involved in some way."

Daddy folded his arms across his chest, and his eyes got that look in them—the one that said he was thinking about a case.

"How many boys were out there at the Jonquil House today?"

"Five or six. They go there all the time to drink beer. Do you think they might have witnessed something?"

"Don't know, but it's worth talking to them. Where exactly did you find the hat?"

"It was right there in an area where the ground was trampled. Daddy, I think that hat was in the swamp right near where you found the body. You think Michael had something to do with it? I mean, he got all upset on Friday when he heard that Mr. Marshall was dead."

"Honey, I think it's doubtful that Michael killed Mr. Marshall. He probably lost his hat going out there to look at the crime scene like you and David did. But seeing as you found it, that makes him a potential witness, and he ought to be interviewed. It would probably be useful to talk to the rest of those friends of his. Will you make a list of the boys who were out there this morning?"

Lizzy nodded. "Are you going to talk to them? Because you do realize that I'm going to be dead once they realize I tattled on them."

Daddy laughed. "No, I probably won't be talking to them. I have to give their names to Sheriff Bennett. The crime is in his jurisdiction."

"Daddy, he's not going to take Michael's missing hat seriously."

Daddy sighed. "I know. But I promise I will follow up on this lead. And tomorrow you and I are going to have a father-daughter chat about stuff because I'm not wild about you and David going off into the swamp together."

"If you're talking about the birds and bees, I already got that talk from Aunt Jane."

"So I heard."

Lizzy forced a smile. Daddy could be so lame sometimes. It was time to change the subject and put him on the defense. "So, where are you taking Ms. Chaikin?" she said.

Daddy's cheeks colored. "Uh, well, I thought I'd treat her to some barbecue, and then we're going to see Mr. Nelson's Christmas lights."

Wow! Lizzy hadn't expected that. Was Daddy actually planning to take Ms. Chaikin off into the dark place by the old sweethearts' tree to fool around? No, he wouldn't.

"Uh, maybe I should give *you* a daughter-father talk, huh?" she said.

"Okay, that's enough out of you." Daddy's eyes kind of sparkled as he pushed away from the door. "Now I need to finish getting ready."

"Is there anything else on your mind?"

Lizzy gave him a big smile. "Only this: Don't overdo the aftershave, okay? There is nothing more uncool than a guy who smells sweet."

Lizzy turned and scooted back down the hall and into her room where she immediately called Cassie with the news that Daddy was taking Lark to the lighting display. Cassie's grandfather was the one who put up the Christmas lights every year, and Cassie always helped at the cider stand. Cassie was going to have to be Lizzy's eyes and ears, and Lizzy expected a full report from her friend tomorrow morning.

• • •

When Stone came to pick Lark up, he was wearing a leather bomber jacket, a green plaid shirt, and a pair of relaxed blue jeans. No bulletproof vest, no utility belt, no weapon, no uniform.

He came to her as a man, not a warrior. And the vulnerability that he wore made him all the more dangerous and sexy.

He took her to a hole-in-the-wall barbecue place outside of town called the Red Hot Pig Place. It wasn't exactly the kind of place Lark had expected of him. He'd seemed so serious when he'd knocked on her door, earlier, that she'd sort of expected him to take her to a fancy restaurant.

Good thing she hadn't rushed right out to the mall in Orangeburg and bought a dress for the occasion, because wearing a dress to the Red Hot Pig Place would have been overkill. The place was built out of cinder blocks, and the dining room had wooden tables covered in plastic tablecloths. Paper napkin dispensers and plastic bottles of barbecue sauce sat in the center of every table.

Fancy this was not.

Oh, but the food was to die for. She had never tasted barbecue like this. It was served up as a kind of spicy hash. And the fried cornmeal dumplings called hush puppies melted in her mouth.

They shared war stories over a pitcher of beer. It wasn't exactly romantic small talk or salacious banter. But it was precisely what Lark needed to talk about. And she had to hand it to Stone: He might not be a conversationalist, but he sure did know how to get her talking. And because he reminded her of Carmine Falcone, she ended up telling him things she hadn't told anyone.

After her third beer, when her head was just a little buzzed, she leaned forward and reached for his hand. "I could tell you anything, couldn't I?"

The corner of his mouth twitched. "Maybe not anything."

"No, that's not what I meant. I mean, you could take the worst, most horrible story I could tell, and it wouldn't faze you."

"I've been there."

She ran her fingers over the back of his hand. He was warm and alive. He was real—not just a figment of her imagination, or the sexy hero of Pop's books.

"I don't know why Pop sent me here, but—" She stopped before her mouth ran away with her heart.

He turned his hand over and took her hand in his. "But what?"

She swallowed hard. "I'm glad he did," she whispered.

"I'm glad, too."

"Are you? All I've done tonight is tell you one horrible story after another."

He shook his head. "No, all you've done tonight is make it easy for me to be with you. I'm scared shitless."

She blinked and stiffened. "Of me?"

He shook his head. "No. Of the way you make me feel."

"How is that?"

"Crazy. Out of control. And I'm not even sure how you do it."

"That's just you being horny."

He blushed. It was adorable. She had to be careful with him. He could start feeling things. She needed to bypass the emotions and keep it casual.

"Yeah," he said. "It's been a while since I've been with a woman. But that's not why I'm here."

"No?"

"Okay, so it's only one of many reasons I'm here."

She giggled. Since she almost never giggled, her laughter had to be a sign that the beer was getting to her. "Tell me the other reasons."

He stared at her with a deer-in-the-headlights expression. It occurred to Lark that talking frankly about this kind of stuff was not easy for him.

He finally cleared his throat. "The thing is, you make me feel needed," he murmured in a voice so low she almost didn't hear him above the twangy country music that was playing on the jukebox.

What an odd thing for him to say.

He looked wildly around the room for a moment before he forced himself to look back into her eyes. And then it was like neither of them could look away.

"I do need you," she whispered. "You make me feel safe."

He swallowed. "I know. And that makes me feel good in some way I can't really explain. I never—" He bit off the words. Maybe his mouth was running away with his heart, too.

Old man Nelson had outdone himself this year. He'd probably used more than a million LED lights out in his cornfield, not to mention various glow-from-the-inside plastic ornaments. His display was legendary and tacky and lit up the sky.

Stone parked his pickup on the side of the road behind a long line of other cars and trucks. He took Lark by the hand and pulled her along the road toward the lights.

He remembered coming out here with Sharon, the year after Tyler died. She'd said something about offering up their losses to God, almost as if it were a gift. He didn't understand a word of it. But she'd been so determined to be happy that Christmas.

And now, years later, it almost made sense. He wanted this time with Lark to be good just for its own sake. Maybe he could forget about the past and the future and just live in the moment, for once.

So he focused on the way Lark's hand felt in his—strange and new and different. Sexy.

"Oh, my God, is that a glow-in-the-dark Homer Simpson?" Lark asked as they reached the entrance to the light show.

"It is."

"Wow. Nothing puts me in a holiday mood faster than Homer in a Santa suit. How about you?"

Before he could comment, a teenager wearing a pink hat with long, braided earflaps waved at him from the cider stand. "Hey, Chief Rhodes," she said. It was Cassie Nelson.

Damn. He should have known Henry Nelson's grandkids would be helping with the cider and the Christmas tree sales. There was nowhere in this county where he could really be alone with Lark, was there?

Cassie grinned as her gaze flicked from Stone, to Lark, to their joined hands and back again. "Hi, Miss Chaikin," Cassie called.

Lark stiffened, and Stone decided he didn't want to get into a conversation with Lizzy's best friend. He nodded and said, "Howdy, Cassie," then quickly pulled Lark past the smiling girl and down a beaten path lined with glowing candy canes.

"Do I know that girl?" Lark asked.

"Probably not. That's Cassie Nelson. The granddaughter of the farmer who puts up these lights. She's Lizzy's best friend."

"She called me by name."

"That's hardly surprising."

"How do you figure that?"

"Because we're in Last Chance, and everyone in town knows I've taken off my wedding band. They also know that you were watching me from the apartment above the Cut 'n Curl. And by now, they all know we had dinner at the Pig Place."

"Man, that's a little terrifying." She looked up at him, a thousand Christmas lights dancing in her eyes.

"I'm sorry. If you want to—"

"If you're about to ask me if I want to say good night and go back to the Cut 'n Curl, you're crazy. I'm having fun. It's just that I'm not used to being the center of attention. I'm one of those lurkers on the sidelines who snap photos when people aren't looking."

"I'm sorry. You kind of get used to the lack of privacy in this town. But for the record, I'm having a good time, too."

She took him by the crook of the arm. "I'm glad to hear that." She pulled him down the path between the glittering candy canes. The first lighted scene featured a choir of plastic carolers joyously singing "Grandma Got Run Over by a Reindeer." Grandma, complete with hoof marks on her forehead, was lying in some fluffy stuff that was supposed to be snow. A herd of glow-from-the-inside reindeer somberly looked on.

"Kind of warms your heart doesn't it?" Lark said as she studied the trampled body of Grandma while simultaneously tapping her toe to the sprightly music.

"It's a public service announcement about the perils of imbibing too much eggnog on Christmas Eve," he said, deadpan.

She laughed at his joke, the sound as bright and merry as Christmas bells. She took his hand and pulled him down the path. "What's next?"

"Uh, well, that's going to be hard to explain to a Yankee."

They stopped in front of a thirty-foot Christmas tree awash in hundreds of small garnet-colored lights. A giant banner above the tree proclaimed "Go Cocks" in huge, twinkling letters.

Lark stared at the display and cleared her throat. "What do cocks have to do with Christmas?"

Stone felt his face flame. "Not one thing. But Henry Nelson's entire family graduated from Carolina. They are a Gamecock family, you see. And the school colors are garnet and black, which explains the color of the lights."

"Uh-huh. This has something to do with football, doesn't it?"

"I'm afraid so. Football is bigger than Jesus around these parts."

"Which I guess explains the combination of the Christmas tree and the—"

"Exactly."

She turned and studied him in the garnet light. "So, are you one of those guys who worship at that altar?"

"Yes, ma'am. I'm a devoted Gamecock fan."

She smiled. "I think I like that about you." She turned and headed down the path. He followed, wondering if she was just being kind. Admitting that he was the kind of guy who liked to pop a beer and watch the game on Saturday was probably not the best way to impress her.

They walked on, past a group of Christmas trees patriotically decorated in red, white, and blue; a giant collection of blowup Peanuts characters; a snow globe featuring Tigger and Pooh; a veritable army of glow-in-the-dark toy soldiers all in regimented rows; and finally a lighting display of elves hard at work.

"Is that a real moonshine still those elves are working on?" she asked.

"Yes, ma'am, it most certainly is. I think Henry inherited that still from his hillbilly daddy. He keeps the copper nice and polished, don't you think?"

"And you're not troubled by this?"

"Well, I reckon if I found something like that out in the woods, I might have to call the authorities. But you can clearly see the elves are using that still to make hot chocolate, not white lightning."

He pointed to the hand-lettered sign on the still that made this perfectly clear.

"I didn't know chocolate came out of a still like that. And do elves get drunk on chocolate? Because a couple of those elves look a little tipsy to me."

"Well, you see, necessity is the mother of invention. And the truth is, the church ladies made Henry put up that chocolate sign. The first time he set up his elves, they were definitely making something a little stronger than chocolate. The ladies disapproved. I'm pretty sure Nelson got back by adding the trampled granny to his light show the next year."

Lark rolled her eyes up at him. She was close enough that he could smell her shampoo. His body felt as tight as a piano wire.

She whispered, "I definitely noticed a resemblance between that trampled granny and Lillian Bray."

"Shhhhhh. Don't say that aloud." He pressed his finger across her lips, and his heart took off on a wild flight. He wanted to take her someplace way more private. The time had come to make a move. The thought excited and frightened him at the same time.

He leaned down and kissed her cheek. Her skin was cool against his lips. "C'mon, I want to show you something."

He snagged her hand and pulled her off the lighted path and into the darkness between the lighting displays.

"Oh, man," she said as he guided her across the semi-darkness toward the big live oak that stood in the middle of Henry's field. "You're sneaky, aren't you? You ply me with beer, soften me up with country music and romantic lights, and then you guide me out here into a dark cornfield."

Her tone gave him a moment of doubt, but he decided to bull his way through. If Lark was the kind of woman who wanted a fancy dinner, soft music, and romance, then he was the last guy on earth she was looking for. Given what she'd said last night, he was pretty sure she didn't really want those things, though.

"There's nothing sneaky at all about bringing you out here," he said in his best take-charge voice.

They reached the tree. It was deserted. But off in the distance, he could see a group of teens who had spread blankets on the ground. They appeared to have a cooler and some thermoses with them. They were being unusually quiet for teens.

He pulled his attention away from the kids and the trouble they were probably getting into. He leaned into the trunk, caging Lark between his arms.

The flicker of distant Christmas lights illuminated her face and sparked in her eyes like starlight. She was smiling. Thank God.

He touched her hair. It was soft and short and ran through his fingers like silk. She closed her eyes and took a deep breath. "That feels nice."

She was waiting for him. She was willing. He wasn't going to have to seduce her. He wasn't going to have to work very hard at all.

He gave himself up to it. He dipped his head and met her lips, not even surprised to find her mouth open for him. Their tongues met and tangled. He pressed himself against her, her soft breasts tight against the planes of his chest. This was much better than last night. He didn't have that stupid vest in the way.

He reached for her breast. It was soft in his hands, the nipple hard against his palm.

He couldn't breathe. He couldn't think. Blood roared through his head, pounded in his ears. He made an inarticulate sound, deep in his throat, and she laughed.

"Are you laughing at me?" His voice came out husky.

She caught his question with her lips, and he breathed her in. Okay, good. She wasn't laughing at him. Maybe she was enjoying herself.

She confirmed this when she threw her arms around his neck and wrapped her legs around his hips. Wait a second, he hadn't exactly expected her to do that. She was moving so fast.

But he didn't want to stop her. In fact, he was losing the ability to think. He had, quite literally, never experienced anything quite like this before. It was so hot it burned away his guilty feelings.

He rocked his hips against her, and she bucked against him. Their hips danced until they found a rhythm. He couldn't breathe. She felt so incredible.

And then she made a startling noise deep in her throat, halfway between a growl and a groan.

He completely forgot where he was when she let go of his neck and dropped back to the ground. He thought for an instant that she'd tell him to stop, but she didn't.

Oh, no, she made a beeline for his belt buckle.

He let her. Then it occurred to him that he could go after the button on her jeans. It was kind of amazing just how quickly he was able to get it undone.

He was warm and willing, and Lark was completely into it when his hands made it under her waistband and hit her naked, and slightly chilly, butt.

She'd just gotten his belt undone, and she had to stop for an instant and simply soak up his touch. It was hot and crazy. He was hard everywhere. He smelled like a man. His beard rasped against her cheek, and she couldn't get enough of it. She needed him more than she had ever needed anything or anyone.

Her greedy fingers unzipped his fly. She freed him. And when her hand found him in the dark, she spiraled right out of control. He was perfect. He was a fantasy. She wanted him. He wanted her.

Now.

She kicked off her jeans and wrapped her legs around him. She gave herself to him in the cold and the dark, with people all around them who were not paying attention to the naughty, sexy, crazy thing they were doing.

Oh, thank God, he didn't stop to think. He'd packed away his provincial streak, and he just forged ahead, taking her in a mindless, deep, almost fated way. He filled her up, he completed her, he spoke with his body in a way that was utterly magic and so incredibly hot.

When the climax overtook Lark, and he tried to smother her urgent, mindless cries with his mouth, she understood the earth-shattering truth.

What she'd just shared with Stone Rhodes was hot and crazy. But it was also deep and mysterious. There was nothing casual about it.

Stone wanted to take her home. He wanted to sleep with her. He wanted to hold her and show her that he was not a big horny idiot who screwed women in public without any thought about protection or any other rational, adult consideration.

Damn. He needed to remember that this was supposed to be casual and temporary.

He buried his nose into the warm place at the nape of her neck and took a deep breath. His heart was still pounding, and the musky scent of sex filled his head.

How could he have behaved in such a rash, crazy, unforgivable way? He'd just had the most amazing sex in his life, but the guilt was starting to creep in from every side. It was truly annoying to discover that Lark had been right last night. He *was* old-fashioned.

What if he got her pregnant? He already had a terrible track record on that score. All of his children had been unplanned.

"Uh," he said. "That was..."

She gave him a dozen kisses across his cheek and down his chin. "It was amazing."

"It was..."

"Unplanned and hot as hell. And you loved every minute of it." He heard the amusement in her voice. Was she teasing him?

"Uh, well, but, I'm—"

"Don't." She pressed her fingers across his lips. "Don't apologize. You have nothing to apologize for. You were horny. And even so, you gave me incredible pleasure. It was really good."

He didn't respond to that. Taking a woman upside the trunk of a live oak didn't square with his notion of what it took to be a great lover. Although thinking about the noises Lark made when she climaxed sent a ripple of heat right through him.

He let her go, placing her back on her own two feet.

She ran her hands down over his still-trembling shoulders. "We better get our clothes in order before we get caught with our pants down," she said. "Although the risk of getting caught is part of what makes it so much fun."

"It would be embarrassing to get caught. I could lose my job," Stone muttered as he took a step back and started arranging himself and tucking in his shirttail. Damn. He'd just had some great sex without actually taking off all his clothes. That was a first.

He watched as Lark put herself back together. She leaned up against the tree and began to sort out pant legs and panties. There was just enough light to get a glimpse of creamy skin on well-toned thighs. God, she must be freezing out here. He hadn't even thought about that.

Another wave of guilt rumbled through him.

When they were both presentable, Lark wrapped her arms around his middle and gave him a big hug. "Don't beat yourself up about this, Stone. It was fun. Just accept it for what it was." She got up on tiptoes and kissed his chin.

"It's getting late, and you must be cold," he found himself saying. That wasn't exactly what he wanted to say.

He wanted to take her someplace private. He wanted to get entirely naked with her. He wanted to hold her. He wanted to do a lot of other things, too.

But he couldn't invite himself up to the Cut 'n Curl, and he wasn't going to take her to the Peach Blossom Motor Court or the Magnolia Inn over in Allenberg. He'd already acted like a complete idiot, and he'd taken the worst kind of advantage of her.

He also understood the price they would both pay if anyone saw his truck parked someplace late at night where it wasn't supposed to be. And besides, Momma had taken the girls Christmas shopping, and they would be home by ten-thirty at the very latest. Momma would expect him home. Having kids at home made what he'd just done impossibly complicated.

So he didn't say what was on his mind. Instead he took her by the hand and walked her back into the light.

He delivered her safe and sound to the Cut 'n Curl twenty minutes later. And by the time Haley and Lizzy got home, their arms filled with shopping bags, he'd had enough time to throw his dirty jeans and stained shirt in the washer. He'd also taken a long, cold shower.

CHAPTER 17

David screwed up his courage and headed toward the kitchen. It was barely six in the morning, and he was starving. He'd been hiding out in his room for the last twelve hours, ever since Mom had unleashed World War III right in their living room last night.

Mom was furious at David for lying about being sick. She was even angrier about his black eyes and swollen nose, and the fact that he refused to tell her how he had acquired them.

She was sure that David had been lured out somewhere by Lizzy and beaten up by a bunch of anti-Semites. She was almost right.

She wanted to call the cops, except that the only cop in town just happened to be the father of the girl she disapproved of. David might have appreciated the irony of that, if he'd not been terrified by the way his family seemed to be unraveling. How could Mom think Lizzy and her father were anti-Semites? Somehow Mom's concern transformed itself into resentment about everything. Mom was furious at Dad for having lost his job in Michigan. She was furious about having to move to South Carolina. And she was furious about a lot of other stuff that David didn't even understand.

His parents had argued all night.

They had argued so intently that they had forgotten that David's defiance had triggered the crisis, and they'd let him slink off to his room where he'd tossed and turned all night, listening to Robbie cry.

His life was a nightmare. But at least Lizzy Rhodes thought he was brave. That was something.

He crept around the corner of the dining room and headed toward the kitchen. And skidded to a stop.

Mom and Dad were sitting at the kitchen table. They looked horrible. They were drinking coffee. Dad looked up from his cup.

"David," he said in a hoarse voice, "go wake up your brothers. Tell them they've got half an hour to pack their things."

"What?"

"You heard me. Pack what you need in the way of clothes and any must-have toys. I'll ship the rest when I get time."

"We're going back to Michigan," Mom said.

"We are?"

"Well, you and Mom and your brothers are," Dad said.

David stood there looking at his parents. This was not happening. Mom was not going to break up this family over something stupid like Michael Bennett. If she did that, then the bullies like Michael would win.

He turned away, his stomach churning, and his head pounding, and his nose hurting. What could he do? He was just a kid.

He headed back up the hallway and found Robbie standing there, his eyes round and bright. He'd obviously overheard. David put his arm around his little brother, and they both woke up Jonathan.

"We've got to do something," Jonathan said. "Maybe if you told them where you were yesterday."

David shook his head. "I don't think that will change anything."

"We could run away," Robbie said.

"No, Robbie, that won't work. It's cold outside," Jonathan said.

David stared at his littlest brother. "Well, maybe so, but it would delay things."

"What?" Jonathan said.

"If I disappeared for the rest of the day, Mom couldn't pack up the car and go back to Michigan. She'd have to stay. And maybe she and Dad would talk some more. And maybe they'd realize that we don't want them to split up over something stupid like the fact that the synagogue is thirty miles away."

"You're going to run away?" Jonathan asked.

"No. I'm just going to disappear. You guys go back to bed and pretend to sleep. Give me fifteen minutes to get out of here."

Jonathan looked at Robbie. "David, Robbie isn't going to keep a secret."

"Once I'm gone, I don't care if Mom and Dad know that you guys were in on it."

"Where are you going?"

"I'm not going to tell you that. But I'll be back. If no one finds me, I'll be back by tomorrow."

"You're crazy. This isn't going to stop Mom from moving back to Michigan."

"Maybe not. But it's the only thing I can think of on short notice."

Lark woke up lonely.

She lay on her back in the narrow daybed, her hands behind her head, while she studied the antique tin ceiling above her. Her gaze traced the depressed circles and raised leaf motifs as morning gradually filled the two narrow windows with a watery gray light.

The room was all monochrome and sepia-colored. It perfectly reflected her mood.

She had no regrets about what happened last night. But she wasn't going to kid herself about what it meant. It may not have felt all that casual to her, but she didn't belong here in Last Chance. And Stone was rooted to this place. He had children and a family and a dead wife he still loved.

She had nothing, except a Pulitzer Prize, her cameras, and an appointment to be on a flight to Africa the day after tomorrow.

She squeezed her eyes shut and pushed everything out of her mind except for the memory of Stone's body sliding against hers. Heat filled her. She wasn't ever going to forget him. That was for damn sure. But she couldn't stay here and have him.

And besides, it would be crazy to want more from a man who had yet to stop loving his wife. She'd given him what he needed. He'd given her a memory. Better to call it quits, and move on. She was good at that kind of thing.

Only this time it was going to be hard. Stone would be seared into her memory for a long time to come.

Maybe forever.

She opened her eyes and stared at the ceiling and forced herself to think about Pop. Why had he sent her on this wild goose chase?

"You brought home memories, too, didn't you?" she whispered out loud. What had happened on the eighteenth hole?

And just like that she had the answer. It had been hiding in plain sight all this time.

She threw the covers back and headed into the shower, where she tried and failed to wash away the memories. It was nine-thirty when she arrived at the Kountry Kitchen for breakfast.

She ate her toast and drank her coffee and watched Palmetto Avenue out the front windows of the café. People were headed off to church this morning. So if she was going to get to the truth, she would have to wait until services were over.

She ordered another cup of coffee. Churchgoers were not the only ones up early. The Last Chance Police Department—all two of them—were busy this morning, directing traffic, patrolling the main drag, and keeping everything safe.

She recognized the man behind the wheel of one of the police cruisers as it made its rounds. With each of his slow circuits she wondered if he was glancing up at her windows, thinking about last night. Was he getting hot thinking about what they'd done together?

Or was he just feeling guilty?

At eleven o'clock, she headed back to the Cut 'n Curl

and got into Pop's SUV to drive the short distance to Nita Wills's house.

Stone had seen Lark through the front windows of the Kountry Kitchen as she ate her leisurely breakfast. Every cell in his body wanted to stop the cruiser and head into the café for his usual Sunday-morning coffee.

But not if he had to come face-to-face with Lark in a public place. He needed to talk with her, but not out in the open. And besides, he wasn't sure he could keep his hands off her. The memory of what they'd done in the cornfield had haunted him last night. He felt groggy and confused and as randy as a double-peckered billy goat.

When Lark left the café and headed toward the south side of town, he tried to be subtle about following her, but it was impossible, especially since she didn't go very far— just down Palmetto to Julia and over to Maple, where she pulled to the curb in front of Nita Wills's house.

He pulled in behind her. He understood her motives for wanting to speak with Nita, but he also had very clear orders from Nita's daughter, the mayor-elect. He knew good and well that Kamaria would not approve of Lark staking out Nita's home.

He squared his uniform Stetson on his head and left his cruiser. He approached Lark from the driver's side of the SUV. When she saw him, she rolled down the window and looked up at him out of those big, vulnerable doe eyes. Her face was so pale, the skin beneath her eyes bruised, as if she hadn't slept well either.

He wanted to rip open the door, pull her up into his arms, and hold her. It was all he could do not to act on the urge.

He leaned against the door frame. "Are you okay?" he asked. All thought of confronting her about Nita fled his mind.

She gifted him with a sweet smile. "I'm fine. How about you?" A sudden spark of mischief lit up her eyes.

He honestly didn't know the answer to that question. "I'm...confused."

"That's good. Just so long as you aren't feeling guilty."

Damn. It was like she could read his mind. "But I am feeling guilty."

She looked away, and some of the light left her eyes. "I was afraid of that."

"Damn it, how do you expect me to feel? I mean·I acted like an idiot last night. I wasn't prepared. I didn't use any protection. What if I—"

She tilted her head back on the head rest and let go of a belly laugh.

"Are you laughing at me?"

She shook her head. "No. I'm not. Is that what you're feeling guilty about?"

"Well, yeah."

"Oh, that's a relief."

"But—"

"Look." She leaned into the window frame. "I'm not worried about STDs. Not with you. I suppose you probably should have some concerns about me. But I can promise you that, as far as I know, I'm clean."

"That wasn't what I was mostly worried about."

She grinned up at him. "Stone. I have an IUD."

He felt gut-punched. "Oh."

"I'm a grown-up responsible woman. I may live on the wild side from time to time, but I'm not entirely stupid."

"But that's the thing, last night I was stupid."

"No, last night you were horny. You were a guy. We were consenting adults, and you did what any guy would have done. When are you going to realize that?"

He frowned.

"I know. Your male ego is probably crushed by the truth. But that's what happened. I made a move, and you didn't stop me. So don't beat yourself up about it. And besides, I had a really good time."

"Uh, well, so did I, actually," he admitted.

"I know. So just accept it for what it was and move on. Okay? Don't feel guilty. You didn't cheat on your wife last night."

He felt the sting of her rebuke. Because the truth was, in addition to being shocked by his own behavior, he had felt a little like a cheating husband. Especially when he got home and started doing the laundry.

"Okay," he said, pushing his confusion away and dropping back into police mode. He was way more comfortable when he was behaving like a cop.

"So now that we've dispensed with that, could you explain to me why you're parked out here staking out Nita's house?"

"I'm waiting for her to get home from church."

"I figured as much, but, you know, I think Nita made it clear that she doesn't want to talk to you. And, well, the truth is the mayor asked me to make sure that you don't bother her."

"So you're here in an official capacity then?"

"I guess. Honey, why don't you just let it be?"

"Because I can't. I can't sweep the sad things under the table and take the difficult photos out of the family album.

Pop sent me here for a purpose, and I need to know what it was."

"He wanted his ashes scattered."

"Yeah, but why here? And what happened at Golfing for God that changed his life? I have some theories, but theories aren't the truth. Only Nita can tell me the truth."

"But she doesn't want to talk about it."

"So, what are you going to do? Run me out of town?" Her voice sounded suddenly strident. "Is that what you want? Are you so embarrassed by this situation that you'd just like me to leave?"

"No. God, no. What I want is to sleep with you. All night long. I want to hold you and make love to you, and there isn't anyplace in Last Chance that I can do that without the whole town knowing what I've done and gossiping about it." The words spilled out of him like a river in flood stage.

"Oh." Her dark eyes widened. "Well, I've got a few ideas. We could always use Hettie's river house. I still have the keys. Or maybe we could get a sleeping bag and do it on the eighteenth hole."

"Uh." The flood of words dried up in his mouth.

Nita Wills arrived right at that moment, precluding him from further discussion of this scintillating topic. She pulled her Toyota into the driveway, and Jakob LaFlore pulled in right behind in his Volvo Cross Country. Mayor-Elect LaFlore jumped out of the passenger's side.

"Stone, is there something wrong?" Kamaria called from across the street. "Why is that woman here?"

Stone turned toward Lark. "You stay right where you are. Let me see what I can do to help you, okay?"

Stone headed toward the visibly furious mayor-elect.

But before he was halfway across the street, he heard Lark get out of the SUV. A second later Lark strode right past him, heading in Nita's direction. Nita had just gotten out of her car and was walking up the path to her front porch, her grandsons with her.

Kamaria turned toward Lark and, in a most un-mayor-like manner, told her to leave the premises and never return. When Lark ignored her, Kamaria turned toward Stone and said, "Arrest that woman. She's stalking my mother."

"Uh, well, you'd have to get a court protective order for me to arrest her, Mayor LaFlore. And besides, she isn't stalking your mother. She's just trying to talk to her. Now, why don't you just calm down, okay? And we can maybe talk this through like adults."

The look on the mayor's face told him that he'd probably just stepped in a big pile of horse-pucky. She was going to have his ass in a sling if he didn't stop Lark.

But there wasn't any way he could stop Lark from pursuing this. He'd tried. And failed.

And then it struck him, like a bolt from the blue, that Kamaria was terrified of learning the truth.

"I'm sorry," Lark said as she crossed the lawn, "but I need the truth."

Nita stood on her walk, her eyes flicking from Lark to Kamaria and back again. The mayor was yelling at Stone, which wasn't fair. This wasn't his fault. Stone behaved just like a cop. He went into calm mode, using every bit of his professional training to defuse what was rapidly becoming a domestic situation.

Just as Lark's courage began to falter, a tall man, wearing a gray suit, walked up behind Nita and put his hands on her shoulders. He leaned down and spoke softly. "Momma, I know Kamaria is scared, but maybe she needs the truth."

Nita looked up at the man, her eyes suddenly liquid with unshed tears. "It's going to hurt her."

"She'll survive." He patted Nita's shoulder and then headed off toward the mayor-elect.

"That's my son-in-law, Jakob," Nita said. "He's a cardiologist up at the hospital in Orangeburg, and I think he understands hearts better than just about anyone. He's a good man."

Jakob spoke softly to Kamaria, and the yelling stopped. Nita let go of a long, pensive sigh. "Stone, you might as well come on in and hear what I have to say, too. This is as much about your granddaddy as it is about Lark's father."

Nita turned, headed up the porch steps, and unlocked the door to her house. Everyone followed.

Nita's front room was awash in Christmas decorations, from the big tree in her front window to a village of Christmas miniatures on her coffee table. The smell of pine filled the room, and the furniture was contemporary and comfortable.

She turned on the Christmas lights before she settled herself on the couch. "Sit down, Lark. You too, Kamaria." She turned to Jakob. "Honey, you think you and the boys could get some coffee and sandwiches going?"

"Coming right up," Jakob said as he herded two school-aged boys dressed in their Sunday best down the center hall and out of the room.

"Momma, you don't have to talk to this woman. You can—"

"Hush now. The truth is I do need to talk to Lark. And you need to listen to what I have to say." Nita turned and gazed up at Stone, who had not taken a seat. He stood in the archway, his shoulder propping up the wall, his arms folded across his chest. "Don't you want to sit, Stone?"

"I'll stand," he said, his voice low and deep.

Lark was glad he was there. And she wanted to find time to explore some of those things he'd just said. She longed to sleep with him. To wake up with him. She wanted him so much it was almost frightening.

She turned her attention back to Nita. "On Thursday, I told you what my father always said about the eighteenth hole. You told me you didn't know why. But I think you do."

Nita laced her fingers together and studied the Christmas miniatures for a long moment. When she looked up, there were unshed tears glittering in her eyes.

"I was not quite twenty years old. And Abe Chaikin was the most amazing person I had ever met in my life. He was gentle and articulate. He'd seen a whole lot of the world. He had a sense of the absurd and a deep, abiding love for justice.

"And he was color-blind."

Lark found herself nodding. "Yeah, he was also irascible, difficult, moody, and opinionated."

Nita wiped a tear from her eye. "Yes, I can see that. But I didn't know him for very long. Just maybe ten days all told."

"Just ten days?"

"As long as you've been in town," Stone said.

She looked up at him. He looked oddly grim.

Nita shrugged. "When you're nineteen, it doesn't take much to get swept away."

"Momma, what are you saying?"

Nita stared at her daughter. "Honey, I'm not saying anything you haven't already halfway figured out. So don't argue with me. I love you more than I love life itself, but it's time for me to tell the truth."

Nita reached out and took Lark's hand. She patted it. "Your daddy was a good man. And don't you believe the nonsense anyone says about him having anything to do with Zeke Rhodes's death, you hear. That's not what happened."

"What happened then?" Stone asked.

"Well, for one thing, I fell in love with Abe."

"Momma, no."

Nita stared her daughter down, then continued. "I did. I fell for him. And I let him talk me into things I never thought I would do. I was a good girl. I was the kind of girl who always walked the straight and narrow line between black and white. But he showed me the absurdity of that. And so I followed him into the Kountry Kitchen that day. And I knew it was the right thing to do. But I wasn't all that brave. Love filled me up, and I acted on it.

"But you know, there are people in this world who don't understand about love."

She paused and looked up at the Christmas tree. "I think it's important, especially at this time of year, to remember why we celebrate Christmas." She turned back toward Kamaria. "It's all about love."

"Momma, what are you talking about?"

"For the space of a few days, I loved Abe Chaikin. And because we didn't have anyplace to go that wasn't always watched by someone, we ended up in a sleeping bag out on the eighteenth hole."

Both Kamaria and Stone made surprised noises.

Nita gave Lark a sober look. "By your lack of reaction, I'm thinking that you already figured that out, didn't you?"

Lark nodded. "Yeah. But if you loved him, why did you let him go?"

"Because I lost my faith in love. People were angry about what Abe and I did that morning we had breakfast at the Kountry Kitchen. Can you imagine how they would feel if they knew we were sleeping together?

"A group of white boys decided they were going to teach me and Abe a lesson for being uppity. We got wind of it. Abe begged me to come back to New York with him. He asked me to marry him."

"Why didn't you go?" Lark asked.

"Because I wasn't brave enough. I knew things were maybe a little better in New York, but I knew it would be hard for me and Abe no matter where we went. There was a group of angry people chasing us down, and it just seemed like our future was going to be like that no matter where we went."

Nita let go of a deep sigh. "I was wrong. I was so wrong. But it took me years to figure that out. Lark, honey, this world is messed up, but it's a better place than it was forty years ago. It's not perfect, but it's a better place. And it's better because of people like me and Abe." She looked at Lark and Kamaria. "And because of you girls, too. You don't see the world the same way, and that's a good thing. I wish I had been braver. I sent him away."

"What happened to my grandfather?" Stone asked.

Nita looked up at him. "Honestly, Stone, I don't know. He told me to hide in the Ark. I was buried under a bunch of hay with the barn doors closed when those angry boys came by. I couldn't tell you who they were. But I do know that somehow Zeke scared the living daylights out of them. He ran them all off. They were terrified by something out there. I heard them hollering."

"But how did he—"

"I don't know. If you want the truth, Stone, I think it was his angels. I know that's a little crazy, but that's what I believe. Anyway, when I left him that evening, he was alive. I went home, and Momma was so scared about what had happened that she took me right to Columbia and put me on a bus to Chicago where my aunt lived. I only heard later that Zeke died that night. I don't know how."

Nita turned toward Kamaria. "This is the hard part, honey, because about a month after I got to Chicago I discovered I was pregnant."

The silence in Nita's front room was so thick that Lark had trouble breathing.

"Y'all are sisters," Nita said.

"No!" Kamaria stood up and ran from the room, down the hall. In the distance, the back door opened and slammed shut.

"It's going to take her some time to get used to that. I lied to her, you see. She thought my husband was her daddy. And in all the important ways, Terrence was her father. She didn't know Abe."

"Did Pop know about her?"

Nita shook her head. "I never told him. I didn't think there was a place for a family like ours. You know back then, it was against the law for a black woman and a white man to get married in some states. But now, I realize we could have found a place if I'd been willing to try.

"And then I met Terrence, and he changed me. Kamaria

was a few months old, and he taught me the truth about love. He was a good man with a big heart, and he accepted her as his own."

"But she must have known he wasn't her biological father."

"Well, Kamaria knew she was born before we got married, but she just thought we'd made a mistake. We were young, and it wasn't so strange. As it turned out, Terrence couldn't have children, so she was all we had. He loved her until the cancer took him."

Lark nodded. "I'm glad for that. But..." Her throat closed up, and she struggled for words. A hand came down on her shoulder.

Stone. She had almost forgotten he was there. "Pop would be so disappointed that he didn't know Kamaria."

"I'm sure that's right. And I regret that. But maybe we can make amends because you're her sister, and you can tell her about her birth father. And I hope you will."

"I'm not sure she wants to know."

"She'll come around. And you should always remember that you have family in Last Chance. I'm so glad you came here this morning, because I spent a lot of time in church today praying about this. I knew I had to tell you the truth. And I needed to make you understand how important it is to have faith in love.

"I think Abe came to understand this, too. I think he wanted to come back here and be laid to rest in a place where he truly loved. So I'm going to talk to Elbert. Zeke was your father's friend, and I know he would want your father's last wish to be granted."

Lark nodded, tears filling her eyes. It wasn't easy to discover that Mom was not Pop's great love. But then, from the sound of it, Pop probably hadn't been Nita's great love either. The way she talked about her husband was a whole lot like the way Stone talked about Sharon.

"Thanks," she said and stood up. "I think I better go now." She turned and headed for the front door before she came apart at the seams. She'd gone looking for answers, and she'd found them. Now she wondered why the hell she'd done it.

Pop had loved in vain. And it sure did look like his younger daughter might be getting ready to do the same stupid thing. Lark had always been so casual about all her relationships. Love had nothing to do with any of them.

Damn it.

The truth didn't always set you free.

Lark held her head high as she left Nita's house. But Stone could tell by the tension in her shoulders that Nita's story had hurt her.

He caught up with her and put his hand on her shoulder. He didn't have any words. He wasn't good at stuff like this, but he had to make the effort. For Lark. She needed someone right now. And he couldn't imagine a more awful, messy situation.

She was alone in the world and had just discovered a family that was divided on whether she should be invited in. That had to suck.

"You're not okay," he said.

She shook her head.

"C'mon. I'll take you someplace."

He kept his hand on her shoulder, conscious of the tiny bones beneath his palm. He guided her to her SUV. "Give me the keys."

She dug in the pocket of her jeans, fished them out, and handed them to him. He opened the door and helped her into the passenger's seat.

When he sat in the driver's seat, he took off his Stetson and threw it in the back. Then he called in to the county dispatch and told them he was taking the rest of the day off. He turned off his radio, then fired up the SUV and drove it back to the parking lot at the Cut 'n Curl.

Downtown Last Chance was practically deserted, so he didn't think anyone saw him walk Lark up the stairs to the apartment and shut the door behind him.

She turned around and spoke in a shaky voice. "Did you mean what you said?"

"Uh, you mean that stuff about wanting to sleep with you?"

She nodded.

"Yeah. I did. Dropping you off last night was one of the hardest things I ever did."

She stepped closer and wrapped her arms around his middle. His utility belt and vest got in the way, but it was still nice to have her leaning on him. He felt useful holding her up.

"You're provincial," she said.

He buried his nose in her short hair and inhaled. Her aroma raced through his brain, unleashing a chaos of longing within him. "Provincial?"

"Yeah. It's one of the things I like most about you."

"Well, I guess I'm glad you like something."

"I like a lot," she said against his shirt.

He tilted her head up and kissed her briefly. Then he pulled back. "Momma has the girls for the day. I'm free until this afternoon. I have to be home early because of

Haley's Christmas play. But I've got a few hours. We can sit here and drink tea and talk. You can tell me how you're hurting. We can swap war stories. There isn't anything you're feeling right now that would scare me away. Or we could not talk, if that's what you want."

She looked up at him and pressed her fingers against his lips. "I want more than talk. You can start by taking off the weapon and the vest, and then we can see where it goes from there."

She didn't have to ask him twice.

CHAPTER 18

Lizzy had taken her phone into the bathroom, which meant she was talking to David. Or maybe Cassie, but Haley was pretty sure it was David.

Which was why Haley leaned up against the door and listened. Lizzy was talking in a low voice, but Haley heard enough to know that her big sister was planning to meet someone out at Granddaddy's golf course.

Haley waited until the phone call was almost over before she scooted into the living room, where Granddaddy was watching the Atlanta Falcons football game. Granny was in the kitchen fixing the dumb ol' shepherd costume that Haley was going to have to wear for the play at church later. The hood on the costume was too big and flopped down into Haley's eyes.

Haley sure hoped Granny could fix that because it was bad enough that the stupid costume itched. And she was going to be so embarrassed when Maryanne messed up her lines.

She pretended to watch the football game as Lizzy came into the room, pulling on her big red sweater.

"Hey Granny," Lizzy called as she hurried into the kitchen. "Is it okay if I go over to Cassie's house for a little while? Her mother is acting all weird again."

Granny looked up from the sewing machine. She was wearing a pair of little half-glasses that made her look kind of funny. "You know, Lizzy, it's not right to talk about your elders like that."

Lizzy rolled her eyes. "C'mon, Granny, you know as well as I do that Mrs. Nelson is goofy. And Cassie says she gets all weird and sad this time of year."

Granny nodded. "It's depression, honey, not goofiness. And she's on medication for it."

"I'm sorry, Granny. But Cassie calls her goofy all the time."

"Well, I guess it's not easy having a mother like that. You need to be back home no later than four o'clock, you hear? Haley's play is at five-thirty."

"Do I have to?"

Granny gave Lizzy one of those grown-up looks. "Yes, you do. She's your sister."

"Yes, ma'am," Lizzy said.

Haley didn't really blame Lizzy. The Christmas play was going to be lame.

But at the same time, Lizzy not wanting to be there made Haley feel kind of sad and lonely. She'd been feeling that way all day, ever since this morning, when the Sorrowful Angel had left the house with Daddy. She hadn't come back. Neither had Daddy, even though he didn't really have to work on Sundays.

Sometimes he came home and watched football with

Granddaddy. Haley liked those Sundays. She would sometimes sit on his lap and watch with him. But not today.

Daddy was working today. And Lizzy was going to
hang out with Cassie. Maryanne was practicing for the
play. And the angel was missing suddenly. Haley felt a
little bit hollow, like one of those chocolate Santa Clauses
that she always got in her stocking.

Thinking about Santa only made her feel worse. She
really was having her doubts.

"All right, honey, you can go to Cassie's, but you need
to be back on time. Is that clear?"

"Absolutely. I promise." Lizzy turned on her heel and
headed for the door. Haley followed her out onto the porch.
It had gotten cold outside. Maybe cold enough to snow.

Although right now the sun was shining.

"You're not going to Cassie's, are you?" Haley said.

"Shut up, Haley. You're such a brat sometimes."

"You're going to Granddaddy's golf course. I heard
you tell someone that the door to the Ark is always open."

"You remember what I said the other day about Granny's teacup?" Lizzy hissed.

"Yeah." Haley realized right then that maybe she
needed to apologize to Granny about the teacup, if for no
other reason than Lizzy would stop bringing it up.

"Well, you keep your mouth shut, you hear?"

"Okay, Lizzy, but you better not be late."

"I won't. But I don't get what the big deal is. I mean,
you're just a shepherd. When I was in third grade, I got to
be the angel."

And with that, Lizzy hurried down the porch steps and
up the street toward their house. Lizzy's bike was in the
yard, but Lizzy went inside first.

Haley stayed on the porch and watched. A few minutes later, Lizzy came back out. She had her backpack and the extra quilt from the foot of her bed. She stuffed the quilt into the basket on her bike, and then she headed off in the opposite direction from Cassie's house.

Lark rested her head on Stone's chest, listening to his heartbeat. They lay tangled in the sheets, and a wedge of afternoon light came through the windows. Lark watched the dust motes dance on the air while she listened to the even rhythm of Stone's breathing.

She raised her head and studied him: the resolute angle of his jaw, the rugged lines at the corner of his eyes, the firm arch of his brow, the crooked place where his nose had been broken.

He was a study in peaceful repose. A tiny, satisfied smile curled the corner of his mouth.

That little upward spiral made her heart ache. She had told him everything about Misurata and Jeb. He had listened to every horrible thing she had to say. He'd taken it all. And he was still lying there sated and smiling in his sleep.

Man. She'd let her emotions run away with her, hadn't she?

He cracked an eye. The little curl at the corner of his mouth deepened as consciousness returned. "Hey," he whispered and ran his hand through her hair.

In the past, this was the moment when she would deliver the standard speech—the one about how things were going too far too fast. But she didn't want to do that this time. She wanted to say something else altogether.

But he wasn't ready to hear it.

He wasn't ready to love her. Not really. He still thought about his wife. He still loved her. And after what she'd heard about Sharon, Lark knew she couldn't compete. Sharon had sounded like a cross between a saint and an angel.

His expression sobered. "Darlin', are you having regrets? Because that would be funny, given what you said the other night about my being old-fashioned."

She plastered a smile on her face. "No regrets," she said. And really she didn't have regrets. Not for sleeping with him, anyway. And maybe not even for falling in love with him. But she would definitely regret leaving him.

He looked at his watch, which rode military-style on the inside of his left wrist. "It's getting late. I have to get home. Haley's play at the church starts pretty early because they're just little kids."

She nodded. This was good. She didn't have to give any speeches. He would do it for her. He would remind her of the things she wasn't a part of.

"Are you really okay?" he asked.

"I'm fine. I just have a lot on my mind, you know. I'm supposed to be on a plane to Africa day after tomorrow. I hope Nita convinces your father to let me lay Pop to rest as quickly as possible. I need to get back to DC and pack and get ready. This was..." Her words faltered. She wanted to say it had been fun. "Fun" would be the right word for a casual encounter. But this had been earth shattering.

"You think you're ready to go back into the field?" he asked, poking her right in her most vulnerable place.

She met his gaze. "Shooting photographs is what I do. It's what I am—a mirror on the world. I'll be fine. I just need to get back to work. This was...fun." She forced the word out. It turned to ashes in her mouth.

He sat up, his face unreadable. But the fire in his eyes slowly flickered out. He didn't say anything. He took her little adult speech stoically.

They had both gone into this with their eyes open.

He got out of bed and started collecting pieces of his discarded uniform. He headed into the bathroom and closed the door behind him.

A minute later, the shower started up.

Lark pulled the blanket around her shoulders and curled up in the bed, watching the dust dance in the sunlight. She felt empty-headed. Empty-hearted. Empty.

He wore his T-shirt and uniform pants when he left the bathroom, and she watched him put on his vest and then his uniform shirt. He was kind of obsessive about his body armor—just like the marines in Afghanistan.

He crossed the room and sat on the edge of the bed. He leaned down and kissed her cheek. "You're not ready to go back to Africa. Don't go running there because of me, or Nita, or your father."

"That's not the reason," she said. The truth was she didn't have any other place to go.

He pressed his lips together. "I should probably have my head examined for acting like some kind of horny teenager these last couple of days. I should have stopped you last night. You called me old-fashioned, and I guess I am. I should have been more adult about this. But, well, the thing is, I enjoyed having sex with you. It felt good. And I haven't felt that good in a while. It was...fun. But—"

"Good. We're on the same page," she said before she heard what came after the "but." She knew what he was about to say. She was his transition woman—the one who helped him get back into the world of the living. Every broken heart needed someone like that. She knew this truth going in. She had no right to be upset now. None.

He gave her shoulder a squeeze. He sat there for a long moment, and she prayed he would just keep his mouth shut.

Luckily, he was down with that program. A minute later he was gone, and Lark turned her head into the pillow.

Damn it, why did he have to be so articulate, even with his silence?

A kind of creeping numbness filled Stone as he descended the stairs at the Cut 'n Curl. Something had just happened between him and Lark. Something good. Something real. But it hadn't ended right. He knew that the minute he'd turned up the hot water in the shower and it hadn't pierced the cold that had crept through him.

Lark was leaving. He had known that from the start. They had been honest with each other.

So why was he feeling so empty?

He strode across Palmetto Avenue, heading toward Maple Street, where he'd left the Crown Vic. He squinted into the late-afternoon sun and reached for his sunglasses, but he'd left them in the cruiser. A cold wind was building, and it smacked him across the face.

The sun and the wind made his eyes water. A tear leaked out of his eye and fell down his cheek. He didn't bother to brush it away.

He felt so alone. So utterly alone.

He thought back to the things Aunt Arlene had said a few days ago about there being a hole in the middle of everyone. Well, if that was the case, his hole was getting bigger by the minute. Pretty soon it would be black-hole-sized and it would suck in all the light.

He couldn't keep Lark here. But he wanted her to stay.

There was only one thing that might tether a wild, untamed thing like her. He'd have to love her.

But he didn't. He had feelings for her. He was certainly in lust with her. But he didn't love her.

Not like he'd loved Sharon.

For goodness' sake, he'd only known Lark for ten days. How could you learn to love someone in just ten days? It was impossible. He'd loved Sharon from the time they were kids. He'd loved her for years and years before he'd married her.

He reached the cruiser and yanked open the door. He threw his hat onto the passenger's seat and then he slammed the door behind him.

Damn. Damn. Damn.

Lark knew all this, didn't she? She knew it was impossible. She was all about being casual. Not holding on too tight.

Stone sucked at that. He always held on too tight. Always.

He rested his head on the steering wheel. Lark was not his soulmate. His soulmate was buried out in the cemetery adjacent to Christ Church. He forced air through the knot in his throat.

He'd always thought that having Miriam identify his soulmate for him had been one of life's biggest blessings. Sharon was such an amazing person. She had given him children. She had loved him even though he often didn't deserve it. She had held things together, even in their darkest moments. They had forged something good together.

Now Miriam's forecast felt like a prison. How does a person move on to love another when he has already loved completely?

He didn't know.

And knowing the truth about himself, how could he keep Lark here? She deserved to be loved completely. She deserved to be loved for her own self, by someone who wasn't always making comparisons or feeling guilty all the time.

He fired up the engine and headed home. On the way, he turned on the radio and discovered that David Raab was missing. The call had come in just after lunchtime, when he'd had his radio and cell phone turned off. He checked in with county dispatch and learned that the boy had probably run away from home. The Allenberg Sheriff's Department and Damian, Stone's deputy, had been searching for him, but so far David hadn't turned up.

Stone's gut twitched, and his parental sixth sense kicked in. If David was missing, Lizzy had to know about it. He flashed on Jane's comments from yesterday. He sure hoped the town was paying attention. It didn't take much for a girl to get herself into trouble.

Damn. He'd been thinking with his pecker these last few days.

He felt the hole in his middle get a little bigger and wider.

Stone pulled the cruiser to the curb outside Momma's house. He was still in uniform, but with this new development, he would have to bypass the civvies. Finding David was as much his duty to the community as it was something he needed to do as Lizzy's father.

He got out of the cruiser and headed inside.

Mayhem greeted him. Haley was wearing her shepherd costume and practicing her lines. Over and over again.

Daddy was in a deep brood. Apparently the Falcons had lost. Badly.

Usually Momma would be serene as only Momma could be. But the minute Stone walked into the kitchen, he knew something was terribly wrong.

"What's the matter?"

Momma stared right at him. "Well, I can think of a lot of things that are the matter. The fact that my phone has been ringing all afternoon is just one of them."

Well, of course. He hadn't been thinking, had he? Not after Nita had dropped her bombshell, anyway. He'd simply shut down his rational mind. "Are you going to scold me and ask where I've been all afternoon?" he asked. Shame prickled him from his toes to the top of his head. It made his body feel cold and itchy at the same time.

Momma's stare turned intimately maternal. Her eyes burned with some emotion that Stone couldn't quite decipher. She wasn't exactly angry or embarrassed or worried. It seemed to be some odd amalgam of all those things. It was bad enough to feel guilty for taking so much pleasure in Lark's body, but to realize that he'd caused Momma grief, had shirked his responsibility to the town, and had become the object of gossip was almost more than he could bear.

"Honey, everyone has been so worried about you. You abandoned your cruiser on the side of the road. You left it unlocked. And what with Jimmy turning up dead, and David Raab going missing, well, the town is in an uproar."

"So you know about David."

Momma's jaw hardened. "I just heard about it not more

than ten minutes ago. If I'd known he'd run away earlier, I never would have let Lizzy go out."

The guilt turned into fear. "Where is she?"

"She went out about four hours ago. She said she was going to Cassie's house, but I just checked. She's not there. She was supposed to be home almost half an hour ago."

"Damn." He turned around and took a step before Momma called him back.

"Where are you going?"

"To look for her. I'm pretty sure that, when I find her, I'll find David, too."

"Haley's play is in about an hour."

"I know, Momma. But I have to find David."

He turned back toward the door that led into the dining room. Haley stood there, looking utterly adorable in her shepherd outfit. He felt this sudden rush of love for his child. It came from both the inside and outside and gusted right through him like it had been blown on a sudden wind.

She had stopped rehearsing her lines. She stood oddly highlighted by the chandelier, almost as if she were wearing a halo. She looked kind of somber. It was a little scary to see an eight-year-old with such a serious face.

She was the spitting image of Sharon.

"I promise I won't miss your play," he said. His voice came out rusty.

She nodded. He squatted down to be on eye level with her. The headdress of the costume hid her hair and flopped a little over her right eye. "I promise."

She nodded again and then glanced up for an instant. It was as if she were looking at something in the corner. She nodded a third time and looked back at him. Her brown eyes were filling up with tears, and her lips were quivering.

His heart started to shatter in his chest. Lark was right, he'd been ignoring his little girl. How long had he been in this funk? He needed to get out of it.

"Uh, Daddy," Haley said.

"What, sugar beet?"

"I gotta tell you something. It's really, really important."

"Okay." He wanted to tell her that it needed to wait. His gut was twisting with worry over Lizzy. Some sixth sense was telling him that he needed to find his other little girl before dark fell. But he couldn't walk away from Haley. Not when she had a look like that on her face.

"You need to forgive," she said.

"What?"

Haley flicked her gaze to the corner and then back. She nodded again. As if she were nodding to someone else. "You need to forgive. I think you need to forgive me about the angel. Or maybe you need to forgive the angel. Or maybe it's because I broke Granny's teacup."

"What?" Momma said from behind Stone.

Haley looked up at Momma. "I'm really, really sorry. I knocked it off the shelf a long time ago, and then I buried it in the backyard and lied about it. It wasn't the angel who broke it either. It was me."

Momma didn't say anything. The teacup had been missing for a good two years. Everyone had figured that one of the girls had broken it.

"Honey," Stone said, "the teacup isn't very important. I'm sure Granny will forgive you for it. It was wrong to fib about it. But we still love you. And we forgive you. Okay?"

Haley frowned. "Uh, I guess." Her eyes flicked to the corner and back again.

Stone turned to look. There was nothing there.

"You don't see her, do you?"

"The angel?"

"She's there. She's been with you all day. I don't know why. She's been acting kind of weird the last couple of days. And she really means it, Daddy. You need to forgive. I'm not sure who. Maybe Lizzy."

A strange thought occurred to him. "Sugar beet, do you know where Lizzy is?"

Haley nodded solemnly. "She's with David at the golf course. She took a blanket and a backpack with her when she left."

"Haley, did you know she wasn't going to Cassie's when she left?" Momma asked.

Haley looked down at the carpet, a picture of abject misery. "She said I was going to get spanked because of the teacup. She said she was going to tell you about it if I tattled on her." Haley's body went rigid like she was expecting corporal punishment to be inflicted at any minute.

Stone let go of a deep breath and pulled his little girl into a fierce hug. She wrapped her hands around his neck, and he buried his nose into the corner of her neck. The damn costume was scratchy as hell.

"C'mon, Hale, let's go get your sister and drag her back to church for your play."

"Stone, do you think you should take Haley with—"

"I'm not worried, Momma. Lizzy is a smart girl. If she took a blanket out to the Ark it's only because it's gotten pretty cold outside. My guess is that David left home without much preparation, and Lizzy is a Girl Scout. She probably took him food, too, if I know her.

"I'll bring them both back to church. Wouldn't hurt David to be exposed to shepherds and angels and Jesus in a manger. Although I'm sure his mother will be upset about it. Honestly, Momma, the woman is a bigot. She told me in so many words that she didn't think Lizzy was good enough for her son. I have a feeling this disappearing act was his way of telling his momma to back off."

Stone scooped Haley up into his arms. He turned toward his mother. The worried look on her face was gone. Her eyes looked unusually bright.

"Something's come over you, son. I hope you embrace it." Momma blinked a couple of times. "Now, go on, get your daughter and her beau. But just remember that we can't have a Christmas play without a shepherd."

"*Let us now go even unto Bethlehem, and see this thing which is come to pass,*" Haley said in a big stage voice. "I don't think I'm going to forget my lines." Then she rested her head on Stone's shoulder. She was still holding on to him like she wasn't ever going to let him go.

Maybe Haley wasn't all Sharon's creation after all. Haley held on to things real tight. And so did he.

CHAPTER 19

David propped his head up on his hand and stared down at Lizzy. The kids back in Michigan would probably laugh at him, to see him lying in a hayloft in a barn that looked like Noah's Ark. But this was where he wanted to be.

"You can't go back to Michigan," Lizzy said, looking up at him with those big eyes of hers. The afternoon was getting old, and the light kind of slanted in from the clerestory windows. Lizzy's hair was rimmed with golden light, as yellow as the hay.

David wanted to raise his camera and capture the moment, but he resisted. He would have to press this into his memory. Because it was probably the last time he would ever see Lizzy Rhodes.

Earlier today, when he'd jimmied the window in his bedroom and escaped from his parents, his plan to make them stop and see reason seemed so clear-cut. He hadn't intended to stay away for long—just long enough to put the fear of God into them.

But it was cold out here. And his emotions were calmer now. If his parents were going to split up, nothing he could do would stop it. And, in the end, he'd wind up back in Michigan because that's where Mom's family was.

He was going to lose Lizzy. No matter what. And it made him ache, especially since she had come to him the minute her church services were over. And she'd stayed and talked with him all afternoon. He'd poured his heart out to her, and she'd listened without judgment.

"You know I don't want to run away permanently. I just want Mom and Dad to think about what they're about to do."

"It's going to be okay. You stay away tonight and maybe your folks will realize how stupid they're being. I know how hard it is to fit into a new place, but you're doing okay. People like you on the school paper, and you're good with your camera."

He touched the camera that hung around his neck. It was pretty funny how a week ago he would have been okay about moving back to Ann Arbor. But not now. Now he wanted to stay. He wanted more adventures with Lizzy.

He wanted to kiss her again. He'd been thinking about that all afternoon. This might be his one and only chance. So he leaned in and touched his lips to hers. A hot reaction hit his body, and then, to his surprise, Lizzy opened her mouth.

Wow. That was nice. It was a real kiss. He wasn't sure what to do with it, but he improvised. Lizzy did, too. It was kind of wet and sloppy and interesting as hell.

He forgot about how miserable and scared he was feeling.

After a time, Lizzy turned her head. He backed off.

They stared at each other, and a deep red blush crawled up her face. He had a feeling his face was red, too.

Lizzy pulled her cell phone out of her pocket and checked the time. "Oh, crap, it's almost four o'clock. My grandmother is going to bust a gut. The brat has her Christmas play tonight, and I have to be there. Are you going to be okay out here?"

"I've got a blanket, a flashlight, and some granola bars. What more could a guy ask for?" Her warm body next to his?

He stomped on that thought. Lizzy wasn't that kind of girl, and he wasn't that kind of boy. They'd already gone as far as they were ever going to go. And tomorrow he would probably be in the minivan heading back to Ann Arbor.

Lizzy headed for the loft's ladder. "It's going to be quiet out here tomorrow and the next day because of Christmas, but I expect the workmen will be back out here on Wednesday. I'll try to get out here tomorrow afternoon with some food. It might be hard. Christmas Eve gets real busy."

"I'm not going to hold out that long. I only intended to spend one night away from home," he said, following her down the ladder.

They got to the barn door, and he was just about to move in for another kiss when they heard a noise outside.

She frowned and put her finger to her lips, then turned and peeked through the crack in the barn door. Her sharp gasp told David that Lizzy was surprised by the identity of the unexpected intruder.

She moved away from the crack in the door and motioned for him to get his camera. He stepped to the small opening.

Two men were standing on the artificial turf of the eighteenth hole. One of them was Sheriff Bennett. David didn't recognize the other man, but he was old and walked with a cane. Lizzy made a motion for him to take photos, but he opted against it. His digital SLR might not have a mechanical shutter, but it still made a noise every time he took a shot.

David took Lizzy by the hand and pulled her deeper into the shadows of one of the empty stalls. "I don't want to make any noise with the camera," he whispered against her ear. Her hair feathered against his cheek. He was completely aware of her hand in his.

"Listen," she whispered. "That's Lee Marshall, the father of the guy who died in the swamp."

David turned his attention to the voices outside the barn. It was hard to hear what they were saying until one of them shouted, "Goddamn it, Billy, you killed my boy."

Lizzy tensed against David's side. They looked at each other in the dim light. What the hell? The *sheriff* had killed Jimmy Marshall?

David pressed his finger across Lizzy's lips. "Listen," he mouthed.

The sheriff spoke. "The coroner is going to rule Jimmy's death a suicide, Lee. I don't know what gave you the idea that I committed murder."

"Because Jimmy was found out on that old hunting trail that leads to the Jonquil House."

"So?"

"Jimmy hated the swamp. And I doubt that he'd ever been on that trail in his life. But your daddy used that trail all the time. That's where we took Zeke Rhodes, all those years ago."

"Are you admitting something, Lee?"

"Don't you play dumb with me, boy. I already talked with your daddy, and he told me that you know all about what happened forty years ago."

Sheriff Bennett let go of a high-pitched, crazy-sounding laugh. "Yeah, well, you and the old man should have kept your traps closed. You know, Lee, this is a mess of your making, not mine. I'm just like my father, cleaning up your messes."

"What do you mean?"

"I mean Jimmy came to me a week ago and wanted me to arrest you for what y'all did forty years ago. Now, you can see why I didn't want to do that. I mean, there's an election coming up next year. How do you think it would look if I had to explain how my daddy covered up a brutal beating, and all because the high-and-mighty Lee Marshall was involved. I don't think it would go over too good. I'm sure the folks who want Stone Rhodes to run against me would have a field day."

"Jesus, Joseph, and Mary, you killed my boy because of an election? You bastard."

"Lee, he was going to tell everyone about what happened. I was going to be forced to arrest you. Don't you get it?"

"What? Jimmy was my son. My heir."

Sheriff Bennett chuckled darkly. "I don't think that mattered much to him. Jimmy told me that he was committed to winning back Hettie's love any way he could. He said Hettie wanted him to take charge of this town and clean the skeletons out of the closet. I'm telling you, Lee, I did you a favor."

Lee Marshall let go of a sound that could only be called a wail of anguish. And then all hell broke loose.

The sounds of a scuffle ensued. Then before David could figure out what to do next, the two men crashed into the barn door with such force that they broke through and tumbled onto the beaten earth of the Ark's floor, just a few feet from where Lizzy and David were hiding.

Sheriff Bennett's gun was out of its holster and each of the men had a death grip on it. They were rolling around grunting and struggling, wrestling over the gun.

David was so scared he thought he might pee his pants. He prayed to God to let him live while he simultaneously clutched Lizzy's warm, warm hand. It didn't matter who won the wrestling match. He knew with a dead certainty that he and Lizzy had heard too much. Both of these men were murderers.

Beside him, he heard Lizzy whisper her own prayer. Only instead of calling on God, Lizzy was mumbling something about angels.

Lark pulled the SUV over to the side of a red clay road that bisected Route 70 just north of Golfing for God. She was going to walk the rest of the way, since she was planning to trespass and engage in what was probably a felony. Pop wanted to be laid to rest on the eighteenth hole, and there was no good reason not to comply with that request. Once his ashes were scattered, no one would know the difference.

Except for Lark.

She could take some small comfort in the fact that she'd done Pop's bidding one last time. Now was the perfect time for a drive-by funeral, too, while Stone was occupied with Haley's play.

A knot lodged in her throat as she headed down the

side road and tried without much success to push thoughts of Stone to the background. She was getting out of Dodge. Now. Tonight. Before any more grass grew under her feet. She would commit her crime and run like a thief in the night.

She didn't want a long-winded good-bye. For all intents and purposes they'd said their good-byes this afternoon. Hell, they'd said their good-byes before they even started. Her words had been clear. She'd told him the score going in. And he'd listened.

Unfortunately, her heart hadn't listened at all.

But she would get over this. She'd be like Carmine. Carmine never committed. If a female love interest got too close, he hit the road. In that respect, she and Carmine were a whole lot alike.

Lark turned onto the main highway. It was almost dusk. She needed to hurry if she wanted to catch the light at the golf course; she'd have to use her flashlight on the way back. She wanted to click a snapshot of the eighteenth hole before she left. Maybe she would start a family album with it.

She was about forty yards from the parking lot when she realized that the county sheriff's car was parked there. A gray Lincoln Town Car was parked there, too.

Just her luck. She'd come to commit a crime, and a convention was under way at the intended scene. She halted in her tracks and was trying to decide whether to go or stay when gunfire erupted in the distance.

Many years of training took over. She hit the deck hard and covered her head. This time she didn't flash back to Misurata, but her pulse and respiration redlined. She felt vulnerable there in the drainage ditch by the side of the highway. She needed to find cover. She needed to call for backup.

She reached for her cell phone only to realize that she'd left it in the console of the SUV, connected to the car's USB dock. Damn.

She pushed herself up off the ground and scooted into the woods that edged the highway. The screaming started just as she reached the cover of some tall pine trees. The noise came from off to her right, in the general direction of the golf course.

She crouched there for a long moment, gulping down breaths as her heart raced. She needed to get back to the car.

But someone was in really bad trouble.

Her hands shook as she tucked Pop's ashes into her camera bag. She ignored the tremors, took out her Nikon, and affixed the telephoto lens. Then she slung the bag diagonally across her shoulders so she could rest it against her back. The bag was bulky, but she had years of practice lugging it through war zones.

She moved through the pine needles in a crouching run, careful to muffle any noise her bag might make and to keep at least one tree trunk between her and the frantic screams that seemed to be coming from Noah's Ark. She had her camera in her hands, ready to go. But her stomach was churning with fear.

She emerged from the pines near hole number three, Moses in the bulrushes. Something very odd was happening to the light. She glanced up at the sky. It seemed to be boiling. A cloud was literally forming right out of the blue, and the temperature was dropping. The light was very bad. Any photos she shot would be crap.

Nevertheless, she hurried through the plague of frogs, sprinted past the Tower of Babel, then Jonah and the whale, and finally made it to the eighteenth hole. She crouched behind the statue of Jesus. Not that the fiberglass would give her that much protection against anyone with a gun. But it hid her from view, and allowed her to peer into the darkened maw of the Ark.

The doors were open. She could just see a body lying in the opening. A pool of blood was spreading out from it.

A dark vortex of fear gripped her. She couldn't move. Her heart hammered in her chest. She slumped against the fiberglass of the statue and mumbled, "God help me."

Lizzy lost it the minute the gun went off. David cursed under his breath. Until she'd started screaming, there had been at least a tiny chance that neither Mr. Marshall nor Sheriff Bennett would realize they were witnesses.

But it was too late now. Lizzy was staring at Mr. Marshall, who was lying on the floor with a bullet hole in his chest. He wasn't dead, but he was in pretty bad shape, judging by the blood that was coming out of his mouth.

Everything seemed to slow down in that moment. The sheriff's gun was still on the ground, but instead of going for it, he turned in their direction, his bright, blue eyes going wide with surprise and then hard and dark with anger.

There was murder in his eyes. David couldn't beat this man. He was bigger and meaner and about a thousand times more frightening than his bully of a son.

There was no Justin Polk around this time to save him. David had to do something or he and Lizzy would die. The sheriff was about to turn back to get his gun. David had to act.

Now.

David pulled his camera up to his face and squeezed off a shot. The flash fired, lighting up the suddenly dark evening. The surprising burst of light blinded the sheriff.

David grabbed Lizzy's hand and dragged her screaming from the barn, and he did what any smart person did when facing a bigger and stronger antagonist.

He ran like hell.

Thank God Lizzy was able to keep up with him, because they were running for their lives. He'd seen a lot of action movies, and he knew on some level that running in a straight line was a dumb idea. So he started zigzagging across the golf course. He bolted past the statue of Jesus, then turned a little to the right and pounded past Jonah's whale, then changed directions and raced through a flock of fiberglass sheep.

That's when the shooting started.

Lizzy shrieked again but she didn't stop running. David changed course again, heading toward a phony mountain with the Ten Commandment tablets at its top.

Another shot was fired. It felt like someone had just given him a sharp push in the shoulder. He stumbled but managed to keep running. His right arm went numb, and he dropped his camera. It swayed around his neck, bumping into his chest, chafing his neck. His side was burning.

But he kept going, turning again, heading toward a life-sized Christmas display of Jesus, Joseph, and Mary surrounded by a herd of fiberglass barn animals. There were camels there, too, with bobbing heads.

But everything was getting kind of dark. His vision was blurring. And he couldn't breathe. Then, without warning, his legs buckled under him.

He hit a patch of Astroturf and rolled. He came to rest against the statue of Mary. She was staring down at him with such a pretty look on her face.

Lizzy's face came into his vision. "Oh shit, oh shit, you're bleeding all over the place."

There were tears in Lizzy's eyes, and she was prettier by far than Mary. And way more alive.

He wanted to kiss her again, but his attention was pulled away by the sight over her shoulder. The sky had gone strange with clouds and a light—amazing and utterly beautiful. There was music playing somewhere. Big music, sweet music, gentle music.

He wanted to be a part of it.

There was so much blood. Dark and sticky and it was everywhere. On the rubble of the wall. All over Jeb's vest. His head was broken open.

Oh, God, it was worse than that. His head wasn't really there.

Lark couldn't move. Couldn't think. She needed to run before the next rocket came. She needed . . .

Someone came running past her.

More gunfire startled Lark back to reality. She saw David as he was hit and went down.

And something inside her snapped.

She was on the eighteenth hole at Golfing for God. Misurata had happened months ago. She didn't have a weapon, but she had a camera. She turned back toward the Ark, looking for the shooter. Looking for an angle for her own shot.

Her blood ran cold.

The sheriff of Allenberg County was standing not more

than five feet from where she was hiding with his service weapon in both hands. He was taking aim at Lizzy.

Lark reached into her camera bag groping for something to throw at him, and her hand found the small cardboard box. She pulled it from the bag and hurled it at the sheriff.

Her aim was deadly. The box arced through the air just as Sheriff Bennett squeezed off another round. The bullet must have pierced the box because it exploded in midair, and Pop's ashes swirled up into a sudden gust of wind in a crazy dance.

What the hell? The ashes seemed alive as they swirled around the sheriff like a swarm of killer bees.

He started cursing, and Lark decided it was time to run. She got to her feet and hauled ass across the golf course in a jagged line, heading toward the big crèche where she'd seen David go down.

"Uh-oh," Stone said aloud as he pulled his car into the parking lot at Golfing for God.

"What's the matter, Daddy?" Haley said. Her headdress had kind of fallen over one of her eyes, and it made her look adorable. She had to be the cutest shepherdess in Allenberg County.

"Nothing, sugar beet. It just looks like Sheriff Bennett found David before I did." Which meant the a-hole had found Lizzy, too. Knowing Billy, he'd go tell the world that he'd caught Lizzy in the hayloft with David. Billy was like that.

He didn't investigate real crimes. He just swaggered around and made Stone's life miserable. It was a wonder the people of Allenberg kept reelecting him.

Of course, there wasn't exactly anyone brave enough to run against him. And the Bennetts had been running the Sheriff's Department for decades. People in these parts weren't all that wild about change. South Carolina was pretty conservative.

"What's that?" Haley said, cocking her ear. "Somebody's screaming."

Dread precipitated into Stone's gut. He turned off the engine just as another scream pierced the air. It sounded like Lizzy.

"Crawl in the back and get down. Don't move," he ordered. He was out of the cruiser and had his weapon drawn. He sprinted down the path when a gunshot shattered the twilight.

He increased his speed, pelting past Adam and Eve and into the paved plaza by the point-of-sale area. The eighteenth hole stood just beyond. The resurrected Jesus looked beatifically at Sheriff Bennett, who stood in target-practice stance with two hands on his weapon. Bennett was sighting something across the golf course in the general direction of Mount Sinai and the birth of Jesus.

Just as he squeezed off a round, Lark Chaikin popped up from behind the statue and hurled something. A cloud erupted around the sheriff that looked like his own personal dust devil.

Lark lit out across the golf course in the direction of the tenth hole.

Stone wasn't entirely sure what to make of this situation. And he hesitated for just one moment.

And that moment of indecision proved to be disastrous.

"Daddy!" Lizzy's anguished cry came from the direction of the tenth hole. He saw her pop up by the big crèche at the turn. There was blood all over her.

"Stop right there, Stone," Billy yelled.

Stone turned his gaze back toward the sheriff. Billy was aiming his weapon right at him.

"Billy, what's going on?"

"Shut up. I need to think."

"Why don't you put the weapon away?" Stone aimed his own weapon at Billy, but he was a day late and a dollar short. Billy fired off a round.

Stone's last thought, just as the bullet struck his chest and carried him off his feet, was that he'd left Haley alone in his cruiser. She would be late for her Christmas play.

CHAPTER
20

"Come now, little shepherd, it's time," the angel said.

Haley looked up into the eyes of the glowing person above her. This was not the Sorrowful Angel. This angel had wings and a halo. He burned so brightly that it was almost hard to look at him. He was kind of scary. And that wasn't good, because she was already scared.

Daddy had run off. And people were screaming. And there were loud noises that reminded her of that time when she'd been with Aunt Jane. The angels smited the bad guys that time. She was glad the angels had done that, but she really didn't want to repeat the experience.

"Be not afraid, for I bring you good tidings," the angel said, and unlike Maryanne, this angel got the words right. "Come, we need your help."

Oh, boy. She was no good at helping angels, didn't they know that?

The angel waited, and Haley knew that she didn't have much of a choice. Kids never did.

So she got up from the floor of the backseat and climbed

out of Daddy's cruiser. It was practically nighttime outside, which seemed kind of strange because it had just been daylight a minute ago. It had also gotten really, really cold and windy. The angel put his arm around Haley, warming her.

That was different. The Sorrowful Angel was always cold, but this angel was as warm as a fire. Haley followed the angel down the path and around the bend.

"Be not afraid," the angel repeated, "for I am with you."

It was a good thing the angel said that, because just as soon as Haley could see the Ark, there was another loud sound, like a balloon popping only louder. And that's when she saw Daddy get shot.

"Go to him." The angel pushed Haley forward. "Be not afraid."

Haley hesitated for a minute. Sheriff Bennett was standing by the statue of Jesus on the eighteenth hole. And standing right next to him was the Sorrowful Angel.

She didn't look very sorrowful right at the moment. She looked very, very, very angry. Angrier than even Granny got, and that was saying something.

The wind was starting to blow, and it whipped the dumb old shepherd headdress off Haley's head and tossed it high into the air. "Go to him," the angel repeated and gave her another little push.

She ran toward Daddy. Halfway there, she heard Lizzy screaming from somewhere telling her to stay away. But the angel kept saying that she should go to Daddy.

Sheriff Bennett turned toward her. He had a gun in his hand. And he started to raise it in her direction.

Lizzy started screaming. Someone else was yelling, but she didn't know who. And the angel was standing right next to the sheriff.

Haley was really, really scared, but the angel behind her kept telling her not to be afraid. And in front of her, she could see Daddy lying on the ground. He was hurt bad. And she was scared that Daddy might be going away to be with Jesus just like Momma had.

And then the strangest thing happened. Her headdress fell right out of the sky and right into the Sorrowful Angel's hands. She twisted it up and then used it like a whip, the same way Lizzy sometimes did with a wet towel.

She smacked the sheriff with it, and he kind of stumbled back. And then she cracked it against the sheriff's hand, and he dropped the gun. The sheriff was beginning to look as scared as Haley felt.

Haley took her eyes off the sheriff and ran the rest of the way to where Daddy was lying. She fell down on her knees beside him and started kissing Daddy's face and pleading with him to wake up.

And then the angels came. All of them. Just like before. There was a rush of wings and a flash of bright light almost like lightning, and it was just like in the play. Haley knew all of the narrator's lines:

And suddenly there was with the angel a multitude of the heavenly host.

They didn't exactly come praising God, though. They swooped down on Sheriff Bennett like a bunch of golden-haloed turkey buzzards. They circled around him, and then one of them picked Jesus up off His foundation and threw Him right down on the sheriff.

The sheriff screamed as the statue came flying at him, but once it hit him upside the head, he fell down and didn't move.

The angels circled once and headed back up into the

clouds. All except for the Sorrowful Angel. She drifted over and sat next to Haley and Daddy.

And she started to cry.

Haley started to cry, too. Daddy wasn't moving.

And that's when it started to snow.

Stone wasn't sure where the fog had come from, only that he'd been wandering in it for a while. It was cold and wet against his face and muffled everything around him. He couldn't see anything except for a soft blue flicker that reminded him of a TV set in a darkened room. He chased that flickering light for a long time.

It seemed like he was always chasing that light. Like he'd been chasing it for an eternity.

This must be a dream. He often fell asleep with the television going. The noise made him feel less lonely.

He wearied of the chase; there was no point following that light—it was always just out of reach. He gave up and lay down on some grass at his feet. It was cold.

"You need to get up," Sharon said. "You're not dead, you know."

He relaxed. Everything was okay and back to normal. Sharon was always bossing him around. But that was okay. He enjoyed doing her honey-do chores. It made him feel needed.

He drew in a lungful of freezing air. He needed to move, but he felt complacent.

"You stay here, and the snow is going to cover you up," Sharon nagged.

Snow? In Florida? Not likely.

He opened his eyes. And remembered that he wasn't living in Florida anymore, and Sharon was dead.

It was a crushing memory. It left no room for anything else. Snow pelted him in the face, cold and wet. He squeezed his eyes closed again. His head felt muffled and far away. His ears were ringing.

Why was it snowing?

"Daddy, wake up."

Haley's voice. He opened his eyes again. Haley was leaning over him, tears streaming down her beautiful face. Over her shoulder, he could see Sharon. His wife was crying, too.

And that was weird, because he couldn't remember ever seeing Sharon cry. She hadn't shed one tear even when Tyler had died.

What was Sharon doing here? He was starting to remember. He'd gone out to Golfing for God to get Lizzy and her boyfriend.

"Get up, Stone. You're not dead. Your children need you."

Haley leaned forward a little more, obscuring his view of Sharon. "Daddy, you need to listen to the Sorrowful Angel, okay? It's snowing, and it's cold and..." Her voice wavered. "The sheriff shot David, and Lizzy is crying, and Miss Lark is trying to calm her down. David is bleeding, and the angels came, and I'm so scared. Daddy, you need to wake up."

He closed his eyes again. "Sharon," he whispered.

"I'm here. I've always been here. You haven't let me go, and..." Sharon's voice faded into the whistle of the wind. It felt like a freaking blizzard had just hit town.

He opened his eyes again. The wind was whipping the snowflakes in swirls. In the twilight, the snow almost looked like mist, or even swirling ghosts.

He stared up into Haley's face. Her cheeks were red. Her shepherd's costume was wet. She was shivering.

Memories came flooding back to him. Horrible memories. He pushed himself up off the ground and was assailed by vertigo. Sharp pain knifed through his chest. He looked down at his uniform shirt. It had been torn when the bullet struck him and knocked him back. But, of course, he'd been wearing body armor.

He was going to have a big bruise on his chest and maybe a couple of broken ribs. He touched the back of his head and found a knot the size of a walnut. That explained the vertigo. He was probably concussed.

"Are you okay?" Haley asked. "The angels say you're going to be okay. They say David is going to be okay, too, but Lizzy doesn't believe it."

In the distance, he could hear Lizzy sobbing. And something else.

Lark. Lark was here. She was speaking in calm reassuring words about applying pressure to David's wounds. He should get up and help her. But he couldn't quite make his body work, and Haley had kind of crawled up into his lap, pinning him down.

Haley wiped the snot from her nose on the sleeve of her shepherd's costume. "Daddy, the angels who had wings were kind of scary, and they were really warm, and they smited Sheriff Bennett on account of the fact that he was shooting people. But even before the angels with wings came, the Sorrowful Angel tried to beat up the sheriff. Why did the sheriff shoot David?"

"The Sorrowful Angel doesn't have wings?" The minute he asked the question he knew something inside him had snapped.

"No, Daddy. That's why she's here, see, and not in Heaven. She can't get to Heaven without wings."

All of a sudden the ability to see angels didn't seem like such a curse. Sharon said she'd never left him. And if he could see her, then he could talk with her. He could be with her. He didn't have to move on. He didn't have to change. He could just hold on to her until it was his time to go.

"Tell me more about the Sorrowful Angel," he said, knowing it was the wrong thing to say. He should be asking about the sheriff. He should be taking Haley's eyewitness report. He should be dragging himself over to where Lizzy and David were. Why had he asked this stupid question?

"Uh, well, see she isn't golden-like. She's more blue, you know. And she's cold. The other angels are really, really hot. And they're gone now, but the Sorrowful Angel is still right here."

"Where?"

Haley pointed. There was nothing there. But a moment ago, Sharon had been there, all blue and glowy and bossing him around like she always did.

"She said she's not supposed to be here. Didn't you hear her? I thought you were talking with her. I thought, maybe, you could see her." Haley's voice sounded so small and frightened.

He pulled Haley into his arms and gave her a fierce hug. She wrapped her arms around his neck and buried her cold nose against his neck. "I think I have a picture of the Sorrowful Angel," he said.

"You do? Really?"

"Yeah. I do. I'll show you tonight when we get back home. And maybe she'll talk to us again."

Just then the sound of sirens destroyed the strange, muffled quiet of the golf course. Stone held his daughter and watched the snow falling. He should be doing more than just hugging his daughter and talking about a ghost. But he couldn't muster the strength to get up.

"I guess maybe there is a Santa," Haley said.

"Why's that, sugar beet?" he whispered.

"Because I asked him to please, please, please get me out of the Christmas play and also to make it snow."

"That's all you asked for?"

"Uh, well, I also asked him if he would please find a way to get the Sorrowful Angel to Heaven."

Guilt shivered up his spine, but he didn't have a minute to examine it because Lark came bounding up from the tenth hole and skidded to a stop.

She got down on her knees. Her big brown eyes looked bright and fierce. There were ice crystals sparkling in her hair. And he thought she looked very beautiful and bright like that. The crisis had brought out her color somehow. She didn't look like a little brown bird, the way she had when he'd first met her. Now she seemed like a flare in the darkness. And he almost wanted to gather her up into the hug he was sharing with Haley.

But he didn't exactly know how to do that. She seemed so competent at that moment. So in charge. Like she didn't need him. So instead of reaching out, he tried to push himself up off the ground.

She pushed him down gently. Her hand felt oddly warm on his shoulder. "You've had a head injury. I don't want you to move. I used Lizzy's cell phone to call nine-one-one, and help is on its way. David has been shot but I don't think it's life threatening. Lizzy's applying direct pressure to his wound, and he's sheltered in the Christmas display on the tenth hole. I'm afraid that Mr. Marshall is dead. The sheriff is unconscious but breathing. I used some duct tape I found in the office up in the Ark to bind his hands and feet. I'm going out to the road. I'll flag down help."

She stood and ran up the path. And it occurred to him that Lark was like a sergeant reporting to his lieutenant, or a deputy reporting to the chief. She'd gone into battle mode, and she was seriously impressive.

Obviously, she had conquered her fear. Hell, she'd probably saved David or Lizzy's life with that foolhardy but incredibly brave move of throwing the ashes at Billy. If Stone hadn't arrived right at that moment, Lark might be numbered among the dead.

He couldn't think about that. It was too frightening even to let his mind go there. He clutched Haley to his chest and squeezed his eyes shut. His head swam. It felt like he'd had too much to drink. He had to open his eyes again and fix a horizon just to keep the dizziness at bay.

Just then Damian Easley, Stone's deputy, came pounding down the path followed by the Allenberg County volunteer fire department and EMT squad.

In the mayhem that followed Stone lost track of Lark.

Lark clutched the hot cup in her shaky hands and stared at Damian Easley across the table. The aroma of coffee permeated the atmosphere. She was sitting in the interview room at the Last Chance Police Department, and she was still shivering.

If she had been cold, perhaps the coffee would have

warmed her. But these shivers weren't from the cold. They were the aftereffect of the adrenaline.

She'd given her eyewitness report. She'd hung out with Damian at the golf course for a while. She'd watched the forensics team do their thing, and the coroner take Lee Marshall's body away.

She'd thought about Pop and Hettie and the Rhodes family.

Nothing and everything had changed.

She'd spent ten days here. She'd discovered a half sister and uncovered a mystery. She'd fallen for Stone Rhodes. But she still didn't belong here. She never would.

She realized it the minute she'd spoken with Stone, just before the EMTs arrived. He had been talking nonstop about his wife. He seemed to think that Haley's Sorrowful Angel and Sharon were one and the same.

It was crazy, of course. But head injuries—even minor ones—could make people kind of crazy for a while. Lark had seen plenty of that in the field. Stone would recover. But his current hallucinations pretty much confirmed where Lark stood with him.

And she didn't want to play second chair to Sharon's ghost.

No, she didn't belong here. She belonged on a plane to Africa, leaving day after tomorrow. And after what had happened out at Golfing for God, she knew she'd be okay. She'd found that invincible place where every war correspondent lived.

She handed Damian a card with her editor's name on it. "I'm going to be in Africa for a while, and then, who knows. But if you need me to testify at the trial, just give my editor a call. He'll be able to find me wherever I am."

Damian nodded, and they both stood up. "You're not going to stay? See how Stone is doing?"

"I'll give the hospital a call. You tell him to take care of himself, okay? And I'm sorry about the ashes on the eighteenth hole."

Damian laughed, his smile flashing in his dark face. "Oh, I think Elbert will forgive you for that. From what I heard, the ashes may have saved Lizzy or David's life. You know, it's funny how these things work. Folks will say it was your ashes and a freak wind that saved the day. But I think there's something else going on out there."

"Are you saying you believe in angels, Deputy Easley?"

"Ma'am, I do. And I think you just might be one of them. You have a good Christmas, you hear? And someone will be in touch with you if this mess comes to a trial."

She turned and headed toward the door.

"You driving to DC tonight?" Damian asked to her back.

"That was my plan."

"It's a long way. You stay safe. And if you get sleepy, you stop someplace. When the caffeine and the adrenaline wear off, you might need a good sleep."

Lark nodded and left the police station. As she walked to Pop's SUV, it struck her that Last Chance, South Carolina, was lit up with Christmas lights from Bill's Grease Pit all the way to Dot's Spot. And high above it all, the sky had cleared into a cold, velvet darkness.

A star was shining high above the place. She stared up at it for a long time. It was too bright to be a star. It had to be Venus or Mars or one of the other planets. As she drove away, she could still see it hovering over the town.

CHAPTER
21

Now, Mr. Rhodes, I don't want you to worry about the hallucinations," the doctor said.

Stone sat up in the hospital bed. The doc had a fresh face and looked like he'd have trouble growing a beard. He reminded Stone of the marine recruits he'd trained during the time he'd been a DI at Parris Island.

Hallucinations, huh?

"All your tests are negative for serious brain injury. But concussions can be tricky."

Hallucinations. That's what the docs had said about Haley's visions a little more than a year ago. They said the bump she'd gotten on her head had caused her to see things that weren't there. They said the emotional trauma, coupled with the head injury, had resulted in Haley externalizing the fiction of the Sorrowful Angel.

Now that Stone thought about it, this was exactly what everyone said about Daddy and Granddaddy and even Great-Granddaddy. Every one of them had gone to war. Every one of them had gotten bumped on the head. And every one of them had ended up seeing angels that weren't supposed to be there.

Was this some brain weirdness handed down through the generations, or something else? Like a curse? Or maybe it was a blessing.

He stared at the doctor and felt oddly disconnected. Was it a curse to see Sharon when he longed for her so much?

He was losing it. "Right," he said gruffly. "I'll be fine." What else could he say?

The doc nodded and signed Stone's discharge papers. When the doc left, Stone got stiffly out of bed and dressed in his civvies. His ribs might not be broken but the bruises were mighty painful.

He checked his watch. Daddy and the girls were going to be there to collect him in about thirty minutes. He had time.

He headed up to the orthopedics floor and found David Raab's room. The kid had had surgery on his shoulder. Plates and screws and all that. He'd be in physical therapy for a while.

Stone strolled into the room and came right up against David's lion of a momma. Before he could even talk to the kid, she was right up in his face, pointing a finger at his chest. "This is all your fault. You and your daughter. I told you I wanted you to keep her away from him and you—"

"Mom, shut up."

Both adults turned toward David, who was lying in bed with a huge cast on his arm. He looked unusually pale with an unnatural stain of red across his cheeks. He was probably in pain and running a fever. Poor kid.

"I am your mother. You don't tell me to—"

"Shut it," the kid said again, and his mother actually stopped talking.

"Is Lizzy okay?" David asked Stone.

"She's fine. She'll be here shortly, and I was just checking to see if it would be okay if she came to visit you. And also, I wanted to thank you for saving her life."

"What?" Mrs. Raab asked. She had obviously not been paying attention. David was something of a hero.

"Your son saved my daughter's life. When the sheriff started shooting, David kept his head and got the two of them out of the Ark, where they were sitting ducks. I will be eternally grateful to your son. And I just wanted to let you know that I think you've done a good job with him. He's precisely the kind of boy I want my daughter to be friends with—the kind of kid who looks beyond labels. The kind of kid who knows right from wrong.

"Also, you should know that Lizzy's heart will be broken if y'all move back to Michigan. To be honest, I wish you wouldn't go. You living in our town gives everyone a chance to practice tolerance. And I can't help but think that if we'd been better at it back in 1968, Nita Wills might have followed her heart, and my granddaddy and Jimmy and Lee Marshall might all still be alive. So before you start pointing fingers, just think about that."

He nodded at the woman and turned toward David. "You going to be okay?"

"Yes, sir. And thanks for coming after us. If you hadn't shown up, it might have been bad. And when you see Ms. Chaikin, would you thank her for me? She probably saved my life when she threw those ashes. She was impressive. I guess we never got our interview with her about what it's like being a war correspondent, but we sure did get a taste of what it takes to be one. To be honest, I was terrified. But she seemed to be impervious to it."

Stone felt a pang of regret. He'd tried Lark's cell phone a dozen times, but she hadn't answered. He needed to thank her, too. But he was afraid to see her.

He wasn't sure what to say.

He forced himself to give David a smile. "That's the way it is, David. Sometimes in a firefight you just have no time to think. Instincts take over. And that's where you find your courage."

He left David's room and went back to his own. Daddy showed up shortly thereafter. David's mother relented and let Lizzy visit David for about five minutes. And then they all got in Daddy's truck and headed back to town.

An unearthly shiver seized Stone the minute they turned onto Palmetto Avenue and passed under Santa and his reindeer. He tried to shake away the feeling but it crawled through him. Cold and sort of . . . itchy.

And a thought came to him from out of the blue. "I need to go to church," he said. The words surprised him almost as much as Daddy.

"Son, you've had a head injury. I think I need to take you—"

Before Stone could come up with a good explanation for his request, Haley piped up from the backseat. "He's only doing what the Sorrowful Angel wants him to do. She's been talking to him the whole way home from the hospital, all about how she wants to go into the church. He saw her last night, but he's not seeing her now."

"Haley, why do you always have to make yourself and your stupid made-up angel the center of attention?" Lizzy said.

"Lizzy," Elbert said sternly and gave Liz his scary look in the rearview mirror.

"She's here?" Stone asked. His pulse quickened with the idea.

"Yeah. She stayed with you at the hospital. She always stays with you when you sleep," Haley said.

Lizzy made a noise and rolled her eyes. Stone ignored her. "She does?"

Haley nodded. "Yeah. She really, really wants you to go to the church. She says that she misses it."

"Well, that sounds exactly like her."

Haley frowned. Lizzy sat up. Daddy looked at him as if he'd lost his mind, which was sort of ironic.

And suddenly Stone had a deep understanding of everything Haley had been going through for the last year. He felt another flood of guilt. Would he ever get over this feeling?

"She was always nagging me about going to church," he said.

"She? You mean Sharon," Daddy said. "Not Haley's angel."

Stone didn't respond, and Daddy didn't argue the point. Instead, Daddy pulled the van up to the sidewalk in front of Christ Church.

Daddy eyed the other cars parked along Palmetto Avenue. "Looks like the church ladies are up there getting the place ready for services tonight. You sure you want to go up there? You know how they can be."

Stone nodded soberly. "Yeah," he whispered. Something was pushing him. "I won't be long," he said. But of course, he had no idea how long he would be. He had no idea why this compulsion had come over him. Obviously, the bump on his head had rattled something loose.

He got out of the car and walked up the steps and into the sanctuary.

Dozens of poinsettias graced the choir section and the base of the pulpit. Pine roping outlined the altar and the walls. The sanctuary smelled like evergreen and beeswax.

Lillian Bray was up on the altar fussing with an arrangement of red roses, white mums, and holly. Several other members of the auxiliary were polishing the brass offering plate and altar cross.

His own brother Clay was up there arranging music on the organ.

Memories of another church in Florida assailed him. Sharon had been a devoted member of the ladies' circle. She had been involved in everything and was always a whirlwind of activity at this time of year.

He slipped into the back pew, lowered the kneeling bench, and got on his knees. He closed his eyes, but he didn't pray. He merely wished for Sharon with all his might.

A strange cold came over him, and when he opened his eyes, she was sitting right beside him. A glowing presence.

"You're real," he said.

"Of course I am," she said in that voice she always used when he'd said something supremely stupid.

"I'm sorry. I—"

"Stone, you don't need to be sorry. You need to forgive."

"But I'm not mad at you. I mean I was when you died. I was mad at you for leaving me. But it's not you I'm angry with anymore."

"I know."

"You know?"

"I need to go. I don't want to stay here. But you're keeping me here." She wiped a tear from her eye. Another tear formed right behind it.

"You're crying?"

She nodded. "Do you remember what I used to say about Christmas?"

He nodded, "You used to say we should offer up all that we've lost. You said it was the only way to be happy. But you're not happy. Are you crying because of me?"

She looked at him, tears running down her cheeks. How could Sharon be the Sorrowful Angel? Sharon never cried.

"Stop blaming yourself for everything. Make room in your heart. Start laughing again. Pay attention to your children. Love again. Don't you know that the things you've lost eventually come back to you with love?"

She flickered like a television set. She wasn't real, was she? She was a hallucination, and he was probably talking right out loud to the air. But she was wise. Sharon had always been wiser than her years.

"I've got to go. You've got to offer me up to the light." She got up and kind of drifted down the center aisle of the church. She was wearing her Watermelon Queen dress. The one she'd been married in. Had she been wearing that yesterday when he first saw her?

He couldn't remember. She had been so beautiful in that dress.

Just then Clay started playing "Silent Night" on the church organ. Sharon stopped right before the altar, where a strange golden aura winked into existence. The light hurt Stone's eyes, but even so, he knew there was a being inside that light.

Sharon reached toward it, her face filled with longing. But she couldn't go any farther. She was tethered with an ethereal line that ran from her chest to his.

Every tug on that string made it harder for Stone to breathe.

And Sharon was crying.

His memory turned back to that awful morning when they'd argued about Sharon's wish to attend college. He'd tried to hold her back that morning. And she'd cried. Her tears had surprised the hell out of him. And it hurt so much that his last memory of Sharon alive was the sight of her crying.

He needed to let her go. For her own sake. For himself. And for Haley. He needed to send Haley's angel to Heaven where she belonged.

"You can go," he whispered—halfway meaning those long-ago courses she had cried about on the day she died.

"You can go," he said again, this time giving her a mental push toward the light. "You don't have to stay here with me. Besides, Haley needs you to go," he said, his voice thick. "It's the only thing she wants for Christmas."

The cord between them broke. His chest swelled as he took a deep, deep breath. As Sharon broke free, he immediately felt lighter somehow. She walked up onto the altar, and the angel embraced her, and then they were gone, leaving behind Lillian fussing with her flowers, and Millie and Thelma polishing brass, and Clay playing the organ like a virtuoso.

He rested his hands across the top of the pew and laid his head on them. His head was pounding, and his ribs ached. But he felt so much better.

CHAPTER
22

Lark woke up lonely and late.

She cracked her eye and cataloged the standard Days Inn furnishings: An oak bedside table bolted to the wall, a digital clock that said eleven-thirty, teal curtains edged with gray winter light, a bedspread with a cabbage rose motif that was echoed in the wallpaper border.

The long bureau had a flat-panel television tuned to CNN. She had fallen asleep with the television on, the sound set just above a whisper. The news anchor was covering a story about a kid in some midwestern town who had raised a load of money for toys and gifts for the disadvantaged. The kid in the story reminded her of David Raab—braces; too-large hands; serious, intelligent eyes.

A pang of regret squeezed her heart. She took a deep breath and closed her eyes. She needed to get up. She'd driven for six hours last night—to the Virginia border. She still had a couple of hours to go, and it was almost noon.

She stretched and sat up in bed. CNN had moved on to international news. More news about the tense situation in Africa and the Middle East. It sometimes seemed like nothing ever changed.

She picked up one of the many pillows on her bed and hugged it. She was so tired of recording history for everyone else. She rocked back and forth. This wasn't fear talking. She wasn't afraid of going back into the field. She could handle bullets and mayhem. She could find that invincible place in her mind and fool herself. She had done it yesterday.

She could do it, if she wanted to.

She just didn't want to.

What did she want?

All thoughts led her back to Last Chance, South Carolina, where people genuinely cared about one another.

She thought about Pop as a young man, going there and falling in love. She thought about Nita, who was too scared to hold on to what she wanted. She thought about a certain small-town cop who worked hard to keep everyone safe.

She stopped thinking.

And started feeling. She leaned back against the padded headboard and squeezed the pillow to her chest. It was hard to be rational about Stone. He was in every way her deepest fantasy. A big, strong man who spoke with his body, and not with words. A guy who actually understood all of her deepest, darkest secrets. A family man who cared deeply, but who kind of bumbled his way through it all. He was adorable and serious and sexy as hell. He came ready-made with a big family, and damned if she didn't long for that.

She stared at the ceiling for a long time, sorting through her feelings until she recognized the truth.

She was behaving like Pop.

Nita had been too scared to fight for what she wanted.

And Pop had let Nita send him away. He hadn't been brave enough either.

Maybe that's what Pop meant about finding himself on the eighteenth hole. Maybe it wasn't only about finding love in a sleeping bag. Maybe it was realizing that he had walked away from something really important because he was scared. Maybe he learned something from that.

Lark would never know, except that Pop's version of Carmine Falcone always walked away. But Carmine Falcone wasn't real.

And Stone wasn't Carmine. Stone hadn't sent her away. Yesterday afternoon, he'd told her she wasn't ready to go back into the field. He'd told her he was worried about her. He told her that he'd had fun. She had pushed him away, not the other way around.

Idiot.

She didn't want to run away like Pop and Nita. And she didn't want to go back to Africa and shoot photos of starving kids. She wanted something different. She wanted to be part of someone's family album, as stupid and ordinary as that might be.

She needed to stand and fight for what she wanted. She needed to ask for more. She needed to tell Stone that she loved him, even though she knew in her heart that he loved Sharon more. But if she never said the words, she would regret it for the rest of her life.

It terrified her. But then again, she had a role model in her mother. She didn't remember Mom very well. But when Mom was alive, Lark had been happy and felt loved. Mom had showered love on everyone. Mom had been easy to love, so of course, Pop had loved her.

Terrence Wills had probably been like that, too.

Maybe she could be like them. She could be the person who came along second and was easy to love.

She picked up her cell phone and called her editor and told him she wasn't going to Africa. He begged and pleaded. She stood her ground and told him all about her flashbacks and her fear of the camera's shutter. He refused to take her resignation. Instead he gave her a leave of absence so she could go find herself. Lark found that mildly amusing.

She ended the call and noticed that she had fifteen voice-mail messages, and they were all from Stone. If there had been only one, she would have known he was merely calling to thank her for taking care of David and Lizzy when the shooting started.

But fifteen voice-mail messages said something else altogether. Her finger poised over the redial button. She should call him and explain why she'd left.

No.

No, Stone didn't need her words right now. Right now she needed to act. And what she had to say to him was better said face-to-face. Maybe he would believe it when he found out that she wasn't going to be on that plane to Africa.

Stone sat on a hard folding chair in the Christ Church fellowship hall waiting for Haley's rescheduled Christmas play to begin. The kids were getting ready in one of the Sunday School rooms. All around him parishioners in Christmas finery were greeting one another.

He was here for the duration. After the play came the choir's annual Christmas concert, followed by a traditional evening service. Christmas Eve was the one day of he year Momma got him to church—mostly because he enjoyed the music.

He was sitting down, feeling antsy and out of sorts. Why the hell hadn't Lark returned any of his phone calls? Was she mad at him? He could understand that. They hadn't parted well yesterday afternoon. He'd been too busy feeling guilty and thinking about Sharon. And he'd probably said some crazy things right after the shootings.

Well, he probably needed to let it go. Lark had to be on a plane to Africa tomorrow, so she was really busy. The thought left him feeling deeply depressed.

Yesterday he'd wanted to find a way to love her, but Sharon stood in the way. Now he wasn't sure that was true. He needed to see Lark. He needed to figure this out.

"So, how's your head?" Miriam Randall said as she sat down beside him. Today Miriam was wearing a bright green sweater and a costume jewelry wreath with a bunch of large sparkly stones. She cocked her head and studied him from behind her goofy trifocals.

"My head is pounding if you really want to know. And I'm feeling kind of strange."

"Maybe that explains why you were in church earlier this morning. On your knees. Did that bump on the head knock some sense into you? Have you had a change of heart?"

He grunted a laugh. In some ways it definitely felt like his heart had changed. He couldn't exactly explain the hallucination he'd had in church this noontime, but he'd felt lighter ever since. And more determined to speak with Lark.

"Are you ignoring me, son?"

"Uh, sorry. I'm kind of all over the place."

"I asked if you were having a change of heart?"

"No, not really. I mean not about church." He sighed. "Miriam, Arlene suggested a few days ago that I should consult you on the topic of love." His face burned.

It was Miriam's turn to laugh. "Honey," she said patting his knee, "I gave you marital advice when you were eighteen. Near as I can see it's still relevant, even if you are almost forty."

He looked up. "What do you mean?"

She shrugged. "Exactly what I say, but it's so funny how people always misunderstand me. Now, you take Lark, for instance, I told her she needed to find someone she could talk to, and she thought I was suggesting she find a therapist."

"You mean you really did give her a matrimonial prediction?"

"I'm surprised Lillian Bray didn't trumpet it from one end of Palmetto Avenue to the other. But I think Lillian has the misguided notion that I only hand out advice to good Episcopalians. She's a good woman but just a little narrow-minded."

Stone studied the little old lady for a moment. "You told Lark she needed to find someone to talk to?"

"Yes. But not just anyone. Someone who really understood what was going on in her head. She's quite afraid, you know."

"Yes, I know."

Miriam smiled, but said nothing.

"Miriam, are you saying I should *still* be looking for a crusader?"

"So, you *are* looking? I'd heard that you'd taken off your wedding band. Good. Of course you should be looking for a crusader. Didn't I tell you that years ago? And

ust remember that most crusaders come home disillu-
sioned and maybe even a little cynical and scared. They
need to be reminded of what the crusade was for in the
first place. They need an anchor. That's where you come
in." Something sparked in her eye, and Stone would have
questioned her further if Doc Cooper hadn't taken that
moment to step onto the little stage at the end of the fellowship hall and get the Christmas play under way.

It was a little past six o'clock when Lark finally reached
the town limits of Last Chance, South Carolina. The town
looked practically picturesque in the deep winter night, lit
up from end to end for Christmas Eve.

Palmetto Avenue seemed to have a little more traffic
than usual. It sure looked like half the population was
streaming into the parking lots of the four churches that
dominated the main street. This must be the early crowd.
There would probably be a real traffic jam just before
midnight.

She turned onto Calhoun Street and drove past Stone's
house. The windows were dark. She drove a little farther
down the block. The windows were dark at Ruby's house,
too.

Everyone was probably at church.

But which one?

Probably Christ Church—it was the biggest one
in town and the one that Miriam, Hettie, and Lillian
belonged to. She turned the car around.

Five minutes later, she hurried up the front walk of the
church and opened the door to the sanctuary. The place
was beautifully decorated with pine roping and poinsettias. But the place was practically empty.

"If you're looking for the third-grade Christmas play
it's being held in the fellowship hall," said a little balding
man who was sitting in the choir section. "If you're here for
the choir's concert, you're about an hour and a half early."

Lark asked for directions to the fellowship hall, and a
couple of minutes later she quietly entered the darkened
room.

A little boy wearing a white shirt, clip-on tie, khakis,
and sneakers stood to one side of a raised stage, reading
from a paper. "And there were in the same country shepherds abiding in the field, keeping watch over their flock
by night," he read.

When his narration was finished, out from the wings
came two shepherds herding three adorable sheep. One of
the shepherds was Haley Rhodes, wearing a headdress and
a painted-on beard. The sheep ran around the stage saying
"baa baa" for a moment and finally settled to one side with
Haley and the other shepherd beside them.

The narrator spoke again. "And, lo, the angel of the
Lord came upon them, and the glory of the Lord shone
round about them: and they were sore afraid. And the
angel said unto them..."

Out from the wings came a zaftig angel with a gold
halo and cardboard wings. The minute she arrived, Haley
made like she was afraid. The chubby angel spoke. "Fear
not: for...um, uh...um..." She looked out at the audience
like a deer in the headlights. The poor kid was terrified.

Haley raised her head. "Behold I bring you good tidings," she whispered in a voice loud enough for everyone
to hear. A few chuckles could be heard from the audience.

"Oh, yeah, I remember," the angel said, "behold I
bring you good tidings of...um...yeah, I got it...great

joy, which shall be to all people." She hesitated again, and Haley prompted.

"Oh, yeah...For unto you is born this day in the city of David a Savior, which is Christ the Lord. And this shall be...uh...a sign unto you; You shall find the baby wrapped in waddling clothes, lying in a manger."

The chubby angel let go of a relieved sigh, and the narrator took over. "And suddenly there was with the angel a multitude of the heavenly host praising God, and saying—"

Three more little angels arrived on stage and said, "Glory to God in the highest, and on earth peace, good-will toward men."

The narrator continued. "And it came to pass, as the angels were gone away from them into heaven, the shep-herds said one to another..."

The angels exited stage right. And Haley turned to the other shepherd and said in a booming voice, "Let us now go even unto Bethlehem, and see this thing which is come to pass, which the Lord hath made known unto us."

The curtain behind the shepherds rose and there were Joseph and Mary with a manger, and a variety of adorable barn animals.

The narrator read the remainder of the Bible verses as the kids made a living tableau of the first Christmas.

Even Lark, jaded as she was, found herself smiling. She wasn't a Christian and probably never would be, but the Christmas story was always uplifting, especially the part about peace on earth.

The kids got their applause and the house lights came up. She saw Stone almost immediately, as if her eyes were magically directed toward him. He stood up and Haley, still dressed in her shepherd's costume, came barreling toward him. He bent and lifted her up, and gave her a big kiss on her cheek, heedless of the dark greasepaint there.

Lizzy stood next to him, dressed up for Christmas but looking vaguely bored. Stone's family was there with him, too—his mother and father, his brothers and their wives. Only his sister was missing. She was celebrating Christmas in England this year.

Lark hesitated. She didn't belong. What had she been thinking? Had she been thinking at all?

No. She'd been acting on pure emotion. She'd checked rationality at the door.

Stone looked up and their eyes met across the crowded room. He startled. And then he smiled and his shoulders relaxed.

He put Haley down and turned and headed in her direction. There was a smudge of black greasepaint on his nose. It made him look oddly adorable.

"I came back," she whispered, when he stood before her.

"Why didn't you call me? I've been worried about you. Aren't you supposed to be flying to Africa tomorrow?"

She shook her head and looked up into his handsome face. A face she had been searching for all her life. The words she'd endlessly rehearsed during her frantic drive south suddenly clogged in her throat.

It didn't seem to matter. It was like he knew what she wanted to say without her having to actually say it. He reached out and pulled her up into a kiss so hot she almost lost her mind. Something had changed in him. He wasn't holding anything back anymore, and the kiss took her to a place she didn't even know existed.

And when the kiss finally ended the parishioners started applauding. Not just his family, but half the town of Last Chance, South Carolina. There were even a few shouts of "bravo" from a couple of the members of the Christ Church Ladies' Auxiliary.

Haley separated herself from the rest of the family and raced up to them. Stone let Lark go long enough to catch Haley and pull her up into his arms. Her brown eyes were lit up, and there was a big smile on her face.

"Miss Lark, you're right about Santa."

Lark laughed. "Yeah, maybe I was."

"No, really. The angel is gone. She's gone to Heaven. I'm sure Santa did it—and maybe he had some help from the angels. They definitely made it snow."

"How do you know the angel is gone?" Stone asked, his voice just a little hushed and strange.

"I just do," Haley said. "It's the only thing I really wanted for Christmas."

Stone turned toward Lark. "Will you come home with me and share Christmas? I don't want you to go to Africa."

Tears flooded her eyes. "I was coming back to tell you that I don't want to go. Just like Pop, it seems that I've fallen in love right here in Last Chance."

"You were? You have?"

She nodded, and the tears fell down her cheeks. She couldn't say anything more. But it was okay because Stone knew what she meant. He didn't need her words. He could read her like an open book.

He pulled her up into his arms, where she shared a little space with Haley. "I love you, too," he whispered in her ear.

And that's all she needed to know.

READING GROUP GUIDE

Discussion Questions for
Last Chance Christmas

1. People light candles and put up lights at Hanukkah and Christmas. How is the idea of lighting up the dark played out as a theme in *Last Chance Christmas*? Do you think Lark's profession as a photographer is important to this theme? How?

2. Aunt Arlene tells Stone that every person has a hole inside them. Do you agree with this philosophy? If so, where does this hole come from? If not, why not?

3. How does the theme of "letting go" play out in the novel, not just in the main love story but in the subplots as well?

4. Have you ever been the object of prejudice? How did it make you feel? Discuss how the town of Last Chance initially treats Lark and David. Do you think

people in town were fair to them? Do you think Lark and David handled the prejudice well? How were their strategies different from Abe Chaikin's strategy in 1968?

5. At one point in his life, Stone's wife, Sharon, tells him that he needs to give up his losses to God in order to be happy. She tells him that the things you've lost come back to you with love. Discuss how this idea is related to the traditional Christian story of the birth of Christ.

All's fair in love and

literature...

LAST CHANCE BOOK CLUB

Please turn this page

for a preview.

Savannah White pulled her twelve-year-old Honda into Aunt Miriam's driveway. She set the parking brake and studied the old Victorian house through the windshield. It had seen better days. Mauve and gold paint peeled from the shingles and gingerbread woodwork, the porch steps sagged, and the azaleas along the front porch were overgrown, even if they were in full springtime bloom.

She studied the azaleas for a long moment. Savannah had only visited Aunt Miriam in the summertime so she had never seen the azaleas bloom before. The bright pink blossoms were a reminder that she was taking a huge risk. Savannah had no idea if she would even like living in Last Chance year-round.

Of course no one knew yet that she planned to stay. If she had announced her plans, her ex-husband and his parents would have done everything in their power to stop her from leaving Baltimore with her son, Todd. But leaving for a few days to attend a funeral was acceptable. A death in the family trumped everything.

She turned toward Todd. He sat in the passenger's seat completely engrossed in a video game. His brown hair curled over his forehead, and the tip of his tongue showed at the corner of his mouth as he concentrated. His eyelashes were still amazingly long for a boy, but his skin was so pale that he looked like one of those teen vampires from *Twilight*, albeit a slightly chubby one.

"It's time to put the game away," Savannah said.

Todd didn't acknowledge her request. Tuning her out had become a pattern.

"We have to go now. It's time to meet Aunt Miriam."

No response.

She reached over and took the game from his hands.

"Mom," he whined, "I was just about to win that level."

Savannah turned the damn thing off and tucked it into her oversized purse. "Sorry, kiddo, we're here. It's time to join the real world."

He rolled his pretty brown eyes. "Aw, couldn't I just stay in the car?"

"No."

"But I didn't even know Uncle Harry, and I'm sure Aunt Miriam is just some dumb old lady."

Savannah ground her teeth. "You will show respect to Aunt Miriam, is that clear?"

"Yes. But I hate it here."

"You've been here for five minutes during which time you've done nothing but zap zombies."

He rolled his eyes. "Mom, *Semper Fi* doesn't have any zombies. I was shooting members of the Imperial Japanese forces occupying Iwo Jima."

Savannah stared at her son. "You know that World War Two is over and the Japanese are our allies now, right?"

Todd crossed his arms over his chest and sank back into the seat. "I'm not going to some dumb old funeral."

"The funeral isn't until tomorrow. And you will get your butt out of this car and go be nice to your aunt Miriam or I will put your PSP in a microwave and nuke it."

"You wouldn't. That would blow up the apartment and kill the microwave."

"Don't bet on it, kiddo."

"If you did that Dad would buy me another one and Grandmother would yell at you."

And that was the problem, right there.

She drew herself up into full-out mommy mode. "I don't care what your father or grandmother might do. You are with me right now, and you *will* get out of this car. Right now."

He gave her a sulky look and then opened the car door.

She did the same and stepped out into a balmy March day.

"I've never seen a house painted puke green and purple before," he said.

"It's not *that* bad."

The boy wrinkled his nose in disgust. "It's hot. Are we gonna stand here looking at it all day?"

The muscles along Savannah's shoulders knotted, and the headache she'd been fighting since they crossed the South Carolina border was beginning to actually throb.

Just then the front door opened with a bang, and a white-haired lady wearing a blue polyester pantsuit and a pair of red Keds appeared on the porch. Dark, almost black, eyes peered at Savannah through a pair of 1960s-style spectacles festooned with rhinestones. "Well, look who just turned up pretty as a daisy. C'mon up here, sugar," Aunt Miriam said, opening her arms.

Savannah took the rickety porch steps in two long strides and gave Aunt Miriam a bear hug.

"Oh, I'm so glad you came," the old lady said.

Savannah pulled away and looked down at her great-aunt, noting the changes recorded in her face. Her apple cheeks now drooped a little along her jawline. Her skin looked pale and papery. Even the ever-present twinkle in her eyes was dimmed by time and sorrow. Savannah felt a sharp pang of regret that she had allowed so much time to elapse between visits. Aunt Miriam was getting old. Savannah wished with all her might that she could turn back the clock.

"I'm so sorry about Uncle Harry," Savannah said.

Miriam nodded. "He was as old as dirt. And sick these last few years. I know at the end he just wanted to lay his burden down and go on home." Her voice wavered.

Savannah gave Miriam another big hug and whispered, "I'm sure he did. But I know you would have liked him to stay awhile longer."

Miriam pushed back and wiped a few tears from her cheeks. "Enough of this maudlin stuff. Let me see that boy of yours. Last time I saw him, he was no bigger than a minute."

Miriam turned her gaze down into the yard where Todd slouched. Savannah's son had assumed the preteen position—arms crossed and disinterest written all over his face.

"Hmm," Aunt Mim said, "he's a big boy, isn't he?"

Savannah sighed. "Yes, he is."

"Too bad he doesn't live around here. I'm sure Harlan Murphy would be all over you recruiting him for Pop Warner football."

"Really?"

"Oh, yes, ma'am. I think Todd would make an excellent center."

Savannah filed that information away. Todd probably had no interest in playing football. But Savannah was determined to get her son off the couch and out into the fresh air. Last Chance had lots and lots of fresh air.

"Well, son," Miriam said with a wave, "c'mon up here and meet your old aunt Mim. I know you don't remember me."

The boy walked slowly up the stairs and stoically allowed himself to be hugged.

"Y'all come on in," Aunt Miriam said, once she let Todd go. "I've got cookies and pie and enough food to choke a horse. The casserole brigade has been doing overtime these last few days. To be honest, I got so tired of Lillian Bray trying to take charge of my kitchen that I shooed them all away this noontime. They mean well, I suppose, but a whole day with Lillian is enough to try even the most patient of souls."

She turned toward Todd. "I'm sure you're hungry, son."

Todd nodded. Todd was always hungry.

"Well, come on, then, I'll show you the way to the kitchen."

A burst of cool air greeted them in the hallway. It took a moment for Savannah's eyes to adjust to the dark interior. The house had changed little in the eight years since her last visit. To the right stood the formal dining room with its gleaming mahogany table and chairs upholstered in light green moiré. The china closet filled with blue willowware still dominated the far wall. She could practically smell the ham and butter beans that Granny had served on those dishes all those years ago.

She turned her gaze to the left. The front parlor still contained Victorian settees upholstered in red velvet and striped damask silk. The baby grand piano, where she'd practiced endless scales and learned Beethoven's *Moonlight Sonata*, still stood in the corner between the bay window and the pink marble fireplace.

She closed her eyes and breathed in the scents of lemon oil and beeswax and memory. This house had once belonged to her grandfather, Aunt Miriam's older brother. And Savannah had spent most of her summers here. Those had been happy times, for the most part.

Miriam came to a stop beside the oak stairway. "Oh, there you are. I called you to come down five minutes ago," she said as a dark-headed man of about thirty-five two-stepped down to the landing and leaned into the newel post.

He hooked his thumbs through the loops of his Wranglers, lazily crossed one cowboy-booted heel over the other, and assumed the traditional western pose. Too hard and rangy to belong to the house with its 1940s cabbage rose wallpaper, lace doilies, and china figurines, he looked like he'd just stepped out of a grade B western.

He gazed at Savannah with a pair of sexy eyes as blue as Bradley Cooper's, and the corner of his mouth tipped up in a craggy smile. "It's been a long time," he said in a deep drawl.

She blinked a few times, taken by her visceral reaction to the obvious twang in his drawl. And then recognition flashed through Savannah like the Roman candles Granddaddy used to set off on the Fourth of July.

"Cousin Dash," she said, "you still sound like a Texan."

Dash's gaze did a slow circuit of her body, and she felt

naked as a jaybird under his intense inspection. "You've grown up some since I saw you last, *princess.*"

"Don't call me that," she said through gritted teeth. "I'm not ten years old anymore." Granddaddy had called Savannah princess until the day he died, but in Dash's mouth, the word came out as a twisted insult.

"No, I guess not." His eyes flashed to Todd and back. "And I see you've become a momma."

She turned toward her son. "Todd, this is Cousin Dash. When he was fifteen, he put a snake in my bed and blew up my favorite Barbie doll with a cherry bomb. I'm sure he is very sorry for what he did. And I am very—"

"Did the Barbie doll melt?" Todd asked.

Dash chuckled. "As I recall, it blew apart in about a dozen flaming pieces. But yeah, it melted."

"It was my favorite, Twirly Curl Barbie. And—"

"Cool. What kind of snake did you put in the bed?" Todd asked.

"A garter snake, entirely harmless. Scared your momma to pieces, though. You should have seen her running through the hallway in her baby doll nightie. It was the—"

"Dash, I really don't think we have to rerun our entire history for Todd's benefit, do we?" Savannah said.

"If we're talking about the past, princess, it's because you raised the issue."

Aunt Miriam entered the fray. "I declare, I you two sound just like you did when you were children. Now both of y'all act like the adults you are and c'mon back to the kitchen and have some dinner. I've got one of Jenny Carpenter's pies. A cherry one, I believe."

Dash flashed a bright smile in Miriam's direction.

"Yes, ma'am, I will try to behave. But no thank you, ma'am, to the dinner and pie. I have errands to run up at the stable. Aunt Mim, will you be all right if I leave you with Savannah for a little bit?"

"You go on, Dash. I'm fine," Miriam said.

He nodded to Savannah. "Welcome back," he said without much enthusiasm. Then he strode toward the front door, his cowboy boots scraping across the oak floor. He stopped at the rack by the door and snagged an old, sweat-stained baseball hat bearing the logo of the Houston Astros. He slapped it down on his head and turned toward Miriam. "Don't wait up. I'll probably be late," he said, then turned toward Savannah. "Princess." He tipped his hat and headed through the open door.

"Dash, don't slam—" Miriam's admonishment was cut off by the loud bang of the front door slamming.

Todd spoke into the silence that followed. "He's really cool, isn't he?"

Oh, great. Dash Randall was the last person on earth that Savannah wanted as a role model for her problem child.

THE DISH

Where authors give you the inside scoop!

♥ ♥ ♥ ♥ ♥ ♥ ♥ ♥ ♥ ♥ ♥ ♥ ♥ ♥ ♥

From the desk of R.C. Ryan

Dear Reader,

When my daughter-in-law Patty came home from her first hike of the Grand Canyon, she was high on the beauty and majesty of the mountains for months. Since then, it has become her annual pilgrimage—one that fuels her dreams, and feeds my writer's imagination. I've wanted to create a character with the same passion for the mountains that Patty has for a long time, someone who experiences the same awe, freedom, and peace that she does just by being in eyesight of them. And with JOSH, I think I finally have.

Josh Conway, the hero of the second book in my Wyoming Sky series, is truly a hero in every sense of the word. He's a man who rescues people who've lost their way on the mountain he loves in all kinds of weather. There's just something about a guy who would risk his own safety, his very life, to help others, that is so appealing to me. To add to Josh's appeal, he's a hard-working rancher and a sexy cowboy—an irresistible combination. Not to mention that he loves a challenge.

Enter Sierra Moore. Sierra is a photographer who comes to the Grand Tetons in Wyoming to shoot photographs of a storm. At least that's what she'll admit to. But there's a mystery behind that beautiful smile. She's come to the mountains to disappear for a while, and being

rescued—even if it is by a ruggedly handsome cowboy—
is the last thing she needs or wants.

But when danger rears its ugly head, and Sierra's life
is threatened, she and Josh must call on every bit of
strength and courage they possess in order to survive. Yet
an even greater test of their strength will be the courage
to commit to a lifetime together.

I hope you enjoy JOSH!

R. C. Ryan

RyanLangan.com

♥ ♥ ♥ ♥ ♥ ♥ ♥ ♥ ♥ ♥ ♥ ♥ ♥ ♥ ♥

From the desk of Anna Campbell

Dear Reader,

Wow! I'm so excited that my first historical romance with
Grand Central Publishing has hit the shelves (and the
e-waves!). I hope you enjoy reading SEVEN NIGHTS IN
A ROGUE'S BED as much as I enjoyed writing it. Not
only is this my first book for GCP, it's also the first book
in my very first series, the Sons of Sin. Perhaps I should
smash a bottle of champagne over my copy of SEVEN
NIGHTS to launch it in appropriate style.

Hmm, having second thoughts here. Much better, I've
decided, to read the book and drink the champagne!

Do you like fairytale romance? I love stories based on
Cinderella or Sleeping Beauty or some other mythical

hero or heroine. SEVEN NIGHTS IN A ROGUE'S BED is a dyed-in-the-wool Beauty and the Beast re-telling. To me, this is the ultimate romantic fairytale. The hero starts out as a monster, but when he falls in love, the fragments of goodness in his tortured soul multiply until he becomes a gallant prince (or, in this case, a viscount, but who's counting?). Beauty and the Beast is at heart about the transformative power of true love—what more powerful theme for a romance writer to explore?

Jonas Merrick, the Beast in SEVEN NIGHTS IN A ROGUE'S BED, is a scarred recluse who has learned through hard and painful experience to mistrust a hostile world. When the book opens, he's a rogue indeed. But meeting our heroine conspires to turn him into a genuine, if at first reluctant, hero worthy of his blissfully happy ending.

Another thing I love about Beauty and the Beast is that the heroine is more proactive than some other mythological girls. For a start, she stays awake throughout! Like Beauty, Sidonie Forsythe places herself in the Beast's power to save someone she loves, her reckless older sister, Roberta. Sidonie's dread when she meets brooding, enigmatic Jonas Merrick swiftly turns to fascination—but even as they fall in love, Sidonie's secret threatens to destroy Jonas and any chance of happiness for this Regency Beauty and the Beast.

I adore high-stakes stories where I wonder if the lovers can ever overcome what seem to be insurmountable barriers between them. In SEVEN NIGHTS IN A ROGUE'S BED, Jonas and Sidonie have to triumph over the bitter legacy of the past and conquer present dangers to achieve their happily-ever-after. Definitely major learning curves for our hero and heroine!

This story is a journey from darkness to light, and it allowed me to play with so many classic romance themes.

Redemption. A touch of the gothic. The steadfast, courageous heroine. The dark, tormented hero. The clash of two powerful personalities as they resist overwhelming passion. Secrets and revelations. Self-sacrifice and risk. Revenge and justice. You know, all the big stuff!

If you'd like to find out more about SEVEN NIGHTS IN A ROGUE'S BED and the Sons of Sin series, please visit my website: www.annacampbell.info. And in the meantime, happy reading!

Best wishes,

Anna Campbell

♥ ♥ ♥ ♥ ♥ ♥ ♥ ♥ ♥ ♥ ♥ ♥ ♥ ♥ ♥

From the desk of Katie Lane

Dear Reader,

One of my favorite things to do during the holidays is to read *The Night Before Christmas*. So I thought it would be fun to tell you about my new romance, HUNK FOR THE HOLIDAYS, by making up my own version of the classic.

'Twas four days before Christmas, and our heroine, Cassie,
Is ready for her office party, looking red hot and sassy.
When what to her wondering eyes should she see
But the escort she hired standing next to her tree?
His eyes how they twinkle, his dimples so cute,
He has a smile that melts, a great body to boot.

There's only one problem: James is as controlling as Cass,
But she forgives him this flaw, when she gets a good look
*   at his ass.*
He goes straight to work at seducing his date,
And by the end of the evening, Cass is ready to mate.
Not to ruin the story, all I will say,
Is that James will be smiling when Cass gets her way.
Mixed in with their romance will be plenty of reason
For you to enjoy the fun of the season.
Caroling, shopping, and holiday baking,
A humorous great-aunt and her attempts at match-making.
A perfect book to cozy up with all the way through December,
HUNK FOR THE HOLIDAYS will be out in September.
For now I will end by wishing you peace, love, and laughter.
And, of course, the best gift of all… a happily-ever-after!

Katie Lane

♥ ♥ ♥ ♥ ♥ ♥ ♥ ♥ ♥ ♥ ♥ ♥ ♥ ♥ ♥

From the desk of Hope Ramsay

Dear Reader,

I love Christmas, but I have to say that trying to write a
holiday-themed book in the middle of a long, hot summer
is not exactly easy. It was hard to stay in the holiday
mood when my nonwriting time was spent weeding my
perennials border, watching baseball, and working on my
short golf game.

So how does an author get herself into the holiday mood in the middle of July?

She hauls out her iPod and plays Christmas music from sun up to sun down.

My husband was ready to strangle me, but all that Christmas music did the trick. And in the end, it was just one song that helped me find my holiday spirit.

The song is "The Longest Night," written by singer-songwriter Peter Mayer, a song that isn't quite a Christmas song. It's about the winter solstice. The lyrics are all about hope, even in the darkest hour. In the punchline, the song-writer gives a tiny nod to the meaning of Christmas when he says, "Maybe light itself is born in the longest night."

When I finished LAST CHANCE CHRISTMAS, I realized that this theme of light and dark runs through it like a river. My heroine is a war photographer, who literally sees the world as a battle between light and dark. When she arrives in Last Chance, she's troubled and alone, and the darkness is about to overwhelm her.

But of course, that doesn't last long after she meets Stone Rhodes, the chief of police and a man who is about as Grinch-like as they come. But as the saying goes, some-times the only way to get yourself out of a funk is to help someone else. And when Stone does that, he manages to spark a very hot and bright light in the dead of winter.

I hope you love reading Stone and Lark's story as much as I did writing it.

Ya'll have a blessed holiday, now, you hear?

Hope Ramsay

Find out more about Forever Romance!

Visit us at
www.hachettebookgroup.com/publishing_forever.aspx

Find us on Facebook
http://www.facebook.com/ForeverRomance

Follow us on Twitter
http://twitter.com/ForeverRomance

NEW AND UPCOMING TITLES

Each month we feature our new titles
and reader favorites.

CONTESTS AND GIVEAWAYS

We give away galleys, autographed copies,
and all kinds of exclusive items.

AUTHOR INFO

You'll find bios, articles, and links to personal websites
for all your favorite authors—and so much more.

GET SOCIAL

Connect with your favorite authors, editors, and
other Forever fans, and share what's important to you.

THE BUZZ

Sign up for our monthly romance newsletter,
and be the first to read all about it.

VISIT US ONLINE AT

WWW.HACHETTEBOOKGROUP.COM

FEATURES:

OPENBOOK BROWSE AND
SEARCH EXCERPTS
•
AUDIOBOOK EXCERPTS AND PODCASTS
•
AUTHOR ARTICLES AND INTERVIEWS
•
BESTSELLER AND PUBLISHING
GROUP NEWS
•
SIGN UP FOR E-NEWSLETTERS
•
AUTHOR APPEARANCES AND TOUR
INFORMATION
•
SOCIAL MEDIA FEEDS AND WIDGETS
•
DOWNLOAD FREE APPS

BOOKMARK HACHETTE BOOK GROUP
@ WWW.HACHETTEBOOKGROUP.COM